Penguin Crime Fiction
The Night Lords

Nicolas Freeling was born in London in 1927 and spent
his childhood in France. Before taking up writing he
worked for many years in hotels and restaurants, and
from their back doors got to know a good deal of Europe.
When *Love in Amsterdam*, his first novel, was published
in 1962 he stopped cooking other people's dinners and
went back to Holland. His second and third novels,
Because of the Cats and *Gun before Butter*, were
published in 1963. His other crime novels include
Valparaiso, *Double Barrel*, *Criminal Conversation*, *The
King of the Rainy Country*, *The Dresden Green*, *Strike
Out Where Not Applicable*, *This is the Castle*, *Tsing-Boum*,
Over the High Side, *A Long Silence*, *Dressing of Diamond*,
What are the Bugles Blowing for?, *Gadget* and *Lake Isle*.
Many of these are published in Penguins.

Nicolas Freeling

The Night Lords

Penguin Books

Penguin Books Ltd, Harmondsworth,
Middlesex, England
Penguin Books, 625 Madison Avenue,
New York, New York 10022, U.S.A.
Penguin Books Australia Ltd, Ringwood,
Victoria, Australia
Penguin Books Canada Ltd, 2801 John Street,
Markham, Ontario, Canada L3R 1B4
Penguin Books (N.Z.) Ltd, 182-190 Wairau Road,
Auckland 10, New Zealand

First published by William Heinemann Ltd 1978
Published in Penguin Books 1980

Copyright © Nicolas Freeling, 1978
All rights reserved

Set, printed and bound in Great Britain by
Cox & Wyman Ltd, Reading
Set in Times

To The Police Judiciaire

1. Sunset

Henri Castang, at the end of the day, drunk with fatigue and with a tension too long maintained and too brutally released, was driving home through rush-hour traffic. The job was done: he had gone without free time for a fortnight: the one idea in his head was to get home to wife, shower, supper, bed. Then why stop? And what a place to stop in! It was forbidden to park on the bridge. A lot Castang cared for municipal police regulations . . .

The bridge was a strung bow, a taut and graceful arc of stressed concrete crossing the railway. Castang bumped the scratched dusty police car up onto the pavement, gave the door a kick and leaned his elbows on the parapet. Below him forty shiny steel ribbons and the spider-web ladders of overhead cable showed the way to the freight yard; and Paris, some hundreds of kilometres further. Behind him a rushing stream of tin cans paid him no heed. Their jagged owners, if they glanced at him at all, thought he had had a heart attack – or the Renault had; much the same thing and no affair of theirs. But in front of him the sky was full of setting sun.

A winterset: the huge sky was a hard bright blue. On one side, over the city, was a piled mass of white cloud, static, painted all over with pale gold. In the very centre, straight above the railway lines, was one stab of pure bright gold that scorched the eye. The left side, over the interminable suburbs, was scribbled over with fragile lace of a warm bluish grey: God smoking a huge beautiful cigar from Celestial Cuba. The thin veils broke as he looked at them: beyond, tiny islands of white and gold, high and far, promised silence, a glad peaceful tomorrow.

Castang knew no cops who looked at sunsets. He couldn't remember when he last did so himself. For nearly five minutes he leaned on the parapet and breathed in and out. When he got back into the car he kicked it straight out into the traffic without signalling, so that the onrushing queue of baa-black-sheep braked in frenzy, klaxonning furiously and hanging out of the window as they overtook to scream, 'Crucify him.' Again cop, he didn't give a roger for the rats. At the red light he lounged back and stared ahead, languidly insolent like a chauffeur in a Rolls-Royce.

On the quay, bordering a disused canal and pretty with poplar trees, where he lived (a Good, Bourgeois, Frightened district) he locked the car and gazed again for a moment. The sky had gone pale. A lame-brained huge jet plane, like a bewildered pterosaur, lumbered sadly down towards the airport. Poor thing! In its belly, more poor things. There was a silver thumbnail of new moon. Castang felt insanely happy at this new manifestation of good fortune, as though he had drunk the goldfish bowl full to the brim with champagne and then swallowed the goldfish out of sheer insolence. He turned to go into his house; got the fright of his life. The vast, serene pile of cloud seen ten minutes before, whitey-gold as the Pope's triple tiara, was marching dread and mighty across the eastern sky; one immense incandescent flame of pale orange. As the population of France goes, Castang was highly unsuperstitious, but he shuddered and his hand feeling for latchkeys in the pocket made an instinctive sign against the evil eye.

Vera, his wife, who was peacefully reading a magazine, looked up keenly.

'Finished at last? Hallo! Have you met somebody you thought was dead?'

'It's finished,' sitting down and kicking his shoes off. 'Something like that. I'm tired, I suppose. I saw heaven and I saw hell. I saw God in the middle, come to judge the living and the dead.'

'There's nothing very odd about that,' said Vera who had a theological cast of thought.

'I suppose not. God was smoking a very big Cuban cigar.'

'You saw the sunset,' said the woman of rapid understanding. 'I was studying it too. You've had a hard time. Are you getting your days off now?'

'Yes, unless some idiot holds up a bank.'

'Let's go somewhere with no telephone. There's potato soup.' Vera's potato soup was Slav, like her. One got a big bowl, and three little bowls, with chopped chives, and little soldiers of fried bread, and rashers of bacon, grilled crisp and crumbled up. It put heart back into Castang. He wished he'd had a shower. Vera sniffed rather, and it was probably his socks, but she was too polite to say so.

'How's your baby?' he asked.

For she had been paraplegic for three years after an accident. She had re-educated herself, helped by much female bloody-mindedness, into walking; could manage now short distances without crutches, and as though in celebration had managed to get herself pregnant for the first time. Now in the third month. It had given Castang a whole new sense of responsibilities and a different awareness: he was not ordinarily given to looking at sunsets.

'It's quiet, and comfortable.' She would not be ostentatious. She was knitting a lot, but there was no display of tiny garments. Not going to lever a vast belly all over the place, either. Everything was going to be undramatic. Breath-control exercises, a nice change from birth-control; there would be no sweaty groaning or clutching of bedposts. Plainly, it was Castang that would create all the uproar. Life as a cop was not yet reconciled to the blushing-father bit.

They would sort it out, the way they handled all their problems; together. There were things about being a cop that he did not tell her; mostly she guessed at them, and passed them over in a tacit agreement. Most of what had happened in the last ten days she knew. She knew the two sides of a policeman's

9

existence; the arrow that flies by day, and the quieter, more sinister knife in the dark.

There was not much to tell her about the English family: she knew all about that, understood it perhaps better than anyone, had been instrumental, perhaps, in disentangling it. She knew all about the property speculator too. She knew about the last brush – too close – with violence. It was best so. This was what being married meant. Indeed without this confidence in each other, they could not have stayed married.

'I'll have a shower,' taking the gunbelt off, carrying his trousers into the bedroom to put on a hanger. Castang the meticulous. Won't last much longer, he thought. Place will be full of babies and nappies and whatnot. An end, finally, to a tidy, careful, egoist existence.

He sat on the bed to peel plaster strapping off his body; the itch was driving him dippy.

'Healing,' said Vera, studying the angry red scar just above his liver. It was; he knew from the itch, and had looked when Fausta changed the strapping: no, he wasn't going to tell Vera about that detail.

'It needs a day or two's rest,' he said. 'We're going out to-morrow night, to celebrate.'

'Are we? Where?'

'To your friend Monsieur Thomas. We've both earned that. He'll be an unwilling but lavish host.'

'That adds edge to appetite,' going off to do the washing-up. She wasn't smoking at all, because of being pregnant. He was smoking much too much. This was all wrong but she was going to be placid about it. 'I'll make some coffee, shall I?'

Yes, that was a good idea, before he tumbled down asleep under the shower.

2. Sun also rises

It had been a green winter: they were the worst. There had been a heavy premature fall of snow, and up to Christmas it had frozen hard, but this had all melted and left a dense tangle of muddy boots and wet smelly umbrellas: it had hardly stopped raining since. A real February filldyke; the river valleys brimmed with floodwater, topped by an offensive layer of fog. Castang caught a streaming cold, a rarity with him, and gave it to Vera who was not best pleased. The very mildness of the temperature lowered resistance, the fug smelt bad, when one could smell anything: the rain that fell was not clean, but greasy and polluted, and left stains on Vera's windowpanes. Commissaire Richard seemed in a perpetual bad mood. A heavy crop of crimes in the senseless-violence category did nothing to tax his brains but laid a strain on his nerves. There was the usual Press outcry about incompetent police forces which persecuted the public without protecting it.

March the third dawned much like the sixty days that had gone before it; grey, oppressive, smelly. Castang, whose cold had passed the disgusting stage and dwindled to only one pack of paper handkerchiefs per day, got up and went to the office with resignation. A vague prayer went up to police divinities (it was hard to believe that God took any interest) that it be a quiet day. He had three reports to write, all unsatisfactory, on three different holdups of three small suburban banks. One had no sympathy whatsoever for the banks, who kept opening these idiotic corner-shop branches and leaving them insufficiently protected. No sympathy for the bandits, though at least half of them were pathetic imbeciles armed with toy pistols. No sympathy for anyone but himself, who had to get through a mass of paperwork.

Concentrated upon all this – an individual one metre sixty-eight in height (who had measured him?) with light-brown hair (how long since the individual had washed it?) whose features had been dissimulated under the roll neck of a loose dark green pullover – Castang failed to notice a vague lightening of the spirit, which somehow disinfected the work in hand. It wasn't until he came out of the door to go to lunch that he noticed that the sun was shining. Not just a watery gleam, but a true sun in a clean sky. Lunch was only the 'plat du jour' or cheapest menu in the pub opposite; stewed bacon and lentils with endive salad, a morsel of cheese and a cup of coffee, tax and service included with a quarter of mineral water, and his table-companion was Lasserre, never a stimulating person, but the sun made all the difference. He was digesting in some contentment when the phone on the bar rang and the boss said, 'Castang' – might have known it was too good to last.

'I want you,' said Richard's voice.

The Commissaire was drinking a cup of vervain tea. Richard didn't eat in pubs. His secretary, the seductive Fausta, provided material as well as spiritual refreshment; a delicious vision bringing scrambled eggs. She had a camping-gas stove in the outer office, and made a rather snobbish ritual out of it. It was a quarter past one and lunch was now over.

'Whip smartly out to Thomas,' said Richard, sweeping crumbs into the wastepaper basket, 'peculiar things are happening on his parking lot.'

'Oh hell – why me?'

'A variety of reasons,' bland. 'He asked for you, seems to think you'd be anxious to do him a favour.'

'Trust him to get a lot for sixpence. Vera did him some drawings and he thought he was doing her a favour,' with a snort.

'He seems too to be in a muddle with some English people and you do speak roast-beef.' It is extraordinary how quite sophisticated Frenchmen remain convinced that the English are nourished exclusively upon sirloin.

'What's it all about?'

'I've not the slightest idea,' said Richard more blandly still. 'Vampires by the sound of it. He gabbled. Corpses appearing

12

and disappearing. He wants discretion, so he was unconscionably discreet. You're such friends, doubtless he'll open up. No Press, he begs in terror. Go and unruffle him.' Resignedly, Castang went.

One might think that the Police Judiciaire would be unlikely to send an officer running fast to investigate a vague tale of vampires, and one would be quite right. But though Thomas is a common name, there is really only one in France, because in all France there are only a dozen three-star restaurants, and only one of these is called Thomas.

This small and exclusive club possesses much leverage. Not perhaps strictly speaking 'political', but getting three stars in the first place had more to it than just being a good cook. You see to it that you acquire influential friends. Having got them, you take pains to keep them. Castang was far from being an influential friend, but every little helps. Vera, a semi-professional graphic artist of accomplishment, had made some drawings for new menus and sold them to Monsieur Thomas, pretty cheap.

Richard, who moved in golf-club circles and made a very good imitation sometimes of the dynamic business executive, might be an influential friend. That wasn't any of Castang's business.

The sun had dried the roads and sparkled on the drops clinging to hedges. The green shoots of daffodils showed yellow at the tips, the thin haze of tiny leaf was on the willows. Everybody in France who had the slightest sense had invented pretexts for stopping the dismal tasks they were engaged in, and rushed to the garden. On the outskirts of the city the little municipal vegetable-plots, dear to Vera's heart, were a bee-hive. Castang felt the pleasure and wellbeing, absent for too long. He was going to enjoy the vampires.

Three-star restaurants are found in unlikely places, and can show a splendid contempt for scruffy surroundings. If the wine is really good, it needs no bush. 'Thomas' lay on a main road, but at the end of a dreary and cement-dusty industrial quarter, a few kilometres outside the city, which had almost swallowed the original village. From the outside, an utterly undistinguished house. A word with the local mayor had seen to the planting of a few weedy-looking trees to insulate it from the main road. At the back, however, was a large terrace whose glass doors and roof rolled back in fine weather, and a big parking lot, pleasantly broken up by fruit trees, still bare.

Castang parked his dented and smelly Peugeot. This was where vampires had been flitting about? – he saw no sign of any. He studied the parked cars. Usual clientèle of elderly Germans in beige Mercedes sedans, French show-offs in Jaguars – salesmen – Americans in self-drives and plenty of pederasts of all nationalities in aggressive sports coupés with deep baritone exhaust-notes. There was a black Rolls-Royce with GB plates: ho ho.

Mr Thomas was certainly agitato, to come rushing out in that way: whatever form the vampires took they were bad publicity.

He was a youngish man, with a pleasant, slightly cheap face. He had charm, humour, and amiable conversation. His was the scarlet Ferrari at the end; a piece of conspicuous consumption to encourage customers into the same.

Three-star restaurants are a family business: a husband and wife, a pair of brothers, and there must be a strong personality, even if as occasionally happens this is a notorious phony. This wasn't it; the real Thomas was the father, a cook of great imagination and talent, now an old gentleman of seventy, still an enormous presence in his kitchen but otherwise never seen. He had always hated customers and never went near them. The restaurant had been ruled by Mother, a formidable biddy like a champagne-granny, who had succumbed to brain haemorrhage a year or so ago. The son, a nonentity but a good front-man and adroit publicity hound, had inherited enough of Mum's business sense to step into her shoes.

Castang and he shook hands.

3. How a butcher buries his grandmother

They sat at an obscure table by the service entrance, behind a barrier of flowers and fruit. There was the unmistakable perfume of the very best which is found nowhere else.

'Have you eaten?' enquired Monsieur Thomas.

'Yes,' said Castang before he had thought of saying no.

'Never mind – another time,' very rapidly. 'Something to drink?' half-hearted.

'Yes please,' with firmness. Thomas jumped up and held a whispered confabulation with a head waiter; returned beaming. A commis arrived with two glasses, another with a half-full bottle. Much flourish of white napkins; stylized hieratic gestures: monsignori blessing the incense in the ritual of Pope Pius the Fifth. Castang knew perfectly that the bottle had been sold to a customer who had not finished it: the name on the label was flamboyant, the vintage superb. He admired this skilful mix of flattery with economy.

Monsieur Thomas chose his words with equal felicity: his explanation was brief and witty.

Funeral customs in France are the subject of strict municipal regulations, which differ from one community to another. It can happen that several enterprises in funereal pomp are allowed to practise in open competition within the community. The prices at this moment have at least a likelihood of being within the bounds of reason. In other, especially smaller towns, a monopoly exists, and by connivance with municipal authorities you may only bury your relatives with the aid and comfort of officially approved standards of hygiene. The price of which is exorbitant and the profits immense.

A venerable lady chose inconsiderately to die within such a community. Her grandson the butcher, shocked by these immoral practices, the more because they were his own, permeated moreover by the French principle that there is no such thing as a

15

small economy, took action. Possessing a splendid new Volvo station-wagon, frequently used for the surreptitious transport of black market carcasses, and thinking like a sensible man that one piece of meat is much the same as another, he decided upon the illegal removal of granny, who would thus enter a better world at less expense. Briefly, granny got stuffed in the station-wagon.

Castang was enjoying the wine; it was excellent.

Quite naturally, the butcher had decided on the way to have a little light refreshment before tackling sterner matters, and chose these hospitable premises. Most unfortunately evil-minded persons, lurking in the neighbourhood, stole the station-wagon, all unaware of granny enshrined therein.

Mr Thomas sobered down for the next bit. That damned butcher, ramping about the place howling at the top of his voice, was execrable publicity. One could understand his torment. He had to balance the loss of a brand-new Volvo (and if he didn't report it, Mr Thomas, in the interests of his customers and himself, certainly would) against embarrassing queries about granny. Where was she now? Tipped somewhere in a ditch; no, it wouldn't do. Avarice conquered shame, as it always does. It would be in the paper, and the neighbours would snigger, but hell, they'd all have done the same in his shoes. So would the mayor. It would quickly be forgotten. A relatively trivial fine for flouting the Public Health Authority regulations was a lot less bad than being unable to claim on the car insurance.

Castang said he quite understood, including annoyances caused to Mr Thomas. It was however no matter for the Police Judiciaire. Car thefts, non-declaration of decease to the competent authorities; these were grave misdemeanours, but concerned the local gendarmerie. He would try to expedite justice. This was nice wine. While he was about it, what about the payments due to his wife for her drawings?

'The drawings are lovely. I'll write you a cheque right here. You do see, these are wonderful for her, too – our menus get taken as souvenirs, and religiously kept, all over the world, and with her signature on them, you do see, Castang, marvellous

16

opening for her. But there's worse, much worse. I count upon you.'

'Ah yes, the roast-beef brigade. I'd forgotten.'

'I haven't. But I had to explain the other first. You see, the damned English woman in the middle of lunch has forgotten her handkerchief, goes to look in the car, and lets out the most unmerciful yell ever. There's a body in the boot! As though that wasn't bad enough the butcher starts up all over again. Thought it was his granny . . .' He writhed at the memory. Customers who paid his prices thought themselves entitled to every kind of outrageous behaviour, but corpses on the parking-lot . . . 'I got on to Richard straight away; the gendarmerie simply don't want to know. And neither do I!'

'All right, I'll see what I can do. Where are the English?'

'In the little banquet room. Didn't want to eat any more; one can hardly blame them, I suppose. I cancelled their bill – but it's no fault of mine, damn it. How am I to keep it quiet? – a dozen wretches in here will rush to sell the whole tale, madly distorted, to the Press. I'm livid. Now look, Castang, you come out here with your wife, and have whatever you please, and you're my guests, and moreover I'll pay her the whole agreed sum, but for the love of heaven see to it this goes no further.'

'Well, if you'll just give me that cheque now,' said Castang agreeably, knowing well that otherwise they'd never get a smell of it. He would never again have a whip hand. Thomas got his cheque book out, unhappy, but bravely concealing it. Oh, what an awful day. But if the gutter Press came here he'd know how to deal with it. Whereas the cops were capable of leaking the most dreadful nonsense if one didn't take pains to keep them sweet.

'Sue the butcher,' suggested Castang, pocketing the cheque.

'I would,' said Thomas vindictively, 'if there were any way of doing so without covering myself in ridicule. I'll never lay eyes on him again, thank God. No loss; my father wouldn't buy so much as a rabbit's egg from the horrible twister.'

Castang had managed to get two whole glasses out of this remarkable bottle and felt mellow. He looked around the restaurant. Despite momentary upheavals, screams and suchlike, the company was sunk in the pleasant lethargy born of gluttony felicitously sated. No sign of nervousness or anxiety. And these English people had a corpse in their car. A homicide cop had, however, seen corpses appear in weirder places. PJ business, no doubt of it, but hardly likely to be a great burden. They were tourists, and if someone had got rid of a corpse in a hurry it would be some place outside his area! Still, be on the safe side.

He looked at his watch: it was only five past two.

'Anybody pay and leave early? Or in a hurry?'

'One or two. Locals mostly.'

'Whom you know?'

'For the most part, I think.'

'I'll want identifications. Wherever that's not possible, the most exact description possible from whoever served them, their cheques or credit card details, photostats.'

'That's easy. And the people here now?'

'No need to upset them. When they pay, ask politely for them to leave their names and addresses; routine police measures, blahblah. Have a headwaiter take a discreet note of the numbers of every car that's still in the lot, since I've nobody here. No problem about the butcher – whoever pinched the wagon will dump it the second he discovers granny. The gendarmerie'll handle that, and I'll look after these English. Okay?'

'Emphatically okay. Show you the way, shall I?'

4. Anglo-Saxon disapproval

The restaurant was a pleasant, unassuming room with a lot of green plants, full at the moment of spring flowers, in good taste because it was in no taste at all. The 'little banquet room' was abominable. It dated from the time of Mother, and was in a

18

false Louis Quinze of whitened and gilded wood, upholstered in brocade of just the wrong shade of pink. The table for eight persons was laid but had no flowers; both formal and dead. The little bar at the end was empty, and few sights are more depressing than a closed bar. A round table in one of the two window embrasures was laid with a coffee service and a dish of petits fours, and on the banquette sat the English, in freezing attitudes, hating everything. Plainly, someone's dog had misbehaved itself beneath the table.

It was a family of four. An elderly gentleman, something over sixty: a fattish comfortable woman, something under: a young woman of twenty-six or -seven, plain but with good features: a young man twenty-fourish. All looked constrained and corseted, but Castang wasn't seeing them at their best. He hadn't expected to; few people when first faced with a PJ cop look anything else. He introduced himself in his odd but workable English and asked permission to sit in one of the little armchairs.

Mum was the spokesman; she would be the possessor of awkward but correct French, with the passports and the travellers' cheques in her voluminous crocodile handbag, inspecting the rooms before taking them.

'Our name is Armitage. We'd like to know how long we're expected to stay here.'

'It's best to think of it as a breakdown. I know, a Rolls-Royce doesn't. But that is the way it works. Like to tow the car into the garage, and the specialist looks. The mechanics diagnose quickly, we hope. Maybe we need a spare part. We try to get that without delay. So now – two twenty. Maybe today, if we are lucky. More likely, I have to say, tomorrow by lunchtime.'

'Oh dear. What – here?'

'Better in the town. The garage, you see, and the mechanics. But it's a nice city,' said Castang smiling. 'I realize, and I am sorry to interrupt your holiday. Now this moment I can give you no answer for sure. I know nothing yet. I am told you found a body in your car. Who is that, where does that come from, how does that come where it is? This may be very easy to find out, it may be more complicated. But in any case, there are formalities. My superior, the Commissaire, is the authority; he only can decide. I gather all the facts possible, I report to him. Perhaps he would like then to see you, perhaps not. We wish to give you the least trouble possible. But, I am afraid, this is the minimum.'

'I see.' There was a silence. With some hesitation, she decided to play her high card. 'Perhaps I should tell you at once that my husband here is Sir James Armitage, a High Court Judge, in England. You must realize that his word in any matter would be absolutely unquestionable. It strikes me that if he were to put his word to a statement, if need be I suppose in writing, for your superior, that would be an end to the matter.'

'I see.' Castang put his pen down, outwardly placid, thrown inwardly into consternation. Tile number one has just fallen off the roof. Missed me narrowly. On all building sites in France there is displayed a notice: *port de casque obligatoire*. Luckily, he was wearing his helmet.

'And what would be the essence of this statement?' cautiously.

'Why,' in some irritation, 'that we know nothing whatsoever about these questions you asked, obviously. This, uh, who it is and where it comes from. And that, frankly,' flatly, 'is enough to satisfy any police authority. We quite realize of course, none better than ourselves, that the police have their work to do. But this, I mean, this abominable discovery is purely coincidental. Our car has been parked in the open. The affair concerns us no further.'

He picked his pen up again.

'I don't want to irritate you,' he said gently. 'I know that official phrases are detestable. "It will all be gone into at the proper time" – yes, of course, and why should you be bothered? Certainly. I am the servant of the law. Sir James – I am sorry, is that correct? – understands that, like you say; nobody better. The rules of evidence. We have here a death, unexplained. Perhaps accidental. But at the least it has been sought to conceal that death, to disguise or falsify the circumstances, and this is serious. The law here prescribes that the Procureur, er, the

20

Attorney-General of the region, or his substitute, shall inspect. If he is not satisfied, which appears probable since there is no explanation offered, he shall ask a judge of instruction to open an enquiry. The police, ourselves, shall be charged with that enquiry. The Commissaire shall decide the course it should take. Until this is done, I cannot help you. You must help me. That is clear, I believe.'

Another silence. The trouble with being a law-abiding citizen is that you have to abide by the law, and a great bore this is. Quite.

'I suppose there's something in what you say. Please understand this, then. If we do as you ask, it is reluctantly, and under protest. We shall have to make up our minds whether there are grounds for official protest. Certainly we shall lose no time in contacting the consular authorities, in requesting their presence at any official transaction, and in notifying our embassy, which will see that the proper steps are taken.'

Tile number two, with a bang on the helmet but glancing off. He felt angry enough to be sure of one thing: the cops weren't intimidating anybody. He started to write, rather slowly.

'I take note of your protest,' he said indifferently, 'as of your appeal to your rights. They are legitimate. They will be scrupulously respected. The procedure will create delays, probably, in the administrative process.'

The judge, who had been looking out of the window like a man bored by all this, turned his head and shoulders in one piece. A long rectangular face. Skin beginning to droop under blue eyes and a chinny jaw. Short silver hair. Healthy skin with a light tan.

'Mr Er, I put a question to you.' Deep hollow voice, accustomed to governing public debate. 'These notes you take – what evidential value, if any, do they have?' Curt but polite; nothing to object to.

Castang smiled, although it was tile number three.

'This is called a preliminary enquiry. Until ordered by the magistrate, no, the notes are not evidence. They are a documentation of any facts apparent to me that may be relevant to a subsequent legal proceeding.'

'In that case,' quite polite, 'don't waste your time writing anything at all. My name and address will be quite sufficient. You sought to impress my wife, and did so enough to provoke her into talking about consuls. I can't see any need for that, Rosemary; as he remarks it would complicate their bureaucracy further.' The blue eye went back to Castang. 'Five minutes with your superior will be quite enough to settle this.'

'Good,' said Castang with brisk gaiety. 'The names and addresses, if you'll be so kind. And the serial numbers of your passports please. Rather like prisoners of war,' in a lucky afterthought. He felt a naughty pleasure at getting the last word.

5. Richard's inalterable good humour

Castang had a wishful thought that when the Rolls-Royce was finally opened there would be nothing there. The daughter (her name was Patience, which he thought pretty, and she would be pretty too if she gave herself a chance) made a face when he asked to be shown the gruesome object.

'I'm not going through that again.'

'Oh, I'll do it,' said the boy indifferently, as though it were a question of putting the dog out. 'Chuck me the keys.' He had not spoken a word hitherto: even his name, which was Colin, Castang had copied off the passport.

'What's your opinion of all this?' Castang tried, as they walked out to the parking lot. A shrug.

'Seems obvious to me. Anybody wants to get rid of an embarrassment, he tries to hook it on to somebody else. The unlikelier the better; it starts a red herring. What none of us can understand is that you should fall for it. While you sit fussing here the real fellow's on a plane to Brazil or something.' It wasn't worth answering.

He opened the boot and stood indifferent with his hands in his pockets. There was about what one would expect in the way of holiday suitcases and overcoats on hangers. Fitted in – it had been flexible enough at the time – in a knee-elbow attitude was the body of a youngish woman with no clothes on. Colin was studiously staring at the sky and pretending to whistle. That pretended insensitivity was just youthful bravado. The whole family would have agreed upon the tactic to follow. Nothing to do with them, and they didn't intend to get involved.

Mr Thomas was hovering about on the terrace.

'Here's the information you asked for.'

'Thanks; use your phone?'

'Come into my office. Er – no further complications?'

Castang didn't answer, shook his fingers loosely from the wrist in the gesture that says 'Ow – hot!'

Fausta put him through; Richard, a good listener, did not interrupt. When his instructions came they were brief.

'Have the car towed in by the local garage. With them in it. I'll have the Parquet and the police surgeon standing by. Autopsy and lab report. All as usual. Who these people are is irrelevant.'

'You'll interview the Judge?'

'I'm looking forward to it.' No signs of intimidation there, either . . .

An idiotic cortège formed, parody of a real funeral. Ridiculous too to see a Rolls-Royce being towed by a breakdown van, the sort of flappy old lash-up one expects to break down itself at any moment. Humiliated, the English were raging, Patience holding the wheel and straining to suit her name. It was of course regulations: still, it could have made no real difference to let them drive it in. Why antagonize these people? Richard had probably done it on purpose, but he hadn't met them!

It was followed by Colin, by himself in a small sports coupé, with skis on a rack at the back. Castang had been disconcerted, he didn't know why, to find the boy on his own, though nothing was more natural.

'What should I do tagging along with them?' asked Colin, looking surprised. 'When I heard they were going on holiday I thought it a good notion. Get some skiing in.'

'You'd arranged to meet here?'

'I came along for the grub,' said Colin with simplicity. 'Pity about that!' His appetite hadn't been spoilt.

Bringing up the rear was Castang in the tatty police car, both inside and outside leaving much to be desired and the ineradicable fearful smell even with the window wide open.

When they finally drove under the arch into the courtyard of Police Headquarters, a building that had been in Napoleonic times a military hospital and today looked like the grimmest kind of lunatic asylum, there was an impressive reception committee. The Parquet, in force – the Procureur's senior substitute, a judge of instruction and his clerk – its curiosity for once whetted. Corpse in the luggage of His Majesty's Judge – wow. How they would behave in analogous circumstances had not crossed their minds. Richard, raffishly smart in a bow tie and sports jacket, flanked by two individuals Castang had never laid eyes on, introduced them with a flourish.

'Mr Martin Greene – the Vice Consul.' Young, thin, a face well shaped for bursting out laughing, but now plainly unhappy.

'The Consul-General is away, I'm afraid.'

'And this,' Richard delighted with himself, 'is Mr Malinowski. Who is an expert simultaneous translator and officially recognized interpreter.' A little neat man in a black suit, bald and flexible, with a little black beard and confidential neat little face, perfectly adapted for whispering into people's ears. Whee, thought Castang: he has worked fast to set all this up. 'So that everything is going to run very smoothly.'

The magistrates, who didn't speak a word of English, bowed politely to their distinguished colleague and retired into a huddle. The English contingent made for Mr Greene, except for the Judge, who stood fast and surveyed operations like the Duke of Wellington on a battlefield. The boot was opened with solemnity.

'Don't expect me to climb in there, do you?' said the doctor crossly. 'Pull her out.'

'Moment,' said Richard, 'Photo.' The technicians, a hangdog group, were relieved to have something to do. The body came out wooden.

'Rigor,' said the medical gentleman unnecessarily. She was arranged, still knee-elbow, on a plastic sheet prepared. Castang, with an increasing suspicion that he was going to get lumbered with a very tiresome enquiry, told himself he'd better watch. The dry white fingers manipulated things, studied face, finger-nails, vertebrae. Limp black hair kept getting in his way. 'Wearing off. Tcha . . . Tcha . . . Thought so . . .' He straightened up. 'Have to look at her in detail. Meantime, homicide. Strangulation. Not manual, not ligature. Arm.' He demonstrated with a crooked elbow how easy it is to strangle people.

'You can confirm that much now?' asked the Substitute. 'That at least leaves no ambiguities.'

Quite. A ligature can be suicide and even an accident. An elbow on the other hand may not be intended to cause death. It's still a homicide. The medical and legal technicalities can wait.

'Very well,' said Richard, still good-humouredly. 'Monsieur le Juge?' It has to be said formally, for the clerk to make the record.

'Instruction hereby opened. Preliminaries, Richard. And if – uh – the gentleman from the Consulate . . . see to that in due course.' Rush off to hide behind some law books. Interpreters are a commonplace, but consuls – embassies: oh dear. A pre-liminary enquiry will doubtless show that this is a nonsense. Disconcerted by the Duke of Wellington, the Parquet left in a hurry.

'We'll go to my office, shall we?' said Richard. 'I hope it's big enough.' Fausta, who must certainly have been looking out of the window, had whipped the chairs from under the bottoms of several cops. She didn't have enough teacups to offer refresh-ments. Mr Malinowski stood just behind Mum and Dad. Richard created a slightly theatrical pause.

'I think, Fausta, you'd do well to book rooms at the Hotel

d'Albion. One night should suffice, I think, since the doctor is going to do an autopsy right away. Castang, you'll take four statements in verbal-process form.

'When the technical findings.' Richard went on, bland as milk, 'are in accordance, the matter's settled.' As though technical findings, thought Castang, were a bunch of carrots you went out and bought in the supermarket. Bloody lucky if they're in accordance with one another, let alone the statements of witnesses . . . 'The Albion is a comfortable place. The adjective "perfidious" is rather out of date, I should hope,' a remark Mr Malinowski glided adroitly past. 'Mr Greene is welcome to assist at interrogations if it be so wished. Which is all, I think, that need be said, at this juncture.'

6. Summaries of interrogation

Even while telling himself it was ridiculous, Castang had an obscure need to apologize; for the dreary exiguity of all the offices but Richard's, for that frightful corridor outside where people would keep using the fire buckets as ashtrays, for the prevalence of obscure items of clothing, calendars with obscenities scribbled on them, the general air of untidiness, incompetence and slipshod ruffianism, all calculated to give the worst possible impression. It was a pleasant surprise to find the family, one after another, politely unaware of all the tat, even when that imbecile Orthez came crashing in in shirtsleeves, braces and a gunbelt much in evidence, both sweaty and objectionable, saying, 'Oh, Sorry,' in his cretinous fashion. One after the other: courteous, patient, a mite condescending, but nothing to complain of.

He didn't try to talk English: one couldn't work orally in one language and write in another; thank God for Mr Malinow-

26

ski. He was able to take refuge in official phrasing, a language worn smooth, but running on bearings. He took the Judge first.

The Honourable Sir James Clarence Gregory Armitage, looking straight ahead down his nose, was clear, precise; one would say professional. The Rolls-Royce had crossed at approximately midday by hovercraft to the Pas de Calais, had motored along the coast road, in a leisurely fashion; he disliked hurry. It had got as far as Rouen, where discouraged by heavy traffic they had stopped in the centre of the town, at a hotel whose name he could not recall. Rather noisy. The car had been put in the hotel garage. Despite wind and rain, they had made a small promenade in the interests of architecture, Norman food – too heavy for his taste – and Joan of Arc. They had crossed the Seine next day, pottered on through the cheese-and-cider country, avoiding the autoroute, lunched lightly in Caen, gone back to the coast to examine the site of the wartime landings at Arromanches, and ended the day at Bayeux, where the car had lodged in a courtyard, and he hadn't felt like eating much but they'd had a good bottle of wine. Next day they'd had a long and tiresome drive, ending near Tours, a very pleasant country house sort of hotel, mercifully lighter food, delightfully quiet, and they'd slept well. And next day they had continued, and this was the result.

No, there'd been no fixed itinerary. They'd gone wherever inclination led them, in their own rhythm. Nothing had been booked. One found rooms everywhere at this time of year, which was partly why they chose it. No meetings had been planned nor had they encountered any friends: all stops had been fortuitous. It had all been more or less new to him. Parts of the countryside were superficially familiar from previous visits, but the womenfolk liked novelty, and what they called 'exploring'. To the best of his knowledge, nobody in either England or France could be aware of his movements, until such time as the picture postcards the ladies sent began to arrive. He grasped the trend of the questioning, and understood the point must be eliminated, but the hypothesis was preposterous.

In general terms, he supposed the dead woman must have

been inserted at Tours. No stop had been made that morning, but in any case forensic science would surely determine that the young woman could not have been dead for longer.

He had not, himself, been near the car boot that morning or the previous evening: he had contented himself with his overnight bag, which for ease of access was kept inside the car. He had needed his suitcase in Bayeux, and since then hadn't laid eyes upon it. Matters of luggage, in general, he left to his wife, who was most efficient.

His son, who had different notions of enjoying a holiday, had only caught up with them here. He didn't know where the young fellow had been, and wasn't curious.

Lady Rosemary Grace Armitage, née Maitland, felt absolutely sure that the traitorous addition to the luggage must have been made at Tours. While settling the bill – shockingly dear – she had entrusted the car keys to a porter person, for the night before she'd had the small suitcase out. The car, that evening, had stood in a parking lot some distance from the hotel. True, the hotel stood in private grounds, but anybody could walk in, and since the parking lot stood in a spot that was not overseen from the hotel, anything could happen. Indeed some time had elapsed. The man had brought the keys back, but had he locked the car properly? There'd been a delay of about ten minutes; Patience had forgotten something in her room. She'd been preoccupied by checking the bill. Her husband invariably left all such details to herself. What about all the other guests of the hotel whose cars were parked? She couldn't quite remember whether she'd checked the lock of the boot. She rather thought she had. But it was an automatic movement, such as one made, or conceivably didn't – without thinking. Perhaps Patience had. She had driven this morning.

No, they hadn't laid eyes on Colin since leaving the ferry. It had been vaguely agreed to meet here at this restaurant if things worked out that way, today, yes: they'd all wanted to taste the food. Such a pity lunch had been spoiled.

Oh yes, these keys. There are three sets altogether – at least she thought so. Patience and herself, who shared the driving.

Sir James dislikes driving, and the more so on the Continent. The other set was she supposed at home: their chauffeur (also gardener, also handyman) must have them. A Portuguese boy, a charming boy. Certainly, most reliable. He must be at home, catching up on the garden. That at least was what had been arranged. He was certainly not in France – what should he be doing there?

Miss Patience Armitage hadn't much to add. Perfectly true, she did go back to her room this morning, for a personal reason. If he must know, not more than ten minutes; she would have thought five. She'd only had her overnight bag. She hadn't noticed what case her mother had had. She couldn't swear to not having touched the boot lock but all she could say was it was most unlikely: she'd popped her case in the car, and it was raining; she was in a hurry. This midday – at lunch there was something she wanted in the boot – a road map – and she'd opened it – yes, unlocked it – and got such a fright she'd just banged it shut again. Let's see, that morning they'd stopped in a village for petrol. But in broad daylight on the street. She herself had gone into the service station for a sec.: her parents had stayed in the car: no, any interference there would be impossible. Of course the business happened at Tours; anything else was out of the question. Well, surely one could tell, how long a body had been dead? But in any case, though there'd been several stops the day before, anything untoward would have been noticed that evening, when her mother's small case was brought into the hotel. It was there that enquiries must be directed, though they'd all understood that their testimony was to establish this point.

'You know,' the voice was apologetic, 'there's nothing fundamentally improbable or odd about any of this.' Mr Martin Greene had been the perfect bystander, never once interjecting or fidgeting, and never once getting under Castang's feet or skin.

'No,' agreed Castang colourlessly.

'I mean, English people are like that, and what here appears strongly marked eccentricity is there accepted as quite normal.'

'Yes.'

'The boy Colin is a cool card. But he's quite outside the scope of your enquiry, wouldn't you agree? It's the Rolls-Royce that is the key. Somebody found it clever – I hesitate to use the word funny . . .'

'What holidays does a judge have, in England?'

'Do you know, I'm a bit vague: I'd have to look it up. All a bit medieval; use these Latin names for their terms, Trinity and Michaelmas. Spring is Hilary I believe. But it wouldn't be that rigid, because they work outside the terms too, to deal with urgent matters. If he'd been sitting in chambers, as they call it . . .'

'Spare me. I'll see if the boys are ready with the car: otherwise you can ferry them back to the hotel?'

'Oh yes, I've mine here. And I'll sort of reassure them, don't you know? English people tend to have a deep-rooted fear of French law. They'll have seen that neither you nor Commissaire Richard are exactly ogres.'

'Yes. Many thanks. Be in touch in the morning? We'll have found out something by then with any luck. Got to get the judge to issue a commission to interrogate, for Tours.'

'Oh yes; quite.'

'Mr Malinowski, my sincere thanks to you – you'll see the Commissaire's secretary?'

'Certainly. I imagine you'll be needing me tomorrow. 'Evening to you both.'

Ten to six. Not bad at all.

7. Broken-Sticks Conversation

Why any sort of desultory chat is in French called broken-sticks talk is a French enigma, but this was a speciality of Richard's.

He read the sheaf of typescript, all properly made out in official shape and each page initialled as true and accurate by all concerned, including Mr Malinowski, coughed, lit a cigar, corrected five spelling mistakes Castang had overlooked, and said, 'Cool enough, the Colin.' In French it's a fish.

'Colin-maillard,' suggested Castang. Blind-man's buff. 'That Greene – he was no trouble – was plainly bothered lest I treat it as insolence: blandly declaring that you can't remember the hotel's name and not being a commercial traveller you didn't bother keeping the bill. But impudence, yes.'

'A challenge. A queen's-pawn gambit. Do you accept it or not?'

'What's the population of Deauville in the month of March? It's a village. Comes under Caen's district, no?'

'Unless the judge insists on checking, I'd say no,' decided Richard. 'It's a trap. Over the last dozen years there've been maybe four cases of crimes involving English tourists and I need only remind you of Gaston Dominici. Each time the English Press worked up an immense hullabaloo about our disregard for human rights and tried to create a diplomatic incident. If the boy provoked us into anything construable as unreasonable interference they'll have us on toast. As it is we'll get accused of a smear campaign against Rolls-Royce cars.'

'That's exactly the way I see it,' said Castang, relieved.

'This girl Patience – pretty name that – her repeated and prolonged visits to the lavatory ... it's the same thing.'

'Yes. I didn't propose to reopen the great pro-or-anti-bidet controversy.'

'There are a variety of small discrepancies. About what one would expect – in your opinion?'

'The judge says they didn't stop this morning whereas there was a petrol stop.'

'And the girl went to the lavatory ... It's within our district. I'll send Orthez, exactly the right job for him. Was the car really left unattended for any length of time? – simply to get it watertight. And all the people on Thomas's parking lot. If the car was really left unlocked. The gendarmerie are in hot pursuit of the villains who pinched Granny, but if you have a naked corpse to dispose of, in rigor or not, you don't choose the terrace outside Thomas to cart it around. Did they find Granny, by the way?'

'Of course they did. The butcher is now claiming that Granny was damaged in transit.'

'And the Rolls?'

'Nothing unusual there. Locks were certainly not forced. Electromagnetic.'

'Does a single key serve all the locks – including the boot?'

'I haven't the report yet. And this Patience – didn't know what case Mum took last night, where is it – Luynes or Langeais? But a minute later she says "the small case". They had of course separate rooms – what drew her attention to "the small case"?'

'I should say that's no more than the result of their talking it over between themselves. They were stuck for an hour in Thomas's beastly wedding suite, and they must have tried to reconstruct the affair between them. "Did I give you the key, dear?" "Yes, don't you recall you couldn't find the toothpaste?"' Richard nodded.

'If three different accounts didn't present at least four glaring anomalies you'd smell a cooked-up tale from afar.'

'To my mind at least they sounded candid. Not Colin of course, but that is deliberately disingenuous. I only wondered whether it was designed to lead me astray from whatever happened at Tours.'

'Start enquiring,' said Richard dryly, 'into what English tourists picked up whores in Deauville, even in the month of March, and every French visitor to Marks and Spencer will be arrested for shoplifting. These photographs,' picking them up. 'Next to useless for identity purposes, naturally.' Castang didn't even look at them. No photographer, and certainly not a police technician, will succeed in making that swollen and distorted face recognizable. Cops look at bones, but the public looks at features. Cops look at ears, which are not altered by strangulation, but this girl had worn her hair long and straight.

32

'Teeth,' said Castang.

'Of course – once we get her back from the path. lab. Obviously, I've called for all the missing-person files, and frankly, anything there would astonish me, so I gave the job to Orthez!'

'The other guests, at Tours . . .'

'Just recall that you're what, under two hours by autoroute from Paris? All those places are love nests. That's the judge's theory. Something goes wrong in the middle of the night. Fellow hides corpse in handily left-unlocked Rolls-Royce.'

'What utter bullshit. He'd put it in his own car, the one he could make sure nobody would search.'

'Say things like that to judges, they always answer "Overtaken by panic".' Neither of them risked confusing the judge of instruction with the English Judge: the two were given quite a different intonation.

'See tomorrow what Tours says,' concluded Richard. 'Off you go.'

Castang went home. The day had been quite long enough.

8. Verbs are also conjugated in the plural

Castang was attached to his town in a sense profounder than that in which a civil servant is attached to his ministry. He was fond of it. Every police officer hopes of course for promotion: he was a principal officer with a law degree, however painfully acquired; he had 'been to school' and had passed the examination to become commissaire; he had the requisite seniority. Technically thus, he was only waiting for some old schnok to retire, in order to be 'named'. But by law any 'agglomeration' of over five thousand inhabitants must possess a commissaire of police. Good word; there are plenty of terrible backwoods dumps that scarcely deserve to be called towns and he didn't have the slightest wish to become a 'village notable': he wanted to stay in the criminal brigades, and promotion within these is a trickier affair. Not being named was a good sign, perhaps, meaning at least that Richard was not anxious to get rid of him. He was content to stay where he was. He had no real roots in this town; he had none anywhere. But he had grown 'fond of it'.

One disadvantage of getting off from work at the usual hour for the daytime shift to end is the rush hour ... Between five and seven in the evening the city, like all others with a medieval foundation, is blocked by cars, and there is nothing unusual in finding yourself inching across a junction for a quarter of an hour on end. Castang, characteristically, attacked this problem in two ways.

He lived, first, in a bourgeois quarter of wide straight avenues with trees, fairly close to the centre. And whenever he could he took his bicycle, and not that stupid car. The bicycle went at the same speed and was less frustrating: at least one third of the time it went faster. One did not just sit and gaze at the tin behind in front, breathing its nasty exhalations.

There were two main disadvantages. The rent was shatteringly high (though his street faced a canal and was both quiet and unsmelly in consequence. Without hypocrisy, it was just as much for Vera as for himself). And riding a bicycle was a dangerous pursuit. Motorists hate bicycles, and do all they can to destroy them and their riders. Daily Castang was tooted at, cursed at, forced into the gutter; actual physical assault with a large powerful metal club, as dangerous as any gun, was an everyday occurrence. He defended himself, sometimes, by getting off at red lights, walking over to aggressors, saying 'Police Officer! Papers!' in his nastiest tone. This was often efficacious, the motorist being as cowardly as he is bullying; a lot. But it wasted his time and energy, and it didn't make the police any more popular. Vera, who went out seldom and never in rush hours, did not really know how bad it could be. A cop is trained to accept the idea of wounds, of death, with a good deal of nonchalance. He declines the verb daily. He, she, or it dies. You die. I die. He has no enthusiasm about dying from a smashed pelvis and a crushed spleen. Castang was glad to arrive at his home without incident. He had no inclination to think about naked young women in the boot of a Rolls-Royce: his own skin was preoccupation enough.

His house was a typical piece of urban European architecture of the late nineteenth century; tall, narrow, ornate and hideous. But built with a splendid solidity and thus quiet. The high windows were generous with daylight and sunshine, and had wrought-iron balconies for Vera's garden, which was undiminished by living in pots. In this honeycomb lived bourgeois bees, busily gathering financial honey. Castang was not popular in the building: they were all quite sure he would turn out to be a waxmoth. Police in the house! Whatever next? Even if there were burglars he would be a broken reed: the police always were. Everybody knew they didn't give a damn . . .

Castang pushed the door open, wheeled his bicycle through the hall, smelling as always of dried, heated dust and dimly lit by a phony Tiffany lamp with sinister little bits of stained glass, and down the basement steps to the cellars. As in all houses of this sort there were a great many cellars from the front where the central heating lived, through a vaulted passage, sort of Bridge of Sighs with barred openings on each side giving obscure glimpses of bourgeois hidey-holes where the moth ate and the rust corrupted, to the back where the dustbins lived; and piles of old newspapers, broken flowerpots, and Castang's bicycle.

In this subterranean rabbit warren lived an aged, toothless and harmless ogre named Monsieur Auguste, extremely hard of hearing and totally gaga. 'Lived' needs defining; he was supposed to have a house of his own somewhere, and presumably slept there, but all day, and every day, he was to be found here in the basement. He was some vaguely-defined relative of the proprietor, who spoke of him with respect, as being venerable and indeed useful. He acted as a sort of superannuated concierge: not only did he look after the dustbins, but he would tinker with locks and leaking radiators; he had a sort of affinity with the electric cabling, which like him dated from the eighteen-eighties. He had a cubby-hole next to the dustbins, spoken of as Monsieur Auguste's Workshop, full of broken door-handles and window-catches in ornately-figured bronze, keys enough to sink a liner by sheer weight, and the component parts of Victorian lawn-mowers, air-conditioners and weighing-machines. He had stopped dead with the invention of the internal-combustion engine: this was an invention of the devil and he would have no dealings with it. Castang consequently liked him a lot. And he was always affable.

'Why don't you open an antique shop?' Castang would ask, and 'It's this wind,' Monsieur Auguste would reply, satisfyingly. Civilization in Europe is greatly impoverished by the dying-out of the concierge.

In the middle of the Bridge of Sighs, under the arch of cankered brickwork, the bare hundred watt bulb burned glaringly, despite fourteen anguished written notices begging one to put it out. Monsieur Auguste had never got around to putting in a time-switch, that perfectly French invention of a bourgeois race that wastes a thousand francs turning the heating too high (the building was always like an oven) but is immensely proud of an ingenious device for paring cheese.

'Monsieur Auguste,' said Castang, his voice reverberating weirdly in the vaults.

'Monsieur Auguste,' bellowed Castang, deafening himself.

He was certainly in the lavatory, for among other embellishments the basement boasted a lavatory, the Victorians being as determined to relieve their bladder upon every possible occasion as the royal family. The mechanism indeed of the water-closet was exactly calculated to appeal to Monsieur Auguste and he spent many hours there. He always left the door open, and if disturbed would appear, bravely decked in braces and long woolly underthings.

The door was half open: Castang gave it a discreet kick.

It opened. Monsieur Auguste was present, hanging by his braces to the pull-and-let-go. 'Oh, hell,' said Castang. I die,

36

thou diest, the naked girl in the Rolls-Royce dies. We die, you die, they die. Castang felt an intense kinship with Monsieur Auguste. We die.

Castang gripped the tiny body, dry and light as a moth, lifted it, unknotted the braces, bore it out into the light: one of the pathetic economies had been to rely on as much of the passage bulb as filtered through the grimy pane over the door. He made a careful if superficial examination, much as the police-surgeon had done that afternoon, looking at eyes and fingernails, wobbling vertebrae cautiously, trying to feel through swollen tissues. He didn't feel happy at all. One would have to go and see the proprietor. This elderly avaricious widow, who concealed her heart in a bag of rusty nails (one of Auguste's hidey-holes, said Vera), lived on the third floor, directly opposite himself. Discretion, at least, could be assured.

9. Never two without . . .

She had a heart after all, the owner. Tears streamed open and spontaneous, heedless of losing face before a tenant, and that the least considered among them.

'He was my brother,' snuffling wretchedly. 'My only brother, and the last link with the old days.'

Castang was pleased at the ray of light. It did occur to him that gaining face with the landlady would do him no harm.

'You can leave this to me, you know. I'll see that it's handled in a way to minimize trouble and embarrassment.' At last the police was going to justify its existence . . .

'Oh, Monsieur Castang, what a blessing to have you in the house.' True, at this moment a flicker of oh-dear-what-have-I-said crinkled the fine mesh of the face, but the old girl stuck to her guns. 'Can it be kept out of the papers?'

'They do do their best to avoid reporting suicides.' It set her off again.

'Oh, Auguste . . . oh, it's not possible . . .' That was what he thought, but he had to find out.

'Has he been complaining of pain?'

'Auguste was only seventy-two,' indignant. 'Cancer is not in the family, Monsieur Castang; we are a hardy race. My father died of pneumonia at ninety: my mother was eighty-five. Auguste was as healthy as a hornbeam. And,' with unmistakable sincerity, 'a very happy man.' Yes, he thought, a little astonished but convinced: that is true.

'I'll have to bring,' clearing his throat, 'the police services here. They'll be, uh, discreet and quiet; I can promise you that.'

'I suppose you do,' thinking about it. 'I'll come,' resolute. 'Don't ask me to go down to that basement.'

'Leave it to me.'

She stood guard in the hall. Two or three of the tenants, seeing her, showed both curiosity and a wish to complain. She made her voice carry to where he could hear it in the basement.

'We're – we've been faced with a little trouble, which Monsieur Castang is very kindly seeing to for me, and I must beg you not to ask me questions. The safety of the house is not in question. It will all be cleared up tomorrow. Please do not alarm the others.'

It was really a matter for the urban security brigade, and Commissaire Favre, but he hadn't wanted a lot of uniformed cops, or the Police-Secours ambulance. He had rung the duty PJ officer, and Richard, who might have grumbled at being dragged out at supper time, but didn't. He could have sent Lasserre but didn't. It was a sort of loyalty that made him valued by his subordinates.

The PJ technicians were inclined to make jokes about a corpse in Castang's famous bourgeois residence but he shut them up. They took the usual measurements and made the usual photographs without a lot of racket. As he'd asked, they'd brought the Safari station-wagon without markings. Monsieur Auguste, with decency and discretion, was removed to the

Medico-Legal Institute (officialese for the morgue) as soon as Richard had taken a look.

'I'm sorry,' said Castang. 'To my mind it's a palpable fake. It's for you to decide. But look at that bruising: I couldn't help thinking . . . here, Martin, give us some more light.'

Richard took his time, giving Castang an uncomfortable moment.

'Yes,' he said at last. 'Path. would have to confirm that, but I agree. The ligature's been put on to mask manual strangulation. Interesting coincidence. If like this afternoon it had been an elbow, path. would detect it but you – we – wouldn't: moot point perhaps but this is unmistakable at the start. Which may make all the difference. Hm, this is your house. I daresay that tiresome as it may be you'd prefer if I left you to get on with it.'

'Perhaps,' said Castang carefully, 'you wouldn't mind saying a tactful word to the old biddy in the hall. My landlady . . .'

'Yes,' said Richard. 'I see perfectly. Don't worry.' And Castang lurked for a minute, while a soothing mutter took place in the hall. Richard was excellent at handling the bourgeoisie. He always looked so gentlemanly, even when called out in the middle of dinner.

Castang found her standing on the step, looking down the street, saying goodbye to Auguste. The door had been latched open to let the stretcher pass. For a moment he wondered why she looked so familiar, somehow so characteristic. Little light came from the hall; the street-lamps were far enough spaced as to throw no more than a diffused light upon the lined old face, the jaw turned and lifted, looking and listening.

He recognized it then. It was exactly the attitude in which Auguste used to stand, immobile, waiting for the dustbin men, to make sure they worked properly and left no mess on the pavement. In the hall if it were raining; if it were fine – as it was now, a beautiful mild spring evening – on the step outside, in an attitude that belonged to brother as to sister, listening and looking. Just the same: seeing nothing and hearing less. Ghosts, perhaps.

Who on earth would want to kill Auguste? Why? It was not a thing he proposed to think about now. Vera, undoubtedly, would be growing anxious. She was too sensitive not to have noticed the peculiar goings-on, and too discreet to come bundling down into the hall to find out. But he must reassure her, and instantly.

And it wasn't a question for the PJ, not until an official medical examination had been made. The 'path.-lab.' (familiar gloomy tool of police investigations) was in fact a department of the University Hospital, and if there were any controversy about a death they could get a very good opinion: the autopsy would be done by the professor, and not by a few casual students or lab. technicians. Castang would think about Monsieur Auguste tomorrow some time.

There were these tiresome English too, hanging about. Damn.

Time had to pass, and pass in a useful and official fashion doing paper work. Despite private urgent requests to make it as fast as conceivable because of avoiding Diplomatic Incidents, Tours could not be expected to send answers much before lunch: a 'rogatory commission' sent by a judge is a ponderous affair at the best. An autopsy was another thing that couldn't be hurried. Monsieur Auguste would have to cool his heels, acutely literal sense of the phrase, till they were ready for him.

Mr Martin Greene, prepared to be long suffering but not, he hoped, for too long, had been armed with instructions and despatched to the Hôtel d'Albion wondering whether in the circumstances the Judge's family would be at all interested in sight-seeing ... His Britannic Majesty's Consul-General had been routed out of bed with a suggestion that a courtesy call might perhaps not be taken amiss, the Honourable James being a distinguished, uh, visitor, uh, involuntary: what did uh, protocol dictate in the circumstances of an Honourable who finds an unwanted, very, young woman in the car? The Consul-General hadn't been any more pleased by the news than anyone else. The judge of instruction was worrying, working himself up by imagining several hypotheses, all involving bad publicity. The famous Secrecy of an Instruction was a legal fiction, and doubletalk: whatever you called it he detested the phrase.

Castang was about the only person involved who was left relatively tranquil but even this didn't last long: his telephone rang.

'Come up here would you?' said Richard with an odd note in his voice. He was alone, smoking a cigar.

'Castang, I'm sorry to pester you. I thought you'd like to know this. I've this minute had a routine notification from Favre's office of a suicide discovered an hour or so ago on your quayside. And no, there's no error, difficult as that is to believe. They found an identity card on the subject, and I phoned to verify. They say they know him. Reille, Joseph Reille. That mean anything to you?'

'Never heard of him – which means nothing at all except that it's not my house,' shrugged Castang. 'Who's they?'

'Avenue Briand, where else?'

'I suppose I was hoping against hope.' The area commissaire, Marchand, was not a friend; certainly not of his, and not even of Richard's. One would get very little out of telephoning. When the public says it loathes the fuzz, Marchand is what they mean. Remote and ineffectual, high-handed and uninterested. With colleagues, notoriously touchy. Trying to get anything done with or through Marchand wasted one's time and energy on any occasion—but now in particular. Castang could guess . . . He had been high-handed last night, and contented himself with an official note sent by the duty officer. A death in the Aristide Briand district was a suspected homicide and as such being dealt with direct by the PJ. A sort of bureaucratic vengeance would now be exacted.

'I'd better check up on it,' sighing.

'That's what I thought,' said Richard. Only a coincidence, no doubt, but the police have an inbuilt dislike of the word and the thing.

10. Three . . .

Something ought to be done about provincial police stations. Especially those in nineteenth-century urban areas. Some hope! Suppose you got the City Sociologist (i.e., somebody in public relations) and the City Architect (almost certainly a brother-in-law of the mayor's wife) to agree to let a cop design a police station. Some hope! You'd get ground fine in the mincer of municipal finance, just the same.

Some Scandinavian countries (of course) have tried to do something about Welcoming the Public. Inside the Town Hall or the Prefecture or wherever they've built a sort of hotel lobby, with reception girls, and carpet on the floor, and plastic palm trees. Very much like banks. As with banks, the public has had the sense to take one look and decide that it's getting conned just the same.

Even in France there are commissaires of police who try; little things like replacing the grey paint with cream and having a few flowers. Commissaire Marchand is not one of them.

Richard had once made a few 'inexpensive recommendations' about the PJ offices. A service note had come back eventually, saying in municipal prose that any break in the uniformity of the building was deplorable, contrary to Standing Orders, and not to be thought of for an instant.

'Very little would be needed,' wailed Vera. 'Scarcely any money. Nine-tenths of taste is simplicity and suitability.'

'Ho yes,' said Castang naughtily. 'I can just see a directive coming down from the Ministry. You will all henceforward show good taste. That easy. Like forbidding the navy to appear on parade wearing bedroom slippers.'

The Avenue Aristide Briand is not too terrible as arteries go. There are trees, and little shops selling pastry or antiques. It's just that the smallest, ugliest and meanest house in it would have to be the local commissariat. It is on a draughty corner, has barred windows up to the first floor, and is painted dark brownish crimson, like drying blood. Why no bars on the upper stories? So that suspects under interrogation can jump out more easily.

The waiting-room was full of public. You couldn't tell which of them had been 'convoked' (ominous word) and which had come to make a complaint: there were plenty of both, and poor them. Castang (one must always be polite) shook hands with a few people he knew by sight and skipped up the stairs to the 'Sûreté Urbaine' office. Mr Marchand's door was tight shut and he hoped it would remain so. Generally it did.

'You had a suicide this morning as it seems, on the canal.'

'Oh yes, that's where you live, isn't it. You had one in the house, as I hear. They just can't hold out any longer,' guffawing at his own wit. 'Nothing to interest you here. Only a clochard.' A clochard is a vagabond, a down-and-out, though neither of these words is technically accurate.

The clochard! Castang's eyes were opened. Quite often they become attached to a certain spot and 'elect domicile' there. Save in the very coldest weather this one lived on the quayside, a hundred metres from Castang. They knew each other well. In a sense they were almost friends. That was to say, Vera and the clochard were almost friends. But towards one another the two men maintained a dignified and good-natured tolerance.

One had to be tactful, here.

'I'd like to know about it. Seeing as you say it's my neighbourhood.'

'I haven't any dossier. Cut his throat, with a razorblade. Got referred to us as a routine death. Boss saw no need for any action on it. Want the report? – not gone to file yet,' scrabbling in the basket.

Brief and bare, to the point of pathos, though Castang was too used to these things to notice that. Agent Bastian Dominique while on duty on the said date was notified by a municipal employee of Parks and Gardens that a dead body was to be found at the stretch of waste ground corresponding to no. 44

(ancient towing-path). Agent Bastian proceeded to the spot and made the usual observations. Death was quite obvious proceeding from a self-inflicted incision in the carotid artery (right) and resulting in extensive haemorrhage causing decease almost immediately, said decease (blood had congealed and was drying) estimated at two to three hours previous or perhaps around dawn. No sign of disturbance or struggle. Subject one Reille, Joseph, date and place of birth as stated, of no fixed domicile and without ostensible means of support, is known to the reporting agent and in the district as habitually camping in this spot. Subject is a known alcoholic, severely physically and mentally debilitated. Ethylic crisis (alcohol) likeliest motive of death. Was known as of peaceable disposition and avoiding others of his species: quarrel or dispute (violent) unlikely and not borne out by evidence. Conclusion, suicide or conceivable accident in hallucination. Disposal: Police-Secours Ambulance called and body removed. Measurements taken in situ. Statement taken from witness (attached). Further procedure: judged needless subject to usual precautions. Witnessed and signed by the Investigating Agent, Dominique Bastian, Third Arrondissement.

Attached was a half page *procès-verbal* from Souche Thierry, Municipal Gardener, attesting to the exactitude of the above. The observations of the Investigating Agent were to the best of his knowledge and belief accurate and confirmed by his own conclusions.

These things get rubber-stamped, either with an 'Inform and Report' furtherance, or a 'Classify', at the discretion of the supervisory officer. Marchand had given it the latter, and an initial. Why let these things hang about? Closed before even being open. It meant that Castang could do nothing, unless Richard . . . which would be going against the administrative grain: Richard wouldn't. If Castang wanted to do anything at all it would be in his own time.

He looked at his watch. He might be wanted back at the office pretty quick but a quarter of an hour . . . Agent Bastian was still on duty and in uniform, so even a quick one in the pub across the street was out. He was a young chap with an open fresh face, but his antennae quivered defensively.

'No trouble, is there?'

'Not from me. And nothing official. Don't bother. I won't be worrying Monsieur Marchand. I might want to see you at home, which is where?'

'La Mouette,' grudgingly, but Castang was an officer, and if he chose to waste everybody's free time . . .

'Personal interest is all. I live on that street. It may not be anything at all.'

'Look, I'm covered, no matter what.'

'Yes, yes,' irritably. 'I may not even bother.' It would be desirable too to see Monsieur Souche while his memory was warm. It would not have cooled this evening in the pub but it would, certainly, have become embroidered. This afternoon, maybe . . .

It was as well for him that he had not dallied, because the telex was in from Tours.

11. Merde, alors!

'Brief and necessarily most superficial checking confirms account your English witnesses in all save microscopic detail. At least three hotel employees involved in baggage handling. For obvious reasons their involvement unlikely, but all conveniently vague for equally obvious horror of embarrassment. Day and night porters admit to handling keys but claim never to have left desk. Underporter who physically handled case claims not to have seen interior of car boot. Quote stood there and got loaded with a heap of junk unquote. Same boy brought out case next morning but claims to have left it on ground beside car. Asked for explanation says quote I received the impression they were the kind of customers who didn't like the car touched unquote. This is supported by other staff who remarked upon fussy and difficult clients but is unverifiable. No presumption can therefore exist whether car was in fact locked during evening and night total period thirteen hours. Car park some distance from main building and screened by trees. Preliminary conversation gave porter staff impression only larceny involved. Upon learning a death involved and investigation homicide shock shown typically expressed as angry defensiveness but no essential change in statements and claims remained unshaken. Tape taken and sent you. My own opinion that hotel staff involvement in high degree unlikely. Written statements will be taken today. Advise discretion continuance investigation ends. Benoît PJ Tours.'

Richard, Lasserre, Cantoni and Castang were meditating on this.

'I know what the judge is going to say.'

'It's a pure technicality, the death coming to light on our ground. Plainly the whole investigation belongs to Tours.'

'One thing is sure and that's there can't conceivably be grounds for supposing the English involved, so they can't be on our neck.'

'What makes you so sure?'

'This whole business with the keys. They get passed from hand to hand, everybody thinks the other locked the boot, consequence is the boot stayed open all night and anybody could have access.'

'How does your assassin have access to this important piece of knowledge?'

'Well, that's for Tours to worry about. All the other customers of that day. Or tradesmen. Fellow who takes the pigswill.'

'How far away is the village or whatever it is?'

'About three kilometres, and the junction with the Tours main road just further.'

'There you are. Any passer-by, anxious to get rid of a body. He thinks of dumping it in the bushes, finds a car open – better still, creates more confusion. Could have happened anywhere between Paris and where is it – Nantes.'

'Hardly. Time factor. At the earliest the death was late the night before.'

46

'Still plenty of time to dump a body. When did the English move off? – nine?'

'Even the English couldn't put a case in the boot without noticing a body there.'

'Don't be so cretinous; the whole point is that the English never opened the boot. They found the case standing there and chucked it in the car. There was stacks of space.'

'The baggage boy's story is consistent. If he left the case by the side of the car and they only found it at the last minute then it's quite likely they did chuck it in the car.'

'Sounds very thin to me.'

'No, there are people like that, who'll accuse hotel help of anything, even leaving scratches round the lock.'

'Like the fellow says the hotel help is out for obvious reasons. It would all point direct to them since they handled the keys. And they were initially questioned under the impression it was just a larceny.'

'Equally obvious that they'll all swear blind they never touched it. No need for collusion.'

'I know Philippe Benoît, enough that he's done a thorough job. He's also told the hotel management to get all the visitors as well as overnighters on a list. Plus the plumber and the pigswill man. I spoke with him last night.'

'People from all over the country, no doubt. One can see the rogatory commissions stretching away ahead into eternity.'

'Until we get an identification on the dead girl.'

'If those damned stupid English hadn't been too lazy to open the boot in Tours we'd never have been stuck with all this nonsense.'

'Since we are stuck with it, what's the use of complaining?'

'Yes but merde, alors.'

'The absolute priority is to get rid of the English.'

'That's right. Or we'll have the Foreign Office and the House of Lords and the Board of Trade complaining, and, and ...'

'Gold Stick In Waiting.'

'That's right. Absolutely.'

'Very well,' said Richard, 'I'll go see the judge. That'll be all for you three. Did you check that suicide report, Castang, by the way?'

'They sent a cop. Who took a look and shovelled it all rapidly into the dustbin. Went back and wrote a report. Whole thing took about half an hour. The report went up to Marchand, who hadn't stirred off his arse, and it took him about three microseconds to stamp it Classify. So that there's nothing to be done. Unless one got very strong grounds indeed. I'll have a word with the witness who found him.'

'Yes, that's all only what one would expect. No reason to suppose he's not right, alas. It was only the coincidence that was troubling. Fausta, get Path. on the phone will you and ask if the Professor can spare me a moment. If that's plain sailing the judge will sign a release. This one could well turn out troublesome, Castang, so make a pious prayer would you? It's been a week too since we had a bank hold-up.'

'One moment,' said Fausta, 'Mr Martin Greene is on the line.'

'Bothersome of him,' unfussed. 'Tell them all to have lunch and that I'll have word by the time they reach coffee. I'll go round to the Albion myself. Hallo – Professor . . .'

Castang fled, uttering pious prayers all the way down the passage. Get off quick for lunch yourself, idiot. He was half-way home before a horrible thought struck him.

Perhaps that young Bastian got it wrong. Or perhaps I misread. But surely the report said right carotid artery front to back. Because the clochard, and that's a thing I'm quite certain of, was left-handed.

I must have got it wrong. Because alors, merde!

12. Pathology, and parasitology

Richard saw his cops out of the door with relief. There were moments when they were exceedingly irritating. Cantoni was a good cop, talented at gangsters and hold-ups, largely because his mentality was so close to theirs. Quite fearless, decisive, very rapid; and alarmingly insensitive. Lasserre, God forgive us, was also a good cop, even if he had the morals of a herring gull and most of the other characteristics too of that disagreeable beast: hard, greedy, noisy, and vicious. Castang was the brightest of them, as well as sensitive and imaginative enough for two, but unreliable because full of soft spots and apt to go dreamy at the wong moment. Bracketed with the Corsican you had a strong team, but they disliked one another ... As for Lasserre ... They detested each other! Castang did well enough on his own, if he didn't fuck it all up through some idiocy peculiar to himself. 'Yes' he said into the telephone.

'Sorry to have kept you waiting,' a voice so desert-dry and studiedly emotionless that one could not picture the man outside his sterilized environment, though Richard knew that he had six children. 'Since I know you to be in a hurry and I haven't yet dictated the report ... Germane in the immediate, your boy was quite right. Gripped from behind in the crook of an elbow, throttled by forearm pressure. Larynx crushed, the subject asphyxiates. A thing that I dare say will interest you – she was nine weeks pregnant. Sedentary worker, secretarial, played quite a lot of tennis. Her teeth are bad; considerably mended, and standing in need of a lot more. Went around a good deal in bare feet. Let's see; blood group, lungs – she smoked rather heavily. Some alcohol present, in fact rather a lot: she was fairly drunk. A copious meal an hour or two before death. Banal meal: shellfish, steak, deep-fried potatoes, salad, cake. Depending on what time she ate, we can put death around midnight. Sexual intercourse between the meal and the death

49

but we can't type the sperm. I won't say there was a struggle; it's too vague a word. She was handled with some roughness; bruising on the upper arms and in thoracic area. Some of it old. Not consistent with rape: she was a willing partner. Is that enough to be going on with or do you want more?'

'Enough for the moment: I have to see the judge. I've got the rough picture, and many thanks. You're finished though?'

'I've plenty to be getting on with. But with this one – yes, provisionally. The text will be with you as soon as it's typed up.'

'Thanks again,' said Richard.

'I've been trying to get you for the last half hour,' said the judge's voice, crossly. 'That girl of yours –'

'She's been trying to raise you,' lied Richard blandly, not allowing any chat about his Fausta. 'I've a telex from Tours and the telephonic résumé of the pathology findings; I'll try and condense those still further for you, shall I?' One talked about having the patience of Job: had Job been afflicted with judges?

He made a long thing of 'seeing for himself'. What was there to see? Due process of law, and separation of powers, and checks-and-balances (a lot of phrases coming glib off the mouths of politicians) – very well, Richard would admit gladly that the judge of instruction should by all means possess the right to control and supervise police investigations. It sounded well. The public rather liked the idea of an upright and scrupulous magistrate keeping a severe eye upon the crooked sheriff. In reality a piece of bullshit legislation whose origins went back to Fouché – Napoleon had had a healthy distrust of conspiracies while he was away, and distrusted his Minister of Police more than anyone else.

Anyhow, *quis custodiet ipsos custodes*, or who guards the guards?

Most judges, indeed, practised a comfortable negligence, and went to some pains not to know things it would do them no good to know. Get a couple of troublesome, tricky little jobs and one had to fall upon a self-important little snip like this, barely out of law school and imagining himself Godsent to keep an eye on Richard's morals! Pure bad luck that Castang's house, ordinarily a hive of bourgeois parasites, yes, but merely comic, should now be giving the same whippersnapper the fidgets. Castang upset, on top of everybody else . . . There were more kinds of parasite than one. Rhinos had a tick bird balanced on their horn or wherever, and sharks had a remora clamped to their stomach, and he, Richard, had to live permanently with a tapeworm whose length went three times round this room.

Even his thirty seconds of daydream had to be punished: Fausta buzzed him.

'There's that tedious consul on the line again.'

'I'll be right round,' said Richard in his normal, controlled voice. He wasn't going to have any consuls clamped to his stomach!

'No, nothing, thank you,' hoping his stomach wouldn't rumble. None of their business if the Commissaire had had no lunch. 'We know nothing for sure, Mr Greene, save the one that this is a bizarre affair and that as yet we know nothing about it.'

'It's that very adjective, Commissaire, that surely makes it plain my compatriots here must lie wholly outside the scope of uh, your enquiries. Bizarre is the last word that could be said to apply.'

'Well, as it happens, there's no argument about it. You don't mind my cigar? I've had no time, you must realize, to establish anything but that we're not going to clear this up within twenty-four hours. The result of summary questioning made at that hotel shows that in all likelihood the car was left unlocked.'

'I've been saying all along, maintaining that those people weren't trustworthy –' began the lady in a xenophobic fashion.

'Shsh, mother,' said Patience.

'We must therefore assume that the young woman was put into the car some time during the night, and we must widen the scope of our research accordingly. Let me make my point, Mr Greene, please. I have no wish whatsoever to keep the family here and they are free to proceed as they please.' Triumphant looks were exchanged.

'The reservation' went on Richard, picking his words 'is

small. It must be understood that the examining magistrate has the right to hear and if need be to summon witnesses. This judge is extremely conscientious and meticulous, qualities which Sir James here can best appreciate – would you like to translate that, Mr Greene?'

'No need,' said the Judge, politely.

'In the event thus of a piece of evidence coming to light requiring confirmation by themselves, perhaps they'd be good enough to tell me where I can get in touch with them.'

'Well,' said Rosemary, a bit fussed, 'it's just – I mean, I suppose that's reasonable but the thing is, we haven't definite plans. I mean Colin wanted to ski, and we thought of staying on the south coast, if the weather's good. Around Cannes, perhaps. But if it was very cold and windy, we thought we might go up to the mountains too.' Colin's face said plainly that this wasn't going to happen if he could help it.

'Where were you thinking of?' Richard asked him.

'I don't know,' airily, 'Val perhaps, or Tignes – wherever the snow's good. Might even slip across into Switzerland,' deliberately provoking, trailing a coat. As though Richard didn't know that all the judges in France can't bring anybody back from Switzerland!

'No problem. I'd suggest a postcard if they didn't take a month to come. We're talking about the coming fortnight – you'll be here roughly that length of time?'

'More or less,' said Rosemary grudgingly. 'The start we've had doesn't exactly encourage us. Places where this happens!'

'You mustn't let that – or me – spoil your holiday, Madame,' so nicely that you'd have bought his secondhand car without more ado. 'A simple telephone call to the commissariat at Cannes or Nice, that won't be a bother to you. Just to say where you'll be over the next three days, and whenabouts you'll be leaving.' A few scratches on the paintwork, that's nothing.

'All right,' very reluctantly.

'Dealing with yourselves is a great pleasure. One has perfect confidence that having passed your word you will keep it.'

'Our Consulate in Nice . . .' began Mr Greene hesitantly.

'Excellent suggestion,' said Richard, disregarding the fact that this wasn't the suggestion. 'It could be embarrassing to go phoning police stations. A word to Mr Greene's opposite number and they'll take care of it for you.'

'That wasn't quite what I – oh well, I suppose so.'

'Let me wish you a pleasant holiday. Should be lovely there now. Don't give any of this a further thought – that's my work.' He was full of love. 'Judges,' whimsical, 'they do like having things confirmed by irreproachable witnesses.' The periwinkle-blue eyes of Sir James Armitage showed no sign of liking whimsy, but the message had been acknowledged.

'We had the car given a wash,' as a parting shot. 'It's outside now. Looks very nice.' He hastened back.

'Telex please, Fausta,' with his mouth full of a belated sandwich known in America as a BLT, 'PJ Nice and Grenoble – no, on second thoughts make that everyone. Relay for all district commissariats. That damn parasite of a judge, didn't want to let them go. Idiot!'

'Suppose they pass a frontier?'

'They won't – it would look as though they'd something to hide.'

'Do you think they have?'

'It would surprise me. But I hate surprises: see to it that I don't get any. Judge wanted them to surrender their passports – think of it!'

'And if they whip straight back home and hold a Press conference?'

'Then there'll have been a miscarriage of justice, which the judge will blame on me. Wouldn't be the first. But that's better than an international incident. All we have now is a waste of public funds. Less bad. Wouldn't you agree?'

'Lot of work,' said Fausta, sighing.

13. Gardening

Lunchtime had been unhappy because Vera, already much upset by a harmless old man's sad and horrid end, felt herself attacked and crushed by the crawling bulldozer of violence and misery. This time it could not be filtered. Just as the tree outside was 'her tree'; this was 'her clochard'. Castang had known this, but underestimated the depth of her involvement and was taken aback at her refusal to eat. It was one more demonstration of – he felt – his clumsiness and insensitivity. He blamed himself, and blamed her, and her pregnancy, and made a sad mess of things all round.

He didn't want to hang around, but did want to get hold of Monsieur Souche, who had left a pickaxe and several heaps of rubbish and other signs of an intention to come back. He roamed about and fidgeted. What were they doing here anyhow? As usual with people who know nothing about gardening it seemed to him that the fellow was just being destructive. The municipal tidiness complex was offensive: it was only a piece of dishevelled waste ground but why must they go fiddling with it? There he appeared at last, still wiping his mouth with leisurely municipal deliberation. Castang adopted the rôle of bourgeois householder seeking enlightenment.

'Ah,' said Souche. 'I don't know what they're going to do. Maybe make it nice. I wouldn't know,' defensively. 'I got to clean out the rubbish. Brambles and such; them old sallies is no good anyhow. Be a good thing.'

'I suppose so. Get rid of the clochards.'

'Well, the one was here won't bother you no more. Dead, he is. Found him myself.'

'Yes, I heard about that.' Time to unmask the batteries. 'In fact it's what I'm here for. Police officer. A few things I'd like to ask.' Souche was startled.

'Told the cop everything this morning. Lost a lot of time, I did. I got no more time. Left a lot of dirty old junk, I got to clear that. I don't want to talk about it. Poor old sod. Oh well, that's life.'

'I want you to leave that until I've had a chance to examine it.'

'Can't do that. Wagon'll be along, see, to pick up the débris. I don't get that done, boss'll want to know what I've been doing with my time, see. What d'you think then? – that I want to lose a day's pay on account of a clochard and talking to a lot of cops?'

'You prefer to come down to the bureau and make a proper statement? I'm trying to make things easier for you, you silly bugger. I want a quarter of an hour, no more, and we'll do that in the pub. I'll take a look then at the clochard's stuff, and afterwards you can do as you please. Right?'

'You give me a paper, see, to say it's official business and you take the responsibility. I gotta have that to cover me.'

'I'll do that. Come along then.' Monsieur Souche picked up his billhook, and held it as though in self-protection.

'You don't want to leave tools lying about. Lot of thieves around here. And it wouldn't be the cops who would bother,' meaningfully.

They sat at a window table: the pub was nearly deserted in the early afternoon.

'Mine's a marc,' said Monsieur Souche with relish.

'Yours is a beer,' said Castang dryly, buying them. 'I want to clear up one main point, I want you to concentrate carefully. Think back and see it. It's this morning, you have come to take a look and see what work there is, so you're walking along the old towpath, right?'

'Taking trouble not to put my feet in no dogshit,' equally dry. 'It's like you say, I'm taking a look. I see him down there in the little hollow behind the sally bushes. He's always there – keeps the wind off, see? I thought, I got to rout you out of that. He's under that old wagon cover: I thought he was asleep still. Even that early in the morning –' with some expressive pantomime involving the beer bottle. 'They're all the same. He's kind of curled up. Then I see this big lot of blood. All soaked into his beard and everything. Razor-blade – what did he want with a razor-blade?' as an afterthought.

'Good; now where are you standing? – by his head or his feet? Which angle are you viewing him from?'

'Ah. First the one and then the other. I'm circling round him, see?'

'Where can you see best from?' patiently.

'Bit of a slope there. Then there's this scrubby birch – that's got to come out, too. I remember holding on to that. Gives you a turn, no matter what. That old scarf of his is all soaked. I'm by his head.'

'So your right is his right. Which side has he cut?' demonstrating ghoulishly with a cigarette held in his right hand. 'Right? Or left.'

'Left,' unhesitatingly.

'You sure?'

'Sure I'm sure. Aren't I standing there? Nasty sight.'

'That cop's report says right-handed.'

'That's right. I mean exact. Right-handed but he cut his left side.'

Castang started again, still patient.

'You're in a tangle. Think again. It happens I knew this old boy. I gave him a cigarette now and again. That's how I know he was left-handed.'

'You're getting me in a muddle,' scratching. 'He cut on the left side, all right.'

'That's easily checked. He's in the morgue – I've only to look. What I won't see there is which hand he used. You say right. The cop wrote down right. Maybe you're both mistaken. Why? Think.'

'No, I'm not,' triumphantly. 'His left hand, he was holding the bottle, that's why.'

'Holding the bottle,' sceptically. 'You don't cut your throat holding on to a bottle.'

'I don't see why not. That's the one thing they never let go of. Had it by the neck, holding it fast.'

56

'In his sleep?'

'What I reckon, he woke up. Had a sup, or maybe it was already empty. Was empty when I saw. He was cold, or he was ill, or something had gone pretty wrong, and he don't want to go on, don't want to see another day. So he finds this blade, and he thinks about it a bit, and – queek . . .' I'll have to look, thought Castang; see if there are hesitation marks.

'Where is this bottle? It'll have his prints on it.'

'It's gone,' said Monsieur Souche. 'I threw it in the canal.'

'Why?'

'I don't know. You find a fellow like that, even if it's only a clochard, you do things instinctive like. I suppose I thought well, it's no good to him any more. What the hell about the bottle, I tell you, I see him, he's the blade in his right hand.'

'You'll go to bat on that, will you?'

'Look, I didn't touch him, not then. I went straight and called the cop. I didn't have to mess around with him to see he was dead. Ask the cop. He was holding the bottle.'

'Were his fingers stiff? Tight on the bottle? Clenched?'

'No, just holding it loose, like.'

'We'll go and have a look at the scene.' Mellowed by a beer, Mr Souche was not too unhappy at being the principal witness.

'You think somebody killed him?'

'Who'd want to kill a poor old drunk?'

'That's what I'd think.' But if the cops wanted to amuse themselves . . .

They stood together, studying the nest of old coats, unpleasantly congealed by a sticky dark mess.

'Clean it all up,' said Mr Souche self-pityingly. 'They never worry who had to do it nor how shitty it might be. Clean it up, they say. It's always me.'

'I know just what you mean,' said Castang. The clochard's house – tent, blanket, cellar and attic – was an old truck tarpaulin, pierced and ripped as though by Sioux arrows, part burned, patched with anything and everything from roofing felt to plastic groundsheeting. The stink was powerful. 'Take a pitchfork to it,' said Castang disgustedly.

On his way back to work he made a détour at the Medico-Legal Institute. It is no longer sinister. It is pedantic, academic, humourless. Jokes about body-snatchers or grave-robbers are out, but out. A faint tinge of gallows humour – strictly involuntary – does still hang about the place.

'Woman found in a car? – means nothing to me. How should I know? What do I care? We're short-staffed, you know. Louise, you know anything about a woman found in a car?'

'He means one seven four. She's not ready yet.'

'I understood that the professor told Monsieur Richard –'

'Easy for him to say. That report's a mile long and it's not typed up yet. Anyway it's incomplete. She's gone over to Stomatology.'

'Who?'

'The Dental Institute,' irritably. 'Something about her teeth. I'll send it over when it's ready. Madame Groult's had surgery on her varicose veins and isn't allowed back for another six weeks: we're very short-st –'

'Yes, I've heard. I'd like to look at the clochard while I'm here.'

'The what? Name for heaven's sake.'

'I can't remember,' said Castang. 'At a guess, one seven six.'

'Oh. Yes. I remember now. Three in one day, that's a bit thick, Mr Castang. Easy for the PJ. Every time they don't know what to do they put a tag on blithely saying 'Do an autopsy' as though it were a couple of slides with blood smeared on, give it to some student saying here, you, do a haemoglobin count.'

It was Monsieur Souche all over again, saying 'All the shitty work is left to me'.

'Nobody's asked for an autopsy as far as I know. Want to have a look at him, that's all.'

'Well, why didn't you say so? Show him, Jean-Paul, and for heaven's sake get the mop at work in here. Policemen in and out; place is like a public lavatory.'

The cut was on the left side, at an angle that could be left- or right-handed. It was small and neat, hardly more than a nick in the artery. One seven six had had a shower, or whatever measures of basic hygiene that terrifying virago insisted upon for all her guests. The blood and the beard had been cleaned up enough to show clearly: no hesitation marks.

Under the Reign of Terror it had been just the same, thought Castang. Citizen Sanson the executioner was always complaining of the shortage of reliable staff. He wrote a dignified bureaucratic letter to the Committee of Public Safety, saying that unless he got a substantial rise in expense money he wouldn't be able to cope with the work load . . .

14. Get the house tidy first

'I hope you had a good dinner,' said Richard.

'I've been gardening. You know, municipal green spaces or the morgue, there's no difference at all. Don't leave dead bodies cluttering up the place, and get that mop that's standing idle over there.'

Richard didn't mind jokes as a rule, but was vexed about lunch being so late.

'Never mind about the garden: let's get the house tidy first. I've got rid of the English and a pest they were. You can concentrate now upon this woman: did you think of picking up the report from path.?'

'It's not ready yet. They're short-staffed and she had to go to the dentist's, and Madame Something's got varicose veins.'

'Ah. I do see; they're always like that. Very well, what about this other, if I can give the judge some preliminary stuff it'll keep him quiet for a bit.'

'He won't like it much. Only a clochard. Just a smelly old drunk. I think it's homicide on the evidence. Say the evidence is inconclusive, or say Castang's over-imaginative, which he'll say both very likely, and I still think two phony suicides within a few hours inside a hundred square metres is a bit much.'

'Your syntax is muddled and your thought cloudy. I get the drift. Let's have the evidence first.'

'A left-handed person holding a bottle in his left hand doesn't cut his neck arteries with his right. The witness, that's this gardener, is resolute. I've notes. I type them up, get him to sign them. Go then to the cop who made the report, see if I get a confirmation. That'll be the best we can do, since we've no photos.'

'Make it a bit stronger for me,' said Richard, as Castang had been pretty sure he would.

'Medical evidence; I don't mean an autopsy because Louise would do her nut and what would it prove? Assume the suicide hypothesis. He's drunk, or cold, or in pain, or all three, and he decided to make an end of it. Do you see him – be it right- or left-handed – able to do it with just one little incision in just the right place? With no wavering, no hesitation marks whatever? Does one ever see a razor-blade suicide, be it throat, wrist or anywhere, without?'

'Quite a fair point,' admitted Richard. 'Better than the bottle. He could have clutched the bottle screwing himself up. Was it empty? – doesn't matter. Drunks of that sort have sudden moments of lucidity and decision. Which don't last. Still not strong enough.'

'Then if we turn it round and look at the homicide hypothesis. Just as a possibility. No more. Say that you've got an old man quiet, by talking to him, distracting his attention, anything. You're strong, you strangle him and lift him up to attach him to the cistern thing with his belt and braces, producing a plausible suicide scenario. Quick, neat, silent, and convincing. Suppose someone else but me had found old Auguste? The point I'm trying to get my finger on is the similarity of method. Put that with the close connection in place and time, and even a judge wouldn't swallow it.'

'A judge,' said Richard, 'perhaps especially this judge, wants something tighter to tie a loose parcel together. Place and time, yes, it's all very well, but an old bourgeois boy who's a bit gaga, an old drunk out on the towing path – poles apart. What's wanted is a causal connection, and what link can there possibly be? That the one even knew the other existed is already a large surmise. You find a suicide which – I agree – is a phony. We wait for the path. report to have a hypothesis supported by medical evidence, but we're already working on a homicide theory. You find another suicide in the neighbourhood, and your mind jumps instantly to the notion that it's a second phony. It's my job not to let your imagination get the better of you. If I say the hell with Louise, and ask for a path. report on a drunk, and they find a painful cancer, and arthritis or something in your other old boy – where are you then?'

Castang was trying; thinking of Auguste alive, blinking in the sun on his doorstep, waiting for the garbage men. Suddenly he felt sure he had it.

'Dustbins,' he said.

The eyebrows went up in dislike of oracular utterances.

'You live in a modern building,' said Castang. 'You put your garbage down the chute, and never give it a second thought. I live in an old-fashioned house. Some of the bourgeois go brazenly down in the lift with plastic bags: others creep furtively down the service stairs with squalid cardboard boxes.'

'Make your point,' unimpressed by rhetoric.

'The bins are always full because people will put stupid things in them, and there are endless squabbles or would be if Auguste hadn't gone to great pains. Newspapers left separately tied with string – you know. He'd put them out on the pavement and watch over them lovingly like baby chickies. The bourgeois are much more frugal than working people, never throw anything away and least of all Auguste, who skimmed the cream off. But there'd still be pickings for a clochard.'

'It might perfectly well be so,' said Richard dampingly, 'but you get no further. Nineteenth-century novel; the Romance of the rag-and-bone man. Auguste found a hoard of gold coins in the dustbin. Your clochard pinched it, hung Auguste on the pull-and-let-go to conceal his crime, was then seized by remorse and cut himself. Scenario worthy of Victor Hugo – I'm quoting the judge. No, continue quietly with your gardening and anything you turn up that creates a definite link between the two would tip the balance, and Mossieu Marchand can have his head washed. Meanwhile synthesize all you can get in the path. report into an identikit that we can farm out; hope that Tours will turn her up, yes; but be well prepared for trouble. These circumstances are highly ridiculous. Ask yourself one question: who, suddenly lumbered with a dead woman, goes careering round the Loire countryside looking for a wastepaper basket until he so handily finds a Rolls-Royce full of these Lord Mayor's Banquet figures? Falls very pat and convenient, doesn't it? Think about it. Send me Orthez in here – no, on second thoughts send Davignon; he's a bit brighter.' Richard shook a schoolmistressy finger as he opened the door. 'Have your housekeeping nice and tidy. You might have to pack your little bag. Nantes, say, or Saint Nazaire.'

15. Letters from Auguste

He worked with virtuous assiduity at the housekeeping, including things that always got put off. Like taking a statement from someone in the local jail, a tedious business. Fellow's been there for three months, and will be there another three, while his instruction proceeds in leisurely fashion. One of those where twenty other similar cases will be taken into consideration at the trial, and the judge has asked for supplementary information. The authorship of this particular one ('nocturnal burglary with effraction or escalade') is dubious, but one will make an effort to pin it on this chap who's in custody anyhow: tidier that way. The police are dilatory about such things: not very fair really, but what they tend to think is that the fellow's there in jug; i.e., he's there when you want him and you don't have to run around the neighbourhood.

Before closing time he still found time to wind a 'deposition' form into the typewriter with its sheaf of carbons, reduce Mr Souche's bucolic ruminations into officialese, and prepare it for signature. Thus he was only ten minutes late getting off. Belt off home, and by the greatest good fortune catch Mr Souche putting his tools away, and get him to sign the thing, with many assurances that it would not prove later on to be a source of vexation.

Castang looked at his own house with longing, but on a nice sunny evening like this – it really did look as though spring was truly here – with everybody in a good mood he did want to get both house and garden tidy . . .

He ran Agent of Police Bastian to earth at home, a little flat that was bright with new wallpaper, and a Madame Bastian, a typist in the town hall, who kindly offered him a cup of coffee. She was rather taken back, the girl, coming in with it to find Castang stretched out on her living room floor pretending to be a dead clochard. Excuses were made with much cheerful laughter. It was the result that counted. No question about it; the gardener's tale was perfectly accurate.

All in all it wasn't more than an hour of strictly unpaid overtime . . . Castang felt quite content. It wasn't until he got all the way to his landing, with his hand actually outstretched to open his apartment door, that the famous last-minute snag overtook him.

Undoubtedly the old bag had been hovering just inside her own doorway, ears astretch to catch his fairy footstep. She always did, before buttonholing him all honey, with some vile tale about the lift breaking down or the roof needing mending. He suddenly felt very tired. Hadn't the day been long enough?

'Won't it do in the morning, Madame? I'm very late as it is.' She was excited, eyes shiny, skinny claw outstretched, ancient-mariner as all hell, portentous and enigmatic beyond even her usual level.

'If you'd just step in a moment – it's confidential.'

Feeling like a rabbit – and she did look much like a stoat – he allowed himself to be drawn nerveless into her domain, where he had only once set foot, the day he signed the lease: her famous 'business-room'.

She really did look odd. Sly; he would have said sexy if it hadn't been so uh, so . . .

'Monsieur Castang, I have made a very strange discovery. My poor Auguste – his funeral must be delayed by this atrocious autopsy.' God, yes, and he'd be expected to appear. He started to cast about already for a good excuse. Must tell Vera to get flowers . . .

'I went to his house, of course, to get things tidy' – ludicrous this echo of his own activities and Richard's idiotic phrase – 'and of course to see to his papers, uh, insurance and so forth.' How gloomy and depressing this place was, and what a contrast to the bright tiny Bastian living room, where everything was vulgar and in execrable taste, but hell, alive. 'And in Auguste's desk, hidden away most carefully, I found these. And they seem to be addressed to you. I haven't read them, of course.' Not much you haven't. 'Just enough to establish that they actually were – well, I had some scruple, since he didn't actually send them, and there is some doubt as to whether it is proper, well, I must admit I was torn between a very natural desire that this house should not be the scene of further scandals, and, well, of course you realize as I do that we must fulfil our civic duties –' Aware suddenly of gabbling, and that anything she said would be too much, she snatched up a thin pile of letter paper, neatly squared off and paper-clipped by her fair hand, and thrust it at him wordlessly. Mesmerised, he took it.

'I'll say no more about it,' she went on in a great hurry. 'You'll know what to do, but I beg you again, Monsieur Castang, I request most urgently that I can count upon your absolute discretion.' Yes, you were much tempted; I do see perfectly. You'd have vastly preferred burning or at least burying – I wonder what they are. Odd! and odd too the strange notions of integrity people have. There are people whose dishonesty runs into millions, who would be most uneasy at travelling three stops by tram without a ticket.

Some strong medicine had been at work to make her give him these. She was still looking sly and sexy. He'd better beat it!

'I'll make a point of reading whatever it is at once, and thinking it over most carefully, and I'll let you know, of course. Rest assured, Madame. You won't think me rude now if I . . .' sidling firmly towards the door.

What the hell? Auguste's secret confession of his double life?

'Supper's ready,' said Vera, 'and I'm sorry for being a tiresome idiot this morning . . . just shows how old-maidish and selfish one can get. The slightest sign of disturbance of one's comfortable little routines . . . Whereas you never have any; little patterns of comfort, I mean. I hope you didn't have too horrid a day. I don't want this to get dried out . . . oh no! No more paper work.'

'Certainly not,' said Castang, resolutely turning it face downward. 'That smells good,' with an enthusiasm sounding slightly forced even to him.

'It smells good,' said Vera bleakly, 'simply because there's a bit of grated cheese on the top which is now under the grill.

'It's only eggs à la tripe. And standby endive salad because lettuces are still so dear. It's just a meal, and it has no importance. It's kind of you to be polite and utter a word of appreciation for the housewife who has taken pains over the stupid grub – no, sorry, that sounds catty. But I don't want to turn into Madame Maigret, who is now exactly forty-five years out of date. I'm here to share your labour and sorrows, if that is permissible.'

'Yes, it is. The timing is right. There's something funny going on in this house and I don't know what. Richard made a fool of me today by inventing a ridiculous tale about a treasure buried in the dustbin. All I can say is there's something there.'

Tripewise eggs are cheap and filling. You make a bit of cream sauce with a lot of sliced onions stewed in the milk. You put sliced hard-boiled eggs in a fireproof dish, pour the sauce over, and add the grated cheese. Castang had a beer; Vera, still a bit disgustedly, water. The dish was messy where her irritability had splashed sauce on the edge, which had then got baked on. Castang finished the salad with a peanut butter sandwich. His knife, scraping the almost empty pot out, made a prolonged querulous noise in the silence that would get on anybody's nerves. Vera got up (getting up and sitting down were still awkward processes) and came back with a new pot of peanut butter and a second bottle of beer.

'Don't be silly,' she said sympathetically.

'Washing-up,' he said in a wooden voice.

'I'll do it in the morning; let that filthy dish soak. What are the papers?'

'They'll look fine going in the file with peanut butter all over them. Anny gave them me. From the expression on her face they're something weird. She says she found them in Auguste's desk. You read them,' pushing his plate away, lighting a cigarette, uncapping the second beer bottle with voluptuous slowness. Vera read the sheets one by one, turning them over as she laid them down so that they would stay in order. Castang smoked his cigarette and stared at the lampshade, which was dusty. Nobody would call her a lazy housewife. She had got remarkably mobile again, but stepladders were beyond her.

'Don't ostentatiously not read them,' she said suddenly. He grinned and picked them up. Worth waiting for. Old Auguste, who had never been a human being, and was now abruptly alive, insistent . . .

Ordinary letter paper torn off a pad; pale blue, good quality. At the extreme edges, bleached. How long had it been since Auguste wrote a letter? Hand written, with a pen dipped in an ink bottle! The square gothic writing of the generation that had gone to school before 1914, with its ornately looped and intricate capitals. Carefully composed name and address; on the other side the addressee.

Monsieur L'Inspecteur Castang, Service Régionale de Police Judiciaire.

One formal line of writing.

Monsieur,
    I feel it my duty to bring to your notice
and that was all. He frowned and picked up the next.
Monsieur,
    The material proof exists and I have seen it
Not several letters, but several drafts of one and the same. The
next was longer.
    I must tell you that I have the certainty of a crime having been
    committed, and I have it on my conscience that
One was anonymous, neither headed, addressed, nor dated.
    If you take the trouble to investigate this denunciation I can
    assure you that your time will not be wasted
It broke off abruptly like the others.
Monsieur,
    No honourable citizen can stand by and see society set at naught
    by the
One only had reached beyond the opening paragraph.
    A crime has been committed and the author enjoys complete
    impunity. This state of affairs no honest man can stand by to watch
    without attempting redress, but the action can only be instigated by
    the constituted authority.
    If you will engage to respect my anonymity I can indicate to you
    the manner in which proof is to be found and I ask no reward but
    to see justice done.

Vera had finished and was stacking the plates in the sink.
Castang flipped through the rest – they told him nothing further
– and counted them. Eleven. The earliest dated nine days ago.
Twice there were two with the same date, and once three. In all
the writing was neat and regular. There was no scratching out,
and no spelling mistakes, faults in punctuation, or bad grammar.
    'Well?' he said with rather an act of being indifferent.
Vera, too; she was studying the faded and shabby curtains,
very cool, calm and collected. Suddenly she started to grin.
    'You were absolutely right. There's been a crime.'
    'There've been several.'
    'And Richard didn't want to know, and went poopoo, and
now he can jolly well eat his waistcoat.'
    'No, you're misjudging him, reading it slightly wrong. He

knows there was a crime. What he doesn't like, nor the judge, nor me, is things one can't prove. What crime? Where, how, why? We know nothing.'

'On the contrary, we – you – now know a great deal.'

'Good. What? Take your time, schematize. I don't say it just to make a pretence of encouraging you. You'll see twice what I can, and I'm not faking in the least.'

'All right. Auguste was badly frightened, wanted to take you into his confidence, didn't know how to approach you, chose this method, found even that too difficult for him. He was an old man and shaky, and he did his best. He must have had the imprudence to confide in somebody. Because he got killed.'

'Confided in the criminal, you mean? Blackmail?'

'Certainly not; that would be right out of character. Perhaps the other way round; somebody confided in him. X. The clochard? Isn't blackmail more likely from that source?'

'A great deal more likely and a great deal more in character, but don't hypothesize. Stick to what you know.'

'He had knowledge, let's say accidental knowledge, of a crime. He screwed himself up, but each time he tried to write it down it seemed wrong: that you wouldn't take it seriously, or that he would be brought into the limelight. He would have ended by speaking to you, but he'd got so into the habit of effacement and was so used to being treated as furniture: he lived in an ever-narrowing compass. His own sister pretended he was gaga, and he was ashamed of being deaf. So he acted gaga and no longer knew how to break the habit.'

'Why did he keep all the different drafts?'

'Because there was a good phrase in each, and eventually by reading them he hoped he would finish by expressing it the way he wanted.'

'Or maybe because he just hated to throw things away. A pity that in all the efforts he never succeeds in coming to the point. A proof exists and he has seen it. Something material, rather than something merely heard or seen.'

'You mean he was killed to get it back, rather than just to stop his talking.'

'One doesn't get very far with that kind of question. People who kill, or are ready to kill, don't necessarily follow a logic that is yours or mine. The person took a biggish risk, coming into the house.' Unless, thought Castang, it was a person whose presence in the house would cause no comment. He didn't say it; that would only frighten her.

16. The wayang dollies

'Meanderings,' said Richard, 'of gaga old gentlemen . . . Proof that they have no value – if one needed any – is that in eleven tries he never once succeeds in giving a single relevant fact.' But Richard was wrong and the judge showed an unexpected keenness.

'They do have value. The death of this old man could have been avoided, a gratuitous piece of violence. An obvious plausible explanation would have been that he surprised some juvenile bandit roaming about trying doors, and was choked to stop him sounding the alarm.'

Richard said nothing. Since when did juvenile bandits go to the trouble of masking their crimes as suicide? But if the man wanted to listen to himself talking . . .

'As I see it,' the judge went on weightily, 'this vagabond was a witness to the assassin's leaving or entering the house. All this jiggery-pokery of Castang's about which hand you use to cut your throat doesn't impress me. The empty bottle, on the other hand . . . the autopsy report will show what alcohol level there was in the blood. I suspect he was in no condition to sharpen a pencil, let alone cut anybody's throat. Where is this autopsy report, anyhow?' testily.

'The woman who types them is out of circulation – varicose veins,' resisting the temptation to make a pun. The judge held his hands up to heaven.

'And complaints are made about the law's delays! The

tribunal judges a case, and thirteen weeks later the clerical branch gets around to typing it up!'

The police judiciaire spent three-quarters of its time typing, but any remark of this sort would be, plainly, otiose.

'We'd better have a search. This came to light in the house if I follow this garbled tale: there may be other interesting discoveries.'

'If the phrase "exists and I have seen it" means anything at all it means he had no physical proof in his possession. Gaga but not that gaga: the old boy took pains with his phrasing. He found it difficult because he wanted to mean exactly what he said. The same trouble exists with all written reports. Jargon phrases are used because they have a precise legal meaning, irrespective of whether they make any sense.'

'Yes yes,' brushing it aside. 'I still think a search . . . that old woman had plainly rummaged pretty thoroughly, but she didn't know what to look for.'

'Neither do we. What proof, and also proof of what? I might suggest a neighbourhood enquiry.'

'Mm,' said the judge. 'I don't greatly care for them, as you know. They absorb an immense amount of energy, bring a multitude of irrelevant trivialities to light, and rarely anything of value. Still, I see your point. Castang's the man. He lives there; he can go about it discreetly.'

'His living there is one good reason why he'll be very unwilling to do it. I'm anxious too to keep him on this business of the English car. I agree about the discretion. I talked to the old woman, and of course she's exceedingly anxious to hush it all up. Some point in that. If our man is connected with the neighbourhood, as the circumstances seem to suggest, we don't want to alert him to anything untoward while we still know nothing. Time enough for a calculated indiscretion to winkle him out when we know he's there. I'll see who I can find.'

Mr Castang was not typing, for once, but sitting at his desk pulling at a lengthened lip over the autopsy reports, which had just landed there with a flump. Pathology, with a zeal he would in other circumstances have found excessive, having sent three together. They had even done the clochard . . . but he realized that this was not so much a desire to be helpful as a handy clinical exercise for the students. The professor had simply picked a classic demonstration, lying so to speak to hand, of the various syndromes observable: malnutrition, cirrhosis of the liver, blahblahblah, down to ingrowing toenails more or less. A whole group of students had been on the job, which accounted for the startling speed. All this stuff about the pancreas told him much, much more than he wanted to know about enzymes.

He found though one solid fact: police bread and butter. Let's see, how many milligrams form the permissible alcohol level when you breathe in a paper bag? Hm, the tolerances varied widely and you got some butcher driving with a blood stream that would knock anybody else flat on their back, but this . . . all one could say was that if the poor old sod had cut his own arteries then he'd been doing the rumba in the same breath. He turned back to the bit about the wound. 'Incision under 2 cm. in length but almost 9 mm. in depth' – a remarkably accurate job!

Auguste on the other hand . . . the initials on the report were those of a staff pathologist congenitally lacking in humour, and what does he go and write? 'Taking into account all the infirmities listed it is difficult to find anything that would have stopped him living to a hundred.'

The quality of the report on the woman-in-the-car was altogether different as was to be expected since the professor did it. Who else would have noticed that she was used to going about barefoot? It cheered Castang up. Admitted, he had known he was working for the police, so there was far less of measurements and figures, and much more external detail. She began to come on the screen!

Not yet a person, but a shadow cast. He found himself remembering, without knowing why, something seen on television: yes, the Javanese shadow play. The dolls used are extremely stylized. Fragile strips of bamboo joined with scraps of paper or silk, so that the shadow cast is a scrawl, abstract, almost haphazard. Yet more lifelike than a marionette made with careful proportions and pains taken over detail. The wayang dollies depended as did the marionette upon the skill and suppleness of the manipulator's fingers, but these scrawled shadows were more sinister and spellbinding. One could not follow the story, told in Javanese or whatever it was called, but the squeaky monotone was oddly like the professor's bleak, unemphatic voice.

'Heavy, lowslung pelvis: legs short, not quite straight, and heavily fleshed. Abundant growth of coarse body hair. She was not all that clean, and while the usual cosmetics were in lavish use a bit of soap and water would not have come amiss.'

The last paragraph, even more.

'Though the facial swelling and distortion and especially the eyes remove all meaning from the phrase, she was an extremely pretty girl. The clumsy morphology, the coarseness of skin and hair do not contradict the impression of abundant vitality but contribute little. No addition of physiological detail conveys the remarkable attraction she undoubtedly possessed. At the risk of being accused of a contradiction in terms there was a freshness upon her, a glow. Neither the absence of anima nor the brutal suppression of that anima can obliterate the traces of this startling fact.'

Only Professor Deutz reasoned like this. Far from him to be mischievous or provocative, or make use of paradox to heighten his argument. Castang felt the seduction that an exceptional intelligence holds for a good intelligence. The man was not searching for effect; he never did. If he said things like this, it was because he had seen them. This is the use of a real expert, to enlarge and intensify our field of vision. You or I walk through a picture gallery, noting as we pass 'Old woman, by Rembrandt', 'Fat woman, by Rubens'. But do so in the company of the real connoisseur, and it will all be quite different!

If Castang had been there with him, able to put the lighting, the sights, the smells, the techniques aside as irrelevant, he could have been shown; he could have seen.

Even with only the dry and uninflected words of a written report he could get some distance.

He had had the shadows of two wayang dollies on his screen, at first flickering smudges, becoming gradually sharper, more distinct. One an assassin, sly and quick, of efficient brutality in removing obstacles blocking his paths to pleasure. The other a victim, a girl with long black hair and bold, crude features, who liked to dance in her bare feet, supple and athletic, with unusually good timing and co-ordination. Yet behind the screen were only dolls, of wood and paper and glue.

Deutz, in the dead and frozen tissues quick no longer, had seen the quick flash of live blood. Turn back the pages of the report; make an effort.

'Wrists and ankles, fine-boned. The hands and feet, of perfect proportion and drawing.' And however blurred the features – 'Ears, of rare beauty. Lips, magnificently modelled.' And the body itself . . . 'Thoracic cavity, large and well-developed. Abdomen sculptural, strongly muscled.' And the rare sardonic touch Deutz permitted himself. 'Breasts: splendid.' Reading backwards, Castang got back to the original superficial observations. 'Race, half-breed (Eurasian) or quadroon: blood from Indochina or Indonesia but I am no ethnographer. Latin skull.' And Castang, taking a look under admittedly poor conditions, had wondered vaguely whether there was something Slav there: him with a Slav wife!

Paper-clipped on was the dentist's report, all in jargon of a stomatological turgidity! Castang ploughed bravely through.

Translating, her teeth had not been good; decalcification, an impacted wisdom tooth, something a bit prognathous. Toolooroo, where was the meat in this? Why had Deutz wanted an extra report? Good, she'd had a lot of work done on her teeth. Normal, no? – important to a girl and especially to this one. Her mouth was too large for her jaw: yes, he could grasp but . . . ho. In the last line came a punch.

'Most if not all this dental work is of a quality I can only call cheap. Some of the decisions taken are ill-judged, to say the least, and the methods questionable. The style of the work is not European, nor, I should say, American. If asked to offer an opinion I should hazard its origin as being English.'

Was she English? And if so . . . what would Richard say to this?

Like Castang, Richard said 'Ho' and read the paragraph again.

'If she was English . . .' hazarded Castang. Richard felt his jaw all over carefully with his hand, like the 'before' man in a shaving-soap advertisement; dissatisfied with existing results. Fail to use Gloop and you'll never be promoted.

'You know? – you're an infernal nuisance.'

17. A trip to the seaside

'This taste of yours for coincidences is downright vicious,' but the word 'vicieux' is a trap and means more 'perverted'. 'First your infernal clochard and now this!' Poor old Castang a pervert.

'Not my fault,' he said defensively, 'if somebody stuffs English corpses into somebody's Rolls-Royce.'

'You expect me to go trotting to the judge and tell him we've discovered the naked-girl-in-the-car had her teeth done in England, so to all intents and purposes she's English. And he asks,' ferociously, 'what intents and what purposes? And what am I to say? Eh?'

'I imagine,' said Castang blandly, 'that it might cross your mind the n.g. etcetera could be in some way connected with or even known to these good folk. She didn't necessarily travel with them. But met up with them let's say by design, since by accident would be another coincidence and we've too many already.'

'Upon which,' with dangerous mildness, 'the judge suggests that we ask the English C.I.D. to investigate this family's background, with a view to obtaining a positive identification of the n.g. Is that it?'

'Something like that.'

'No, we won't do that, Castang, and neither will the judge. Because the C.I.D. won't be pleased at the idea of a lot of loutish French cops who in their view are one and all Corsican gangsters suggesting their precious Judge has whores from Djakarta as his travelling companions.'

'The famous diplomatic repercussions. So we tell ourselves the Judge's family couldn't possibly know whores from Djakarta. Maybe he once worked in Hong Kong or Singapore – they're English, aren't they? – and had an illegitimate daughter he only dares meet when in France.'

'Castang, do not be sarcastic with me, I beg. What you do, quite simply, is make no mention of the Judge. You get the photograph retouched with the eyes and things back to normal. You build the physical description here into something the English can understand. Old Deutz is a marvel at these things, but leave out about the bare feet and the super breasts; the C.I.D. will take us for a lot of sex maniacs. You send the dental chart and the report, which is all in code so won't need translating. On this extremely complete and detailed description, if they can't do it nobody could.'

'They'll love that. Trotting round all the dentists.'

'Don't be ridiculous, boy, it's done every day. Whitewashes us. We know nothing about a Judge; we're asking for an identity, query English, on a dead woman found in circumstances suggesting homicide. That's all they need know. Once we have a name and address, you have a discreet word with that cop you saw in London over the La Touche affair, and get him quietly to look up her antecedents.'

'He's too bright; he'd smell a rat at once. Anyway he's Special Branch. Introduced me to a homicide inspector while I was there, and a right bastard he was. Nothing more.'

'Very well,' said Richard, 'do it the hard way since you must. Instead of sending your identikit stuff to Tours in the ordinary way you go there yourself. Happened on their premises and they've only themselves to blame. They should pay more attention to parked cars. That's what the judge wants anyhow:

the visitors and staff of the hotel have to be checked out. The judge further agrees that the Armitage boy's story, which was vague, elusive and insolent, concerning his whereabouts must be checked. But he doesn't want, officially, to ask Caen to do this. He is though willing that you go, expenses in reason. I'll have a word with Rougerie in Caen to explain your presence in his sector. You go to Deauville. Nice for you – a trip to the seaside.'

'And what about old Auguste?'

'Monsieur Bianchi will look after that while you're gone.'

Monsieur Bianchi belonged to a vanishing race, that of police officers who have no law degree, no fancy diplomas, in fact not a piece of paper to their name, and couldn't care less about this deplorable state of affairs. He had been, simply, a cop for over thirty years, since in fact the war. Because he sometimes mentioned this the younger element (stuffed with pieces of paper) were fond of saying with humorous emphasis, 'Monsieur Bianchi has been a cop since Nineteen-Nineteen.' He had a distinguished war service and in the buttonhole of his grubby faded jacket lapel is a grubby faded piece of silk cord. The younger element do not know what this is, and haven't the least interest: Monsieur Bianchi (with or without sarcasm he is always called Mossieu) does not speak of it. Once or twice a year he puts on his Sunday suit, and a chestful of medals, but not in the office: he is a Companion of the Liberation, and a lot more besides. There is a legend that once, when André Malraux came down to open a culture-shop and make a speech about Jean Moulin, Monsieur Bianchi (who must have been fiercely swigging at municipal champagne) slapped him on the back and addressed him as 'tu'. Many other legends surround him: one is that he never eats, but subsists entirely upon coffee and the hugest strongest cigarettes – Boyards – fabricated by the Seita. He seems to thrive, and is never ill.

Who will replace him when he goes? For people talk to him who shut up like clams in face of the quick-talking, dressy boys. He attracts confidences. He gets through an immense amount of work, and Richard says gloomily, 'The equivalent of Bianchi would be four good women, all at double the salary,' for since he had no diplomas he has never become a commissaire, and is serenely indifferent to that, too.

Adolescents who run away from home, respectable businessmen who go suddenly haywire, wives who take to the bottle, shoplifting or unsuitable lovers; and all enquiries in the interests of families (still a surprising proportion of PJ business) – all this is meat and drink to Monsieur Bianchi. Castang was quite happy. That is to say, he would have been happier still if Monsieur Bianchi had inherited the trip to the seaside, but there; try not to complain. Vera hated his being away, but had the good taste never to show her anxiety. March up on the Normandy coast: be sure it would be as draughty as hell. Meditation was interrupted by Richard saying, 'Since you're going to have a busy day you'd better run along' in an offensively blithe voice.

The photographer raised hands to heaven when asked for something recognizable.

'Don't be ridiculous, she was swollen up like bubble gum.'

'Well, make a drawing, then,' aware that this was easily said. It crops up two or three times a year, the somebody found in the disused gravel pit and decidedly the worse for wear. The 'wet ones' are awful, but the 'dry ones' which have been visited by crows, rats and other nasty beasts are no better. Police art has never got much beyond the level of the retarded folk who add moustaches to the ladies in brassière advertisements. Even if he took the problem to Vera . . .

He did, in the end.

'You don't have to look at this, if you don't want. She's not nice. Efforts at retouching are catastrophic. I don't know – if one tried from the other end, to make a drawing and then photograph that; could one get a better likeness?' Vera looked, clenched her teeth, looked again steadily and then said, 'No.'

'I understand.'

'That's not so bad: you had to get used to it and so can I. But all I could do is an illustration, an imaginative reconstruction. I couldn't get any likeness.'

'Will you try?' She got a piece of paper wordlessly. Without being told she used a lithographic crayon that would photograph well. She made three in the end, cheating them; three-quarter face with a sidelong slanting look.

'Gitane, by Kathe Kollwitz. Dreadful. I can't conquer the problem; I can only sentimentalize it. I can't do any more.'

'No matter. They look like somebody alive, and that's the way anyone who saw her will recollect her. I'll get them copied. Will you pack a bag for me? If I want to be at the seaside in the morning I'll have to start getting some road under my arse.'

'Come back safe,' she said.

'It's not the sort of thing there's any risk in. Even if there were – I made up my mind a long time ago. I prefer to be a prudent, cowardly cop.' It was only a little less than the truth. She knew about the statistics of the Ministry of the Interior. She didn't know, or he hoped not, that you can be prudent as an insurance company, and of a quite craven cowardice, and still be a statistic. You've got to have the disregard for statistics and the ability to walk away from other people's accidents that journalists call the baraka. Like 'a charmed life' it is not a phrase that cops use.

18. Tourangeaux, and Normans

Driving to Tours as a pleasant morning promenade, with a three-star lunch to look forward to, perhaps, is an agreeable prospect. It is different on a drizzly afternoon in March, in a police car, with a gloomy prospect of having to push on all the way to the coast, and Castang had no comforting illusions about 'la douceur angevine'. Though, fond of his stomach, he did promise himself a good supper. The Loire is not a polluted river, and contains fish. 'Nice fish,' said Castang to himself, rather like Gollum.

Tours nowadays doesn't go in much for la douceur angevine

either. It is thoroughly modern; white, rectangular, austere, and of severe morals: Castang's reception at the PJ 'antenna' was about as far from Rabelais and Icy Doulce France as you can get. There was a fine greasy rain and an acrid wind, and you might as well have stayed home in Aberdeen.

He got an adjunct commissaire called Brillant, of an arithmetical turn of mind. Youngish man with thin black hair, both fine and sparse, and a grey pitted face like an old aluminium saucepan; and his chin was blackish with a dent in it, like the saucepan's bottom. He looked at Castang's homework line by line with a red ballpoint between his fingers, ready at any second to take marks off for haste, inaccuracy or laziness.

'Well,' at the end, putting the papers down after mentally awarding a 'fairly good' to the homework, 'I see nothing to quarrel with there. Your pathologist confirms the police doctor's opinion that the woman was killed hereabouts and put in a car. Our preliminary enquiry shows that to be plausible, since that car was standing all night unlocked; the likelier that nobody admits it.

'From now on it's mathematical. That hotel – you've not been there? – is isolated. In a park, the gates of which are some kilometres outside a village, which in turn is some distance off any main road. You have thus a very strong probability that the woman was put there by somebody on the spot. All right so far?

'On the spot, taking staff and visitors as a global figure, are about eighty people. Staff all in all, twenty-five to thirty, living on the premises or in the village. Matter of elimination. A day or so of work, you can probably eliminate all but three or four of the staff, and on average a good half of the guests. You'll be left with perhaps thirty people at whom enquiries must be directed. That might take several months. As your judge, and you, and Commissaire Richard very well know. So what are you doing haring over here? Why all this bustle and agitation?'

'These English people are in provisional liberty – or just plain liberty, rather, since there's not the remotest evidence to point to them. They've gone down to the coast; they might be around for a fortnight or so. If I can get a connection established . . .' His voice trailed off: the eyes of the man across the desk were not encouraging towards illusions.

Brillant stretched a colourless, languid hand out to the photograph and let his eyes fall on it.

'Well, we'll farm this out. Mm, she doesn't look bad. Never easy to do. I remember one that had taken a shotgun blast from close up. And a suicide once . . . fellow put an American army pistol inside his mouth; you know, the Colt forty-five automatic? The face was still there but the head wasn't, if you follow me? The drawing we made was so bad it took three months to identify him as a deserter from the Foreign Legion . . . where were they, before coming here?'

'Normandy; Bayeux. Rouen. A Channel ferry.'

'And according to the dental work you think she might be English.'

'Photo's gone off to all the cross-channel ports. One can always try. There aren't that many tourists, this time of year. If we can get a name to her – airline booking lists. It's very loose. No passport check anywhere now; that frontier's wide open.' Brillant nodded.

'How many English people work in or around Paris? Come to that, how many English people are resident in Normandy, or even here? Ask at the Préfecture – you'll be surprised. And you're thinking of picking up her track along the road? Two hundred and fifty kilometres from here to the coast.'

'She may have stayed in a hotel.'

'Or a youth-hostel. Or a private house. Or some typist's pad in Paris. You're giving this photo to the Press?'

'Richard's not keen, or not yet, anyhow.'

'I don't know that he isn't right. Well,' getting up, 'I'll do what I can for you.'

'Thanks,' said Castang. Brillant of course had realized that he was running after an outside chance, didn't want to say anything about it, and he wouldn't say anything either. The voice was a little less pale, even if the eyes were still like a dead eel's. Castang, who had been thinking of fish for supper, changed his mind and had chicken instead.

'You'll look for her clothes?' he'd said at parting.

'I don't need you, you know, to teach me my job.'

And there were a remarkable number of hedges, ditches, dustbins and municipal garbage dumps between Tours and Caen. Not to speak of two hundred and thirty kilometres. But she'd been alive, surely, when she got to Tours. And not, presumably, barefoot, in the month of February.

Young Colin Armitage had succeeded in being so vague about where he'd stayed the night that he'd had – certainly, no? – something to hide. He must realize – no? – that if the police were to try they'd find it. People will of course say anything to the police: the man caught coming out of a bank with a sack will say happily that he found it on the pavement. They do not expect to be believed. Did Colin?

Much more likely a little trap of Master Colin's. Just to amuse oneself. Give the cops a lot of trouble, knowing they'll find nothing anyhow: it appealed to some people's sense of humour.

'Not in Deauville actually, no. Somewhere around ... I wasn't in the mood for Deauville, I don't know why ... I didn't really look at the clock. A few miles, I suppose ... Well, those roads, you know. They wind in and out. Sure, there were about ten thousand road signs, and they all said Caen ... I've no idea. The Golden Lion or the Red Lion or the Three Legged Lion ... no, I just said lion. First thing that came in my head ... They all look alike, don't they? Wooden beams, check tablecloths, gothic lettering, and Chicken Valley d'Auge, and lamb chops Valley d'Auge, and baked beans too Valley d'Auge: at least, nobody would be surprised ... Sorry, but you know, things like that just aren't important to me. I was tired. I was only looking for a place to kip and have some grub. I didn't go looking it up in the Michelin. Patience would, because it's awfully important how many knives and forks it's got, and stuff printed in red. But I wouldn't ... I read a book. A detective story. I've forgotten its name. The detectives were better in the book than they are in real life.'

Castang hadn't bothered pursuing it. The boy was too obviously enjoying himself. Richard had simply said 'Nice easy job for Orthez, in case we really want to find out. Or for Caen's equivalent. They've probably ten, exactly like him.' And the job had fallen to Castang, instead!

He'd got to Caen before midnight, and a sleepy night porter had let him in, and he'd fallen asleep almost before he'd got the toothbrush out of his mouth. And however ridiculous the boy's tale there was this much truth in it. Castang would himself have been hard put to remember that hotel's name, but for having to keep the bill, for his expense account!

The rain had cleared, the night before. It started again before he got to Deauville, but coffee put him in good spirits.

It is a small, trim, tidy town, with no history, having been invented out of nothing in the reign of Napoleon the Third, and is an odd mixture of very small and very large buildings, all more or less hideous. The Casino is closed save at weekends, and was closed now, but he had no trouble running a managerial person to earth.

'Nothing like this girl, no. The boy? – it's possible. There are generally two or three like that. Not so many English now: they can gamble at home now, and the exchange is against them, too. But there are always a few lurking in hopes of a lucky hit. Without a photo I shouldn't like to go further, but the staff is trained to observe faces, and remember them. A young woman such as this I'd certainly have recalled myself.' No better, and no worse, than Castang had expected.

The Golden Lion though was harder than he had expected, either because there were more hotels open in winter than he thought, or because it was perfectly true that they looked dauntingly alike. This much of the boy's tale was true, that in the early afternoon, after a hurried meal that gave no satisfaction, he alighted at last upon 'The Arms of the Duke', halfway between Pont l'Eveque and Pont Audemer, upon a crossroad with three different signs saying Caen, two saying Paris, and none saying Autoroute; responsible for all this nonsense.

The police, when engaged upon this door-to-door routine, is received much like a commercial traveller pushing a new coffee-pot, and meets haughtiness – 'Our customers wouldn't like that at all' – conservatism – 'We do very well with what we have' – and of course deep suspicion – 'What's the real price, not this nonsense you're quoting me'. Castang was pleasantly surprised to hear the owner, a stout, bald, rosy man looking altogether too Norman to be true, say 'Certainly'. So much for the Norman reputation of never giving a straight answer. He was eating his own dinner placidly, drinking cider, and had the look, rare nowadays, of a man at peace with himself.

'I remember very well; young English chap with one of these little cars. Number Four I think – I can look it up at the desk.'

'Finish your meal in peace. Single room?'

'They're all doubles. We've only ten. By himself, if that's what you mean. Ate alone. Right here at this table. Served him myself. Was fairly late, is how I recall.'

'Ever seen anybody like this?' showing the photo. The man looked carefully, chewed, swallowed, and said 'No.'

'You're always here?'

'Where else? Seven in the morning till midnight. That's this business for you. November, December, I shut the shop altogether, till the New Year. If she'd been here, I'd have seen her all right.'

'Even in a bedroom?' He got a sharp look. 'I'm only asking,' peaceably.

'I'm not concerned with their morals. If a room is paid for . . . You mean did he pick up a girl? Not to my knowledge. Chambermaid might have noticed. You can ask her if you like. In the kitchen.'

'It's possible?'

'It could happen,' wiping his mouth with his napkin and emptying his glass. 'It has happened. Frankly, it worries me less than people who steal towels.'

'You've no night man?'

'Too expensive. I lock up at midnight. Till then the outside door, the wooden one, is shut but not locked. On the glass door there's a bell. People go out for a stroll. The bell alerts me, and if I'm in the kitchen I take a glance through the window there. But it could happen of course that I'm in the cold room, or the scullery. People have been known to help themselves to a drink; there are occasional spots of trouble ... it's easier, cheaper, pleasanter to stand for a certain amount of trouble. That's all.'

'And in the mornings?'

'I'm out because of the market. Maria's here at six to make coffee. My wife's up and about by seven-thirty; that's as early as people leave. She knows what rooms are occupied; I've written it all out the night before. Suppose there are two breakfasts instead of one; Maria'll charge for them.' Castang nodded.

'Where do they keep their cars?'

'Yard at the back. Door through there by the kitchens. The cooks lock up there when they go, say around ten. After that, anybody wants something from the car, they'd have to ask me for the keys. There's no trouble?' sharply.

'None at all. We're checking on this young fellow's movements. If he had a companion it would interest me. That's all.'

'Talk to Maria. I'll be here if you want me. Big fat girl.'

Maria was finishing her dinner, with the cooks and the two waitresses, and Castang occupied ten minutes looking at the doors – wood, solid, with proper locks. No other way out; a snug little place. Remained that classic, the fire-escape. But there were only two floors, and the firedoors were the type that open with a sharp push to a snap bar: he tried them, and they made a loud metallic noise, discouraging to anyone trying to be furtive. The iron treads of the stair led down to the yard, with space for only a dozen cars, at a pinch, and enclosed by high wooden palings. A car motor starting in the quiet of the night would make a racketing echo. On the street side, the ground floor windows had stout wooden shutters.

Maria was unperturbed at his accosting her, and led the way with a bouncing bust and muscular legs up the stairs to room number four, a tidy, pleasant affair of twin beds, chintz curtains and counterpanes, and a little bathroom. First floor, street side. It was sparkling clean and fresh smelling, which inspired confidence in Maria.

'Do it all by yourself?' She grinned.

'In winter, yes. Lot of work, but the boss is all right. Madame helps out. After Easter, another girl for the top floor, yes.' Her accent was strong but there was nothing wrong with her wits.

'Only one question, but I want you to think carefully. One person slept here that night, or two?' She didn't hesitate at all.

'Oh yes. He had a woman with him. Young man, yes? Gone in the morning though – vanished.' With a comic face and an expressive wrist movement. 'No harm. Bathroom's got to be cleaned just the same.'

Castang, who had been quite ready to say goodbye to a fragile and unsubstantial notion, woke up. Was this infernal trip to the seaside going to be worth while after all?

'Feel sure?'

'Of course I'm sure. Bed used, traces of make-up. And a smell,' with the indifference of one well used to smells, both good and bad.

'I bring his breakfast. All alone then.'

'What time was that?'

'Ah, that I can't recall. Ordinary time. Half-past seven, eight maybe – she was gone earlier. Easy enough.'

'Anything you can think of to describe her? – like fair or dark, I mean perfume maybe – hair in a waste bin?'

'Ah, no,' said Maria, laughing, 'I clean, but not with a magnifying glass. What does it matter, to me? She came from another room, maybe.'

'We'll check on it. Try to think, though, now.' But there was no budging Maria.

'No – you mean slippers forgotten, or a comb, or lipstick on a kleenex – yes, often, but not here.'

'Then how can you be so sure?'

Maria shrugged.

'Experience,' she said.

19. Inspector French investigates

He'd found too much, and not enough. The room had been done twice, and crawling about on hands and knees wasn't going to turn up handy hairpins – there were no grounds for getting a technician. However, it was certainly young Colin who had stayed here, and a woman with him.

He came downstairs with the irritable thoughts of a man who has gone to a lot of trouble to discover a heap of useless facts that are certainly inconclusive and probably misleading. The rosy man was in his little untidy office, making rather a thing of being virtuous, be it with the police or the tax-gatherer.

'Here we are.' It was the copy of the bill. Bedroom number four, one room, one apéritif, one evening meal; one half-bottle, one coffee, one calvados, one breakfast, one service-and-tax-comprised total. Monsieur Robert Maxwell. Castang looked at it gloomily. It was perfectly possible that the stupidest sort of coincidence would oblige him to start over afresh, much encouraged by making a fool of himself. Still . . . The filling in of little forms had been abandoned as a meaningless piece of bureaucracy, and nobody looks at passports any more.

Castang turned the bill over, borrowed a ballpoint, and made a little drawing of a long English head with straight hair that fell forward; looked at it dissatisfied. Most English people looked like that.

'Yes,' said the rosy man dubiously, plainly thinking the same.

'You saw the car?'

'One of these little coupés – dark blue, green perhaps. It's difficult to tell at night. I didn't have any reason for noticing it.'

'Of course not,' agreed Castang, hearing a judge of instruction wonder sarcastically how many there were. 'Any mannerism that you can recall?' But that was too much to expect. 'He make any telephone calls?'

'They'd be marked on the bill.'

'Were there skis on the car?'

'Yes,' after some thought. 'Red, or maybe black.' It was close enough, Castang decided. At the worst, rather than look for a probably mythical Maxwell, one could arrange a confrontation, though it wouldn't prove anything, save perhaps the extreme unlikelihood of Colin's having been to Tours.

He sat in the car and thought. He looked at the roadsigns saying Caen. After a while he started the motor and drove back to Deauville. He parked by the swimming-pool, hired shorts and a towel, and dived into the water. He swam half a dozen lengths ponderously, in company with three fat women, two elderly gentlemen, and four giggly children taking turns in diving after an ear-ring. He lay on his back and floated.

The big window of the Deauville pool looks due west, and the sun sinks in it, and on a clear evening dyes the whole interior blood red. Castang stared at the window thinking about Inspector French, whom he had read once in his student days in a virtuous resolve to learn English. That was the way to be a detective! You allowed no fact to escape you, however trivial. After one hundred and fifty pages of minute observation and flawless logic you proved by Euclidian geometry that Mr Crump's immensely elaborate railway-timetable alibi was a phony, and three months later Mr Crump was with all due solemnity topped in Wandsworth, but this fact did not trouble you, any more than wondering what made Mr Crump behave so idiotically in the first place. Castang climbed out and sat on a stone bench. The radiators were on full blast and warmth comforted his damp behind. He dripped peaceably, and wished he were Inspector French.

Colin, if it really were Colin, had something to hide. This might perfectly well be a banal helping of week-end adultery. And it might be the dark stranger, the barefoot girl. But finding out was a job for twelve dogsbodies from the PJ at Caen.

The boy had been here eating his croissant at eight in the morning. He'd been four hundred and fifty kilometres to the south by one p.m. and you didn't do that by going over country roads to Tours. You did it normally and innocently, on the autoroute to Paris and beyond.

Forget about Colin. He has nothing to do with the barefoot girl at all, and his nocturnal companion is no business of ours.

As for the b.g., let Tours worry about her. She arrived there with her own transport, or she was brought. The second, since there is no sign of an abandoned car, the more likely. She may not be English, and somebody with, perhaps, a peculiar sense of humour thought it exceedingly funny to shove her in an English-registered Rolls-Royce.

What would Inspector French make of this? While waiting for the laborious comb-out of everyone who'd been at that hotel on the night in question he'd look for her clothes. Because no policeman, not even French, would believe in anything but an amateur crime. Professionals might well have dead bodies to get rid of, but they didn't go in for complicated games like this. They would tip a body out on a deserted stretch of road, as unceremoniously as the butcher's granny. They would never do anything to draw attention to themselves, and would not dream of fumbling about in a car park hoping for an un-locked door.

A girl's clothes make a small bundle of rags. They can be stuffed into any corner without attracting attention. Since, however, there is something incriminating about them (or why undress her in the first place?) if you are a clever criminal you will think of the possibilities of them being found.

He wanted to shake the whole thing loose. He wanted to sit on the balcony and enjoy a beer and watch the sun go down over Cabourg. He wanted to enjoy himself. If it were the weekend, and the Casino open, he would go gambling. Be reckless, have a good dinner, pick a girl up. Deauville in March seemed un-promising terrain for pleasure, but it was a matter of knowing where to look. Colin had managed nicely!

This was a stupid problem, and he wasn't concentrated on it. His mind kept going round and round the cellar at home, and wishing heartily that Monsieur Bianchi had been sent here. Richard was quite right of course; no cop got sent to investigate

88

his own apartment block, and no cop would want to. It was too much like a doctor being asked to give his own wife a physical.

Being sent here, in fact, had the smell of a manoeuvre. As though Richard had invented a pretext for getting him out of the way.

No, that was nonsense. Richard could and did do such things, but if he sent a subordinate four hundred and fifty kilometres it was with a purpose. 'Instead of all this aimless running about' – one could hear his deliberately-paced and deliberately unenergetic voice, as averse to stupid zeal as Monsieur de Talleyrand – 'stay quiet and give your brains a chance to work.'

And Castang's brains were not working at all. He was tired, and slack from sitting too long in that vile car and smoking too much, and stupidly bewildered. Right out of form, in fact. And the tide was right out at Deauville, and looked as though it would stay out forever. Shake your liver up, boy.

Castang dived back into the pool of languid, slightly overheated water and swam six more lengths as steadily fast as he could, trying to pace himself, to keep something in reserve while pushing the lazy unused muscles harder than they wanted to work.

He ended puffing, holding on to the bar at the deep end with one finger, trying to breathe without a huge racket, while the drumming subsided and the pulse crawled downward. All this oxygenation was supposed to be good for the brain too. Shake up the sluggish, starved grey matter.

Good saints, it worked like the classic dose of salts. Castang's chronic constipation changed to galloping diarrhoea between one heaving, dragging breath and another. With a snap of all his muscles like a trout Castang leapt out of the water. The old gentleman resting in the next lane, an obese and mild soul with a fringe of grey hair and rubber goggles of an absurd bright baby-blue, looked at him astounded. Castang snatched the scrubby, thin-worn hired towel, and bolted for the shower. He turned it on very hot, very cold, and let out a short barking howl of anguish. He dressed in such a hurry that his underthings stuck to his damp skin. He opened the car window against the smell from force of habit, shut it again in a hurry, let go of the wheel to jam a hat over his wet hair. The chill of a March evening after that moist tepid atmosphere: getting rid of one congestion – that of congenital idiocy – he didn't intend to catch another from pneumonia.

He had made a mistake so huge, so elementary that he had only just caught it: he'd got the date wrong. The Casino in Deauville is open at weekends in winter, but not on a Monday. Worrying about Auguste, and thrown out of gear by the postmortem report arriving late – all the fault of Mrs Chose and her varicose veins – he'd somehow lost a day.

Colin Armitage had spent the night here, but not the same night that funny things were happening in Tours. Twenty-four hours earlier.

He'd been lying and why? He'd given a phony name here, and why?

Because he'd had a woman with him. Who?

Inspector French, concentrating upon timetables, would have found all this out much, much quicker. Castang felt a perfect fool.

20. Rope in the House of the Hanged

Everybody who could go home from the PJ office at Caen had gone, and the duty inspector was quite glad to see Castang: a relief from boredom.

'Things are fairly slack, which is to say overworked as hell, but none of it that urgent.' He nodded; the picture was familiar.

'Meaning you spend weeks,' went on the inspector, whose name was Robin, 'working on this cunt who swears blind he picked the gun up off the pavement; it just happened to be lying there. Knowing that when he comes to trial the judge will say tut tut that was naughty, but since you're a poor deprived boy we'll give you six months, and suspend that. What the hell are we doing here? How hypocritical can you get? Did the fellow do it or didn't he? If I've worked my gut ragged proving he did, then what's this crap about society being at fault? Send the fucker up for five years. Nasty object he is; turn your back a second he'd crack your skull and feel happy. Six months suspended! Now he's laughing his head off at me. Because you can't send society to jug; there isn't room. Courts! Why do I do it? – for the money they pay us?' Castang knew the whole story, only too well.

'I spent the day,' he said gloomily, 'running about like an imbecile after a boy who told me he'd been here. So he had, only it was the wrong day, and I fell for it.' Robin's turn to nod and look sympathetic.

'What's it about then – the naked woman in the car? I saw the signal but the boss didn't say what he wanted done with it.'

'Nothing yet; I came hoping to get something to tie it in. The boy was here, and had a woman with him. Nothing though to show it was her. These other English people were in Bayeux.'

'As I understood it all this was supposed to have happened in Tours.'

'Tours is looking for her. But no luggage, no clothes, no car: she could have come from anywhere.'

'Why here?' Robin not in the least interested and no wonder: they didn't want other people's dead bodies pinned on them. Even talking about it was to speak of rope in the house of the hanged.

'No reason, and there's nothing to show she ever was here. I've only the one thing to go on and that's tenuous as hell; she might have been English, by the work done on her teeth. So there just might have been a previous connection. I find only that the boy lied about the day, and gave a false name at the hotel. Okay, that's not even a misdemeanour. But he had a woman with him. I'm wondering who.'

'Ask him,' with some logic.

'He's down in the Alps in some ski place. But that's not it; the old man's an English Judge, and one can't go on at them on a slight supposition. The English would start getting on their high horse.'

Robin nodded, understanding.

'Awkward.'

'It could mean a very long drag, to find out who she is. And suppose these English are mixed up in it somehow. By then they've gone back home. Can you see the judge's face, asked to apply for an extradition order?'

'Haw haw,' said Robin, with no mirth.

'Yes. So the boss said anyhow go up here and check it out. Just in case.'

'I see. Or I don't see; what's this story about this fella who had a woman with him? She was staying in the hotel?'

'I'm starving,' said Castang, appetite sharpened by swimming. 'Let's go have a bite in the pub. Any chance of a nice fish?' reverting suddenly to Gollum.

'There's a place by the harbour that's not bad,' taking his glasses off with a first sign of enthusiasm. 'Don't know about the fish; whole goddam estuary's polluted, but so are we, so what odds does it make?'

Castang agreed with this reasoning.

A nice café, with a lot of old fashioned brass kept well polished, and ridiculous palm trees: he began to feel better. A big fat woman, Norman in all the best ways, said her fish didn't taste of diesel, and if he didn't believe it look for himself, and brought a huge wing of ray raw on a plate. Gollum asked for it to be put in the pot at once. Robin said it was near the end of the month, and he was short in the pocket but if Castang would stand the drinks he'd go for the veal blanquette. They went back to the house of the hanged much refreshed.

'Well now look; this woman with him – she didn't just jump out the window in her nightie. Where'd she go to?'

'What I thought. Must come from somewhere around. Did he pick her up in Deauville or what? Not known at the casino. Distinctive face.'

'Well, let's have a look. Did we get a photo sent?'

'Doesn't matter,' said Castang, 'I've one here,' rummaging in his raincoat pocket.

'If she's a tourist she must belong in some hotel: should be easy to find out – bleeding saints!'

'Yes, she didn't look too good so we faked up a drawing.'

'Yes, I see. It's not bad either. Look – I know this woman!' Castang gave a jump, and his lighter fell on the floor. Robin had started to laugh! He wasn't that drunk surely . . .

'What!?'

'She just walked in here. Said she was a journalist. I tell you the English are nutty, but this heat everything I'd ever heard. Smashing looker, too.' Mellowed by food and drink, and even more by the recollection, Monsieur Robin was laughing heartily at his reminiscences.

'She isn't any more,' soured slightly at all this guffawing.

'So she is,' pulled up a little abruptly. 'I mean, so she isn't. Shit, you know what I mean. But it's queer, though,' studying the picture. 'It's like and not like, but it's her all right. And it's very funny indeed she should be dead.'

'Why?' not seeing that it was funny at all.

'Because she kept talking about death. She was sitting here opposite me. Where you are.'

Had they both had too much to drink? Castang felt the little ripple of blurred vision, of the objects in his sightline slipping for a second out of focus. He shook his head, shutting his eyes for a moment. Robin was still there, staring at someone who wasn't, but who was sitting in his chair.

'As my boss says; kindly try and make your narrative coherent.'

21. Moths around the candle-flame

Castang was extremely interested; it was normal. At last someone who had seen the barefoot girl with clothes on (and presumably shoes), who knew what her voice was like, her movements, her eyes . . . But not particularly surprised; he had felt sure that sooner or later he would run up against someone who had known her alive. That it should be a cop, of all people, was a coincidence to be sure, but not a startling one. People involved in crimes of violence have very often had for some time an aura of violence around them, which may, quite frequently, have attracted the attention of the police. Cops of experience can recognize this magnetic field, often on no more than the base of a few minutes talk.

Nor was Robin an exceptionally good witness. A trained observer, to be sure, but unless switched on, no more sensitive really than anyone with good perception.

'I was on the same shift as now,' Robin was saying, 'and you know how people come into the office with weird tales or phony confessions; airs of mysterious importance. So I didn't take her seriously. Much like it is now, nothing much doing. One's there in case the phone rings.'

Quite: doing a bit of desultory paperwork with no great energy, drinking cups of coffee, with a copy of *True Detective* and a crossword for when it becomes a real drag.

'Said she was a journalist, doing a series about crime, and could she interview me. So I said yes, subject to the usual, you know; anonymous source, no direct quotes, not to be taken as official. She got a shorthand pad out to scribble on and starts in. An oddball – that was evident from the start. I let her press on through curiosity as much as anything.'

'Was she in fact English?'

'She didn't say so but she talked about some magazine, and the television. Spoke quite good French, fluent, an accent but what's the word – colloquial.'

'How dressed?'

'Quite expensively and well, a bit scruffy. One of those Israeli leather coats, silk scarf, dress like a sack but good wool, a blurry swirly pattern stylized in lots of colours, big soft Italian handbag, the shapeless kind, gold chain bracelet. High boots. Nothing extravagant, none of it new, all worn quite casually. So I said well you're English, why come here, I mean this is France. And it was then, already at the beginning, she caught the ear, not so much what's said as the intonation – you know. Said here there was still a death penalty. Well, apart from telling her to go to Spain what can one say? I mumble the usual, about yes but very rarely applied – more's the pity – and suddenly she said "Have you killed people?" So I woke up a bit, thought steady boy, she's trying to be aggressive. Look girl, I say, it happens that people sometimes shoot at us, happy if they shoot straight, and one had better be quick as well as straight. I thought it the usual accusation of trigger-happiness – but no, she says of course, and am I wearing a gun, and can she see it, and handle it, so I took the magazine out and let her.'

'Exciting herself.'

'Boy, you're not kidding. All those jokes about the gun being the penis: she sat there cuddling it so I asked for it back, said no, sorry, that's serious, not for the girls. She gave it back, said nothing, just grinned. Big dark eyes, big mouth, lot of pale pink lipstick, that silvery kind. I didn't feel altogether happy with her.'

'Very attractive?'

'Yes, fantastically. Great wafts of it. Like she could turn it on. Nothing wrong with that, but she says do I approve of the guillotine, and without thinking really I say yes of course, pull the bloody string myself if it was needed, and her eyes got shiny, so I said pretty quick that feelings didn't come into it, but in this job you saw just how bad bad can be and that's it. Didn't want her there all turned on. She asked had I ever been there, and I said no, abrupt, and changed the subject.'

Castang nodded. He had once been, and wasn't anxious to repeat the experience, which did more than spoil one's breakfast.

'She said was there anybody under sentence, because she'd like to interview him, and could I get her in? So of course I said no, and no. She grinned, said she daresay I could if I tried. Like you know, shall I try too? Temperature getting a bit heated.' Castang laughed.

'No.'

'Too right no, not if it was Marlene Dietrich with her candle.' Castang, thirty-seven and a bit young for Marlene, said stupidly 'What candle?'

'Moths around the candle-flame.'

'Yes of course. So?'

'Well, I'm not going to sit there like an idiot with a hard-on, so I said this sounded all a bit cheap to me and over sensational, and gave a totally false picture, and was there anything else, and she said like that "It's interesting to be hand in hand with death." Oh yes, very, and how do you like France, dear, the grub and the old castles and all, and she laughed and said yes she was just a tourist but she liked to keep an eye open for business to mix with a holiday, and this all interests her very much. Yes Miss, sure, but sorry I can't give you an introduction to our local apache tribe, Geronimo would wonder what I was setting him up for. Sorry, I've quite a lot of work, but enjoy your stay in Caen and see you around, I hope. Off she went with no further fuss. It doesn't sound like much, but the way she looked and spoke – I'm not altogether surprised, I mean, about turning up in the car trunk. She was looking for excitement, and chose maybe the wrong time and place. When you meet them looking for trouble, and know they'll find it – you know? – gives you a tiny shiver: these girls are so damn dim. And yet she wasn't dim. And working herself up, maybe, but in a way she knew and could stay in control of.'

'She didn't meet Geronimo – he wouldn't do anything silly like put her in an English tourist's car, however funny he thought that'd be.'

'That's right.'

'On a high of any kind, would you say?'

'Possible, but no sign, and no visible deterioration. Not quite that sort of excitement. There's a type that is their own speed, and doesn't need to buy it in a pill. Hypernervous, yes, certainly.'

'You said enjoy your stay. You got the impression of – I don't know; time to spend, or in a hurry on the way through?'

'Time to spend, I suppose. I don't know – drifting in here; not as though we were part of the regular tourist circuit.'

'All this was what evening?'

'Weekend guard I had.'

'She must have had luggage; almost certainly a car. And was she with anyone?'

'Should be easy enough to check. I've nothing much to do, and owe you for the drinks. I can ring up the hotels,' fumbling on the shelf for a much annotated phone directory. 'Town's easily checked, anyhow: try that before further afield. By her clothes she had money: we'll try the obvious first.'

On only the fourth Robin got something, a voice that answered his routine information query with a long indignant quack, so that Castang reached over for the spare earpiece, but was too languid to catch more than '. . . like to see our money Inspector, as of course you understand.'

Robin shrugged.

'That's nothing; the old bag there complaining about a skipout, but it'll interest you. The night your boyfriend in Deauville is supposed to have slipped a woman in, my girlfriend here, clearly recognizable from the description, didn't occupy her room. Which wasn't relet, and wasn't paid for, so the old skinflint is sore.'

'She leave any luggage?'

'One suitcase.'

'I'll go and look. And thanks a lot.'

'Sounds like you might be back,' offered Robin, 'in which case see you some more maybe. I'll fill the old man in. And thanks for the drinks. The place is on the square there, in front of the harbour – you can't miss it. Give me a buzz, if it ties up.'

'The judge will probably suggest she spent the night with you,' grinned Castang.

'And that I suggested a honeymoon on the Loire, looking at all those old castles by moonlight. Enjoy yourself.'

22. The barefoot girl acquires shoes

The woman at the hotel desk had one of those figures composed of a series of tubes; a large one from hip to thorax, and smaller ones for limbs, but all of perfectly regular diameter. She was most suspicious, and extremely unwilling to hand the suitcase over to him: he had to show his medal, and the fact that he came from another town didn't help either. In her book, people would do anything to avoid paying a bill, right down to getting killed: when she heard the girl was dead, it was plain that to her mind one crime led to another.

'She fill in a registration?' He copied it into his book: Miss Mary Johnson from Egham, Surrey, England. 'Keep it; we might want it photocopied.'

'What's in the case? Anything better than old clothes? I've the right to keep it to reimburse my losses.'

'Sorry. All property is impounded and kept in police custody; that's the law.'

'Then I want a receipt.'

'Oh you can send a claim in, if you like, to the judge of instruction.' Much good might that do her! 'What time was it she came?'

'Early afternoon. Looked at the room, came down a few minutes later and drove off.'

'Drove – she had a car then.'

'Of course she had a car. Parked outside; I'd told her she couldn't leave it there.'

'Can you describe it?'

'Small. Red.' She got a bit cross at finding nothing better to say. 'I couldn't say, really, what make. Not a French car, I think: that I'd have recognized.'

'Was there anyone else in the car? Waiting for her?'

'No no, alone.' With regret. 'I thought she was just going to park. You better not leave yours there, either. You might be a policeman and all that, but I get the complaints.'

Horrible old cow, thought Castang, bearing his prize off to where he could examine it free of prying eyes.

The case for a start was a good one, while not new. Nobody would leave it, even stuffed with old newspapers, just to dodge a measly hotel bill. Certainly she had meant to come back. Why hadn't she come back?

And these were her clothes; yes, enough for a couple of weeks. A jersey trouser-suit, a long skirt, some sweaters and blouses, underclothes and bundled oddments, two pairs of shoes. She might have had more in the car: no overcoat, no washing or make-up things.

All the stuff was as Robin had described it, good quality and quite expensive. Certainly it was the same woman: old inner-tube back there had given a good description. She'd gone – presumably in the car and presumably to Tours – and certainly would have come back: five thousand francs worth of stuff here. He turned the shoes around in his hand. There was nothing odd about them; a small broadish foot with no deformity. Good leather, a bit scuffed. Not on trees but wrapped in a plastic bag. But they were hers: however small a piece of information it was solid. She was no longer the barefoot girl found mysteriously naked and dead in Tours: she was a journalist, or claimed to be: she was as pretty, and attractive as had been guessed: she was neurotic and excitable, and possibly promiscuous. And English; hm, Miss Mary Johnson from somewhere in Surrey sounded so reassuringly English it was probably another phony like the boy. And she had slipped out of one

hotel into another forty-odd kilometres off, and out of that one
– where?

He knew a lot about her already. But not enough, not
nearly enough. This act of walking into a police bureau, and
PJ at that, chattering about guns and death sentences, was
highly obscure.

Her clothes smelt of a dark, rich perfume. Was there any
point in bringing this stuff back to Maria, in the hope of
getting a tighter identification? He decided not. Even if she
remembered the perfume it was not the sort of evidence judges
thought highly of.

But Bayeux, now . . . It was only twenty-five kilometres off, a
lot closer to Caen than Pont Whatever-it-was-called, even if it
were in the other direction. Sixty-odd kilometres; between the
two that was still only an hour's drive. He didn't suppose
there was anything in it, but while he was here the point had to
be checked. If he could establish a contact, of any sort, between
the English family and the barefoot girl before they ever
reached Tours – why then, he was home and dry. Or a connection in England, he thought hopefully, but that was something
needing more thought. The English police had the description,
the photos, the teeth details – would they come up with anything? – they'd had no time yet. Bayeux first, and Tours again
then. A small red car, and right hand drive. Even in Tours, a
large city, there weren't that many. Bayeux is a small place. He
knew nothing about it, but had a picture of a sleepy market
town.

He was making a fine collection of hotel receptionists. This
time he got a youngish girl, who took a look at his medal and
said she'd go dig out the manager.

'Got a room free?' It was ten at night, and the day had lasted
long enough.

'I'm afraid not; we're always full, even this time of year. I
could try phoning for you.'

'You're kind.'

The manager was in his office, wood-panelled and bulging
with paper; a pleasant, and pleasantly intelligent man who

looked shrewdly at Castang, listened politely to his tale, smiled slightly at all the things that – obviously – were not said, and pressed his clean white fingers together...

'I remember the English family perfectly. The Judge, his wife and daughter. Quiet, very pleasant, no trouble. We get a great many English people even now; this is a favourite spot for them. Ate in the restaurant and left next morning – were going to visit Arromanches, I recall their saying. A young woman such as you describe? – no.' He looked at the photo for a long time, for so long that Castang became curious. 'No,' he said at last. 'Unusual type. One wouldn't have missed her. There was something about it that made me hesitate a while, a resemblance perhaps to some person I have seen, possibly, in circumstances I don't now recollect, but here, no. You can try in the restaurant if you wish.' In the restaurant, where even latecomers had reached the coffee-and-drinks stage, waiters had leisure to look at his picture, but all shook their heads.

The young girl at the desk smiled upon him.

'I got you a bed down the road. Not much of a place; still, it's a bed.' She too hesitated for some time over the photo.

'I'm not sure,' she said at last. 'Not a customer; that I do feel sure of. People do come in, to ask questions or buy picture postcards or – or –'

'To leave a message?' suggested Castang. 'Make a phone call?'

'I'm sorry, I really can't say.'

To him at least it was a positive. Two different witnesses, faced with a sketchy likeness at best, are struck, and try to rake about in their memory: Castang felt sure she'd been here, but the cop told him that as evidence this was worthless. Fall in love with a theory – Richard would say – and you'll always find things to fit it with a bit of stretching. Witnesses are stretchable, because they're anxious to please and eager to appear important. Tug at them, ever so little, and if they can make a guess at what you want to hear, that's what they'll dish you out.

Lying in the kind of bed one would not want to share, even with something excessively glamorous, because of deep erosions in the centre, Castang thought, or told himself he was thinking, even as he fell asleep. She went to Tours, anyhow . . .

23. Where to hide a leaf

Castang decided he wasn't going to hang around any further. Somewhere, he felt convinced, Miss Mary Johnson had had a contact however fleeting with the English family. In the cathedral, or looking at the Bayeux tapestry, or in the museum at Arromanches. If the judge agreed to take the question further it would be a job for Robin and his boys in Caen.

The same applied to any previous meeting. Miss Johnson had booked in at a hotel in Caen in the early afternoon, and driven off half an hour, at most, later. The young chap Colin, amusing himself in Deauville, had chosen a hotel at random – or so he said – at Pont Thing, a half hour's ride from Caen. If they spent the night together, some arrangement was worked out at a point within the orbit. But the whole damned thing, he agreed, was built upon suppositions. 'Avec des si, on construit Paris' . . .

Instead of fluttering aimlessly (a moth around the candle-flame) he must concentrate upon a fact; tangible, inalterable; evidential! He knew of only one: Miss Mary Johnson's small red car. For Colin's claim he'd gone to Paris . . . no no no, leave the boy out of it. Miss Johnson, according to the medical evidence, had met her death around midnight and within a shortish space of time had been put into the back of a Rolls-Royce car not far from Tours. Reasonable hypothesis one, that she got there in her own car; two, that her car is around the place somewhere. The police in Tours, besides an understandably leisurely approach to her misfortunes, had not looked for this car: they didn't know it existed. He did.

Castang's arguments were crude. If he could find this car it would be a reward for a long, boring, troublesome journey. It would do him a lot of good in the eyes of Tours, who were unenthusiastic and who could blame them, and who would certainly drag their feet in the hopes of somebody else clearing up the mystery. It would do him a lot of good in the eyes of the police department generally; a race with a tendency to despise what they called 'Intellectuals'. People who do nothing, who 'have ideas'. Their eternal slogan was: 'What use are ideas? One must be practical, always practical.'

The bankers, as Vera called them with hatred.

It would do him some good with Richard too. Richard, mercifully, did not despise ideas, but liked a few practical results too. And had taken a risk, using up quite a slice of credit with the judge. Castang reappearing with a vague silly story about nocturnal flittings up and down the fire-escape somewhere wouldn't please him much. But Miss Johnson's car could be an important stage towards discovering what had happened to Miss Johnson.

Castang's thinking along the tedious road back to Tours was busy.

The assassin had been very stupid in putting a dead body where it would, shortly, inevitably be found with the maximum of noise and commotion. Alternatives; he was very stupid. Or in a great hurry, bundling her away in fear of immediate discovery.

More alternatives; he had an accomplice or he hadn't. If he hadn't, as was surely likeliest, he couldn't have got rid of the car. Abandoned, it would have been found at once. In a country district a strange car is noticed and commented upon within an hour or two. No car had been found: he had therefore an accomplice, who wasn't perhaps as stupid as he was. The car had been hidden.

It is very difficult indeed to hide a car at all efficiently in the country. The number of disused quarries, flooded gravel pits, deep pools in rivers, etc., is strictly limited. You have to know about them, meaning you must know the countryside really well, and you will almost always leave tracks.

It is much easier to hide a leaf in the forest. In the city. It won't stay hidden very long, but long enough for you to vanish.

Castang liked this theory largely because it favoured him the most. He knew nothing about local gravel pits! It was definitely worth a gamble. Tours was a big enough city to hide a car for a longish time, perhaps a fortnight. This one had been adrift a week, and would be noticed any time. If he was going to get ahead he'd better be right!

There are three classic places. A wreck yard, stacked with old carcasses and who's going to notice one more? A garage, whose environs are mostly strewn with cars in varying stages of disrepair waiting patiently for the shop to get around to them; and a parking lot, preferably an airport parking lot. This is best of all, for people leave their cars for vague, often long periods, telling themselves they'll worry about the ticket when they get back. The Tours airport is a little local affair, with no international traffic, and Castang decided to try the town centre first.

He was in fact a lot luckier than he was with the Deauville hotels. Instead of hanging around for most of a working day at the door-to-door routine, it was the second he tried: a tower parking lot in the city centre, with exactly the right anonymity; an automatic entry gate where you take your ticket, and a control only at the exit. Probably there weren't more than half a dozen, but for it to be the second was heartening.

Few people stay more than a couple of hours, for they come shopping. But of those who stay overnight or longer there are always some strangers. A red Toyota with a right-hand drive and English plates had attracted no attention whatever. It hadn't even been broken into. Castang stood gloating over it.

Strictly, he ought to call the PJ, have technicians come, and go over it all carefully, for fingerprints and stuff. He had never once yet seen an enquiry solved or even advanced by the finding of fingerprints. Even the stupidest and most amateurish criminal knows about them, and if he is too distraught to think he will be identified by other means. Castang didn't intend to allow a lot of cops to get their greasy paws on this treasure-trove.

He walked around, looking. The key of course and the

104

clock-punch ticket would have been thrown away. He was taken aback to see the ticket left neatly tucked into the ventilator grille, most conscientiously.

Castang circled, sniffing like a suspicious animal. Over-zealous Officer Boobs Again! There could perfectly well be four small red cars with English plates in the city of Tours, and being caught breaking into the wrong one ... he could see Brillant's face, and the red pencil awarding him a zero. He went to find the parking attendant, in his glass box at the checkout.

'English Toyota – yes, I saw it.'

'How long's it been there?'

'Few days – couldn't say, rightly. Wouldn't pay no heed, less it was reported stolen or something. You think I go round putting chalk marks on them?'

'But you do look from time to time?' said Castang patiently.

'Most nights – whoever is on late. There're two of us, see. Wouldn't believe the things they get up to. Old wrecks abandoned, boxes of every sort of dirty rubbish. Woman left a baby once. Just said she'd forgot it.'

'People leave keys with you at times, for someone else to pick up?'

'Sure. Some that wouldn't trust us not to pinch stuff – I ask you! Hide the key under the car, where anyone who looked would get it.'

'Could it have been there a week?'

'I reckon.'

Back with the car, Castang squatted, felt with his fingertips. And there it was, taped to the inside of the bumper. Had she left it here? Like the suitcase in Caen? For somebody to pick up?

The clock-punch said 9.27 of the day after her death – or the same day if she died after midnight. The assassin – or an accomplice – had brought it here. But why? If to cover up why leave the ticket? And who was the key for, for God's sake? He felt tired suddenly, and no longer proud of his discovery.

Nothing in the inside of the car: just as well, because of pilferers. He opened the boot.

Her car all right: here were her belongings. An overnight bag with her sleeping things and slippers; one of those awkward female bandboxes with a jumble of make-up and jewellery. But not the clothes she had been wearing. No sign of the things Robin had described; the leather raincoat, the boots, the frock with the swirly pattern. Nor her handbag.

Nothing much he could do. Make a note of the registration plate and the tax disc: he'd have her identity anyhow, if the English police hadn't got it already. He'd never had much faith in Miss Mary Johnson!

The glove compartment yielded nothing, not even a garage bill. That was the trouble with women; they shoved all that rubbish in their bag instead of leaving it around for him to find.

He plunged down suddenly and rummaged under the seats; came up with a small tangled bundle, which turned out to be her tights and knickers, taken off in one, certainly by her, or why bury them under the driving seat? She'd made love, it was in the path. report. But where? Who with?

He relocked the car, put the key in his pocket, stumped off irritably to the PJ. Brillant was out; everyone was out. He left curt instructions and slammed off, nowhere near as pleased with himself as he should be. He'd found a heap of things, enough certainly to justify his vagabonding round the countryside of half France, as it seemed now, but none of them made any sense. He was tired. He yawned a lot on the way home, and it seemed a long way.

24. The Night Lords

Richard was out too. Cantoni was out. Damn it, even Lasserre was out – Castang hadn't thought the day would come when he'd be sorry to hear that! He wanted somebody to say to him 'Look my boy, it's dead simple'. Because stupid as it all seemed he felt sure it was simple. Things were. It was the people who were so complicated. That woman who left the baby in the parking tower . . . women simply didn't do such things! Oh yes they did . . .

Curse, he'd forgotten to take the speedometer reading of the police car. The controller would be quite uninterested in what he'd found in Caen, if anything, but was capable of making a never-ending fuss about how much petrol he'd used. The PJ courtyard seemed rather empty, and so did the office.

'Where is everybody?' he grunted at the desk man.

'Oh,' blankly, 'didn't you know? That savings bank got knocked over again. The one in Sainte Claire.'

'That's the third time in six months.'

'That's right. Cantoni's done his flaming nut. They still hadn't put in an alarm system.' And even if they had: the camera was invariably too high, too low, or had run out of film at the critical moment. Close all the banks! Abolish money! Drearily, Castang typed out his report: it all looked even sillier on paper than living through it had seemed.

He hid himself in the corner, as inconspicuous as possible. Nobody must know he was here! This was utterly childish, since the desk man had seen him (but perhaps would think he had gone out again . . . hopefully). The mayor's office would be ringing up, demanding all sorts of information and a few helpful lies for the public (one was reminded of the new Ambassador from America who had said, pleasantly: 'The technique of this job seems quite simple; learning how to mingle cliché with falsehood'). The local paper would be ringing up, wanting more crimson details. Fausta was there to take care of all that; Super-Fausta was better at it than anyone.

When he finished night was falling. Things had returned, more or less, to normal. He stole out with his shitty typescript, which skated over a variety of details like his brainwaves in the Deauville swimming-pool, the moment he realized what day it was. He could hear Lasserre in his office bawling somebody out. Richard was nowhere to be seen. Fausta had gone home. He went home. A policeman going home was after all much like any businessman going home. As you got in at the door you put on the family face: it was all ho ho ho, and have the children been good, and have they finished their homework yet, and what's for supper, dear? You didn't talk about all the filthy tricks you'd been getting up to during the day, so much filthier than anything cops did. He often thought of the man who listened to the long complaint about businessmen getting so highly paid and answered 'It's only fair; look at the horrible work they do.' (Not that this was any consolation.)

He didn't even get mugged on his way home.

Vera by lamplight was a lovely sight. Her oddly shaped Slav face was only occasionally pretty, and sometimes exceedingly plain, but she was quite often startlingly beautiful and was now. She lit up all over seeing him, and would have jumped up only jumping was no longer one of her skills.

'How lovely. I didn't know whether to expect you but there's an in-case in the fridge.' Smacking kiss.

'There's a very peculiar smell in here,' said Castang suspiciously, 'like a pipe. Who's this new lover you've got?'

She looked ludicrously caught out, blushing and mumbling.

'Oh, that must be Monsieur Bianchi. He comes for a sit, and I make him coffee.' Trust the old bastard to organize himself. Of course – his fearful maize-paper Boyards.

'What's his news?'

'Oh, he won't tell me anything about that, but he does tell me the weirdest things. We have long interesting talks. The things I never knew about the police.'

Castang felt slightly cross. He didn't know why. It was as though he thought Vera would be somehow corrupted by a scaly old villain. As ludicrous as it was illogical: Monsieur Bianchi undoubtedly knew a lot that was discreditable, so that his memoirs would be entitled something like 'Forty Years of Police Malpractice'. It was unimaginable though that he should ever write them. And Vera had a remarkable quality of innocence: it was the most striking thing about her, but in no way to be confounded with ignorance. The 'sheltered life' had never set any limits to her vision, and her mind did not sit in a wheelchair. What did they talk about?

'He's a bit of an old maid,' with a remnant of spitefulness.

'Not in the least, and that is a silly mistake to make, which just shows you've never looked properly,' quite tart.

He sat lordly in his armchair, put his feet on the coffee-table, took his socks off and wiggled his toes luxuriously, by way of a face-saving manoeuvre.

'I'm sorry,' he said. 'I was being spiteful. It's good to be home. I'm not just curious; I'm interested. Nobody knows anything about Monsieur Bianchi.'

'He says the police is an elastic cushion between the government and the governed.'

'Ground between the two millstones, I should have thought,' grumbled Castang.

'You can't compare it with other administrations, like oh, the Post Office or the Railways, because it deals in human values and not technical ones. The mistake has been made of letting it get too technical. Elastic – he often uses that word. Compressible, and can be bent, but doesn't break. Technical things are rigid.'

'Can be bent all right,' he muttered.

'No, you're wrong. He says the bit about the evil men do living after them, while the good is interred with their bones is the wrong way round. Contrary to all his experience, he claims: he's known some very bad cops indeed but they left remarkably little trace, and some very good ones who had an influence, a *rayonnement*, he called it, that went on for years after they were gone; retired or even dead.'

'He might be right at that.'

'Elastic too between good and evil. The law is more evil, and criminality less, than the law is able to accept, because "hard cases make bad law," and the police function is to absorb as much of the creaking as possible.'

'All perfectly true, I suppose, except he better not be caught saying it, but this kind of sonorous generalization gets one nowhere; it's like all those clichés about compassion.'

'He says as much himself. All that gassing about social justice and the rights of man; pure beastly egoism masked by sobbing sentimental rhetoric; reading Victor Hugo instead of Baudelaire.'

'Does Monsieur Bianchi read Baudelaire?' amused.

'Oh yes, and especially the art criticism. But I only meant his conversation is interesting. In Venice, he said, the cops were called "Les Seigneurs de la Nuit". '

'Good,' said Castang tasting the phrase, liking it.

'Very bad, I should have thought. The worst kind of political police. He said he didn't know, but he thought they were a pretty bad set of bastards: it was the title that interested him, because what's night?'

Castang was getting interested himself by now.

'So I said to a painter night was just a special kind of light. He said no, night was an ancient spirit of evil. Night is the cholera, he said.'

'Coo.'

'Yes; we had quite an animated discussion. Sun is of no interest without shadow: a human being is like a drawing, can't exist without contrasts: look at this Rembrandt etching, and yes, he said, he knew that and accepted it, and couldn't explain, but that was hatching, there was as much light as dark even in the shadows. So I made a sort of Matisse thing, you know, with big pools of black to enclose the white forms. He looked at it for a long while and then he just said "Indian ink frightens me". Like that.'

'But I think I know what he means,' said Castang.

'I do too. It's in Goya. We got a bit theological.'

He grinned. Vera always did.

'When he went out he turned around quite seriously and said: "Don't go out between sunset and sunrise." I said I never did, and he nodded and said "In earlier times that was understood." He's a good man.'

'I had no idea,' said Castang, delighted. 'Electric light is a good invention, but like most technology obscures as much as it illuminates.'

110

'Don't start again: supper's ready.'

'Ho, ho,' he said five minutes later, with a spoon of tomato soup halfway between bowl and mouth; it was very hot. 'The Lords of the Night. Who'd have suspected it of Bianchi? He never utters ordinarily. All sorts of talents you do possess.'

Vera stopped blowing on hers to say, 'Why is Satan called Lucifer? Why a light-bringer? Is there a black light?'

'I don't know. We lead a very primitive existence. I mean we've had a civilization for only two thousand years, which is very short, and it consists of very simple ideas for the most, like sun is good. Apollo. But that's just one piddling little star, isn't it? And we're beginning to guess about other weird things out there. Black holes – what are black holes?'

'I don't know, and don't want to.'

'And we've only just discovered uranium, enough to know it does some extremely peculiar things. How many more are there – I mean elements – that we still know nothing about? Why not black light?'

'Matter – but matter begins to stop being matter, and then might stop being such a bore. Like maths. As long as one and one make two maths is a bore, but apparently they don't, always. As in art. The simplest definition of art has always been that it's where one and one make three. Perhaps now we will start getting behind Apollo and find out things about God. Pass the bread.'

'Whenever we don't know anything, we say "God knows" in a ridiculously self-satisfied way.'

'That's right. He isn't going to tell, you know. We have to find out. For ourselves.'

'When we don't even know anything much about matter, how the hell are we expected to understand really complicated things, like human beings? We better have more police-men,' concluded Castang frivolously. 'Or more like Bianchi, anyhow.'

'And more like you,' said Vera. 'Looking at flowers, and Indian ink, and drawings of a chair by Van Gogh. And sunsets.'

'Don't go out between sunset and sunrise. He's absolutely right.'

'Yes. Night is what? A trans-uranium element, perhaps. I mean we say crime, vice, folly, and go on trying to work back, ignorance, disease, fear.'

'There are metaphysical elements as well as physical ones. Is this Parmesan cheese in here, or pecorino?'

'I don't know, I took the one that looked hardest. Venice – the police in Venice must have been extraordinary. Why are we so small-minded and provincial?'

'We're just so pitifully ignorant,' said Castang.

25. 'Fair Stood the Wind for France'

'Pitiful ignorance' was demonstrated the following morning by Commissaire Richard, in his attitude of total physical collapse that was a sign of furious cerebral activity. For subordinates, not exactly a danger signal, but don't fall asleep: if you do Satan himself can't save you. He had slumped deep in his chair, tilted it backward, and was holding himself with the instep of his shoe on the desk's edge; his eyes riveted on the far corner of the ceiling.

'This is . . . altogether lamentable . . . The more so as you've built a very pretty case. As to . . . exactly what happened at Tours, it's probably of no great importance as things stand. I'll speak to Philippe Benoît and impress upon him . . . I don't need to remind you that it's not a legal case: your embarrassment about that was apparent in every word you wrote me last night. Which of course I only read this morning . . .' The voice trailed away almost to extinction. There was a long pause, which Castang had the sense not to interrupt.

'Most of my resources are occupied . . not to say wasted . . . in this idiotic hold-up. Yesterday a farmer turning over ground out in Ferrières brought a skull and some bones to light. They don't seem to correspond with the Martinez affair of two years ago, which you'll recall . . . but it's still "under instruction" and makes for a . . . revival of interest. I've had to send Davignon out there.

'All we need now is for some Arab to avenge his family honour out in the backwoods and I'd have to send Orthez! . . . Very well,' coming back with a jolt, 'we must let this simmer in the judge's mind. It seems to me a foregone conclusion that your Armitage boy is concealing most if not all the relevant information, and is attempting to use the heaven-sent respectability of his family connections as an umbrella. Since the girl . . . his sister . . . chose an extraordinary moment to open the car boot and let out an enormous shriek we can perhaps assume that the family had no guilty knowledge . . .'

'If they'd known,' said Castang, 'surely they'd have tipped her – call her Miss Johnson – in the ditch a lot earlier, exactly like the butcher's granny.'

'Just so. I'm given, however . . . to understand that any interference with the Judge or his family would be thought of as a hostile attitude by the British Embassy: it's become a classic syndrome. The judge of instruction has turned up the files of three such in the last ten years.

'We – I'm not speaking of the PJ, I'm speaking of the French Republic – are singularly ill-placed to complain or protest. The English will purr and point to two recent instances in which a close accessory both before and after the fact if not the actual assassin failed to be brought to justice, and protection in high places became a matter of public notoriety. You understand me, Castang, I sincerely hope. The judge thinks as I do. We'd get torn to pieces and put down the shredder.

'Without a really strong material indication the judge won't even give you a mandate to interrogate, let alone arrest. He's a young man . . . and ambitious.

'We don't want to let the matter rot while we speak of its ripening. I see small joy at the moment. Your two main hopes – good, we can forget the English: they aren't going to tell us much! Benoît may turn something up on the car: I'll tell him to make a polite request that this what's-he-called, this Brillant, ceases being distant and toffee-nosed.

'Now you'll see this matter clearer in the morning light. I might suggest to you – isn't it highly significant that whoever left the car in that parking lot left the ticket and the key! Who pulled what wool over whose eyes? . . . you've grasped that I don't have much time or inclination for speculations . . . Monsieur Bianchi has not yet resurfaced, and he doesn't take kindly to being hurried. He works best when left to himself and so I trust do you . . . oh before you go, Castang, Fausta got a signal from the C.I.D. in London. They say they've got an identification. They also say, which I suppose is very kind and neighbourly, they propose to send us a skilled and experienced officer to help in our enquiries. In other words they propose to put the dogleash on us and the muzzle too . . . I mention this to warn you that if you do see any doghandlers approaching do not begin to show any clinical symptoms of rabies, right?'

'What d'you want me to tell the Press?'

'Oh, I should think . . . that they come from that place we're twinned with under some public-relations thing. Cocktail at the Chamber of Commerce. I'll try and get the mayor to do a civic reception at the town hall, though he's in a shockingly bad mood with me on account of this bank-of-Satan getting held up again. I'll show, myself, an accommodating spirit . . . if I should have a moment . . . I want Cantoni: try and find him for me.'

It was typical of Richard to present the piece of news that had annoyed him the most as a final negligent throwaway.

Castang busied himself in composing a closely-worded telex for Tours, and another for Caen, and then dragged out the statement made by young Colin Armitage. He had blurred over the night, and this was central, on which the rest of the family had slept in Tours. According to him he'd driven the following morning to Paris on the autoroute, had a wish to taste Monsieur Thomas's celebrated chicken, guessed that his family might be there with the same aim, and pressed on in the hope of getting Dad to pay the bill.

Which had all sounded perfectly plausible until one realized that he had in fact left Deauville twenty-four hours earlier, after spending the night with a nana. Mm, the nana was flimsy, depending on Maria's 'experience' and the fact that a real, factual nana (been seen, this one) had not occupied her bedroom in Caen.

He'd got this far, sitting swinging his chair like Richard with his toe on the desk, but his chair was a lot less comfortable, when the door opened and Fausta appeared. An exquisite apparition as always, eyes that crinkled up with secret gleeful thoughts, Rapunzel-Rapunzel hair, the astounding mouth whose under-lip went slightly sideways each time her eyebrows lifted. Totally delectable.

'Are you presentable? I've very important visitors for you. You see, the Commissaire has had to go to a conference at the Préfecture.' Evil girl; she was finding this an enjoyable moment.

'Ask the visitors in. Please say to Orthez that we don't want any interruptions.'

The London C.I.D. was represented by the usual Babcock and Wilcox partnership of a homicide chief-inspector and a detective sergeant.

'My name is Larkins, and this is Mr Townsend.' Good careful French, quiet voice, cheerful smile, modest manners. No clichés served. The suits were neither hairy tweed nor the good navy serge shiny in the seat, but winterweight worsted, one grey, one brown. Nothing eccentric, bucolic or at all uncatholic: neither bowler hats nor dirty raincoats. Two quiet, thoughtful, reasonable men who would pass unnoticed here, at home, or in Buenos Aires. Mr Larkins was thin on top but not unduly; Mr Townsend had a long nose: both had the irregular, uneven features that give character to the English face, but no extravagances. Castang brought chairs, and uttered the usual politenesses.

'We say "What good wind?"'

'Oh, the wind stood fair for France. No, that doesn't sound quite right.'

' "Fair stood the wind",' tried Mr Townsend.

'Better, but it doesn't sound very tactful. Henry the Fifth surely, and the Battle of Agincourt is hardly a good introduction.'

'Anyway,' said Mr Townsend, 'Henry the Fifth was an oafish dolt of no interest.'

'They're our stock in trade, as a general rule,' said Mr Larkins mildly.

'The wind,' said Castang, 'is a good one. I'm delighted to see you. We're pretty full up right now, with a lot of enquiries on hand, which explains two things: I'm glad of any help I can get on this one, and by the same token Monsieur Richard asked me to do my best to make your visit comfortable as well as interesting, because he's afraid of not finding as much time as he would wish. He's going to try and join us for lunch.'

They had plainly felt a bit uneasy, because they cheered up.

'Well,' he went on with a welcoming beam, 'don't need to tell you how enquiries of this sort progress; in a slow tempo unless one is lucky. An amateur crime, with some clumsy amateurish efforts to throw dust in our eyes. You'll want to know briefly how I've got on, and I imagine that you haven't come all this way without some knowledge that will save us scratching around in the wrong direction. I've been occupied chiefly with her movements; now if you can tell me something of her antecedents.'

The door opened – oh no; not Orthez, propelled by his inimitable mix of intense curiosity and tactlessness? The one thing thicker than his skin is his wits. An expectant pause and Fausta entered, shimmering, with three glasses of tea; a saucer with sugar lumps, a saucer with slices of lemon. Went out with a slight wiggle.

'What a wonderful girl,' said Townsend, much taken.

'She's far and away the best thing we have around here. Good, she – sorry, this other she – came to a sticky end in the region of Tours, and the worthy colleagues there have no immediate lead, would be obliged to proceed by elimination. In a hotel full of staff and guests, that's a drag. So I've been retracing her steps, hoping for a link that might shed light on her unexplained appearance in the back of a car. I found a trace of her in Caen, so the good people there are going to try and flesh that out. I have a car, which the technical squad is looking at. The clothes she was wearing have vanished: I'd like to find those. This Rolls-Royce car and the people in it, the Judge and his family, appear as a gratuitous red herring. Not sure I've quite the right adjective. Fortuitous? Ingenuous?'

Mr Larkins had got his cue. He had been eyeing his tea, which was in a beer glass, as though wondering why they brought beer to boiling-point here. Now he rummaged in his briefcase, produced a pipe and a tin of Gold Block, and a couple of pieces of paper. He tasted the tea and began to fill the pipe.

'We got an identification on her without too much trouble as it happened – didn't need the teeth chart – we appreciated your very rich complete dossier. Assuming that she was English we made a presumption that she'd left the country recently, concentrated on that, and struck oil quite quickly. She paid for her journey by cheque, so it was plain sailing. A Miss Letitia – no, Laetitia Toth, with an address in West London.'

'Ah,' said Castang smiling, 'I only know her as Miss Mary Johnson from Egham in Surrey.'

'Really? Egham in Surrey? Fertile imagination. Never mind; this didn't sound particularly English though one never knows: however, naturalized since childhood,' looking at his piece of paper, 'the father had some claim on British nationality: Malaysian. Mother was French, oddly enough; says here born in Nice. These are just some brief jottings the Home Office kindly got for us. Parents no longer living. Grammar school education, some desultory further studies, doesn't amount to much. Job with the BBC, script-girl stuff: for the last three years or so free-lance journalist, in which she seems to have been moderately successful. We haven't gone into this at all deeply: we will, naturally, if it appears relevant. In London of course there's a fringe population of this sort which might run into a couple of thousand. No criminal record. Lived alone – more or less – in a small flat out Holland Park way. Nothing noticeably bohemian according to the neighbours: sometimes noisy gatherings of friends or whatnot, but not stuff to make a complaint about.' He broke off to light the pipe.

'Drug taker?' just to be saying something.

'The odd pill, the odd joint, no doubt. Nothing out of the way. However. What brought us here . . . she was killed here, she had possible friends, relations, I don't know; enquiry in Nice might turn up family . . . but,' waving the match out, 'we looked around the flat, naturally. Letters or such. We came across one or two slight oddities. These built up into a picture – oh, very indefinite, but by their nature I felt that perhaps we'd do best to pop over; apart from that being a pleasure, of course . . .

'The Deputy Commissioner agreed. Oh, nothing much in the way of oddities, but she had two undeclared and certainly unregistered firearms. What were they again?'

'An American pistol,' said Townsend, needing no notes, 'thirty-two Ivor Johnson – hence your Mary Johnson, conceivably – and a whacking great Llama forty-five. Loaded, what's more.'

'Well now, men do make firearm collections, even illegal ones, but such a thing is a rarity, perhaps, in a young woman unless she had criminal connections, perhaps? None that we know of, so far, but it seemed proper to determine whether she had any on your side.'

Mr Larkins was the methodical type, who took his time making his successive points, and it was aimless to try and short-circuit him. The pipe was not going to his satisfaction. And Fausta, that rarity among European women, did better than just pour warm water over a Lipton tea-bag.

'Moreover these weapons weren't rusty old wrecks by any means. Nicely cared for. We confiscated them, of course. Ballistics report – one sec – says not recently fired but in all respects ready for use. Bullets test-fired do not correspond to any known crime involving firearms: you see, as you probably know, we have quite an amount of bother with our I.R.A. However, Special Branch give this woman no especial weight, pending a further look at her associates – I'm clear?

'However. She might have terrorist, that's perhaps too strong

118

a word, connotations here? You might have Bretons and folk who dynamite things: the point I wish to make is that it seemed too tenuous, and at the same time too pertinent, just to mumble at you on the phone. Now in her writings,' picking up the third piece of paper. 'As a journalist there is a mass of notes and drafts and carbon copies: I mean this is as one would expect. Relatively sophisticated women's magazine stuff, not just how to get rid of spots or avoid sunburn. Still at any level this is out of key – I quote: "The Luger is the perfect instrument of death which makes it the perfect work of art. The aesthetics are perfectly satisfying because death is the climax" – there it breaks off. Pretty wild for a women's magazine. We thought of fiction naturally: a script, a short story, a novel? – but none of the other material matches this. Either it was a note for something quite fresh or . . . but either way she had a morbid kind of preoccupation with firearms.'

'Or with death,' said Townsend, 'by this or other means.'

Castang said nothing about Robin's experience in Caen, because one paid out line slowly, especially when one didn't have much. Did the C.I.D. gentlemen have anything to say about the Judge? He was wondering how to approach this ticklish subject when there came a discreet knock at the door. He called 'Come in' and Mr Martin Greene's handsome, amiable features appeared diffidently.

'Am I an unseasonable interruption?' he asked.

'No, no.' Castang performed introductions. Mr Greene smiled upon everyone. What a picture they make, he was thinking: the good old firm of Babcock and Wilcox, Bookmakers, in search of a good tip from the trainer. Castang with a horsy look, a little weird but somehow suitable. His collection of hats and caps for all occasions decorated the whole office. As French civil servants went, agreeable, and unusually open. Bright? That didn't count: they were generally bright more's the pity. Nothing much out of the ordinary there. More an independence of mind. Not in any case a person to be put in a bag and carried away with the groceries, and he hoped this Larkins was bright enough to realize that. They would, one hoped, have sent someone good. Could one count on that? In dealing with the detested French they were capable of showing a staggering silliness at times.

'The Consulate has a pleasurable task,' he said. 'I've an instruction to see to these gentlemen's expenses: let me have the enjoyment of inviting you all to lunch.' Everybody protesting for form, and graceful about being over-ruled.

26. Around the lunch-table

Plainly they had expected to see Richard, and been both disconcerted and indignant at his non-appearance. To them Castang was a subordinate, and Larkins was of equivalent rank to a Commissaire, so that they felt snubbed, and would take it as a hostile performance. The consul-man, Green, nice person, had been embarrassed, had worked hard at being conciliatory, but after his gaffe had been at a disadvantage. Now they'd all retired to the Consulate as to a fortress of Britishness and were there drinking tea and conspiring.

Where the hell was Richard? Fausta swore she didn't know: lying in her teeth doubtless but he could do nothing about that. Polite platitudes were all very well around a lunch table, and the English enjoyed this food-and-drink act, but it wore thin. Greene had chosen a folklore place to go and eat, slightly too expensive and a thought phony. Too many knives and forks and glasses, an over-pretentious fuss about the regional specialities. And had plied him rather ostentatiously with drink. The English had knocked back a lot of wine, but it hadn't muddled Larkins's wits, and he had plenty.

They'd had a round table, a big one chosen for five because of Richard being invited. A conference table: the lunch was supposed to put an end to ambiguities.

They let it be plainly seen that they thought Castang was

holding too much back. Less plainly, but at greater length, that they weren't at all thrilled at any suppositions or insinuations concerning the Judge and his family. There'd been curt remarks from both the English cops on this subject. In fact it had been uncomfortably like listening to Richard! – Castang left in no doubt about it: legally, any sort of 'case' against this irreproachable personage was so flimsy one good kick sent the whole thing flying. The mere fact of the body being found in the Rolls-Royce was, to them (and secretly to him too) quite enough to demonstrate this.

'You've killed a person and you're lumbered with the body,' said Townsend, distinct even with his mouth full (must be an English talent).

'You're going to load it into your own car and set off touring with it in the back? Idiotic.'

'As though that weren't enough,' said Larkins in a voice suppressing irony, 'you have the most conspicuous car imaginable, you land in the most conspicuous place one could choose, to wit a three-star restaurant in the middle of lunch, and you there give vent to an enormous scream. The fundamental unlikelihood of all this . . .'

'We must bear in mind that it's the extraordinary circumstances that are troubling Monsieur Castang here,' said Greene soothingly. 'He does have a circumstance that's hard to explain. In trying to explain, one casts about in all directions.'

'He casts about in the obvious direction,' said Mr Larkins, 'to wit that somebody had the fortune to find this car unlocked owing to the misunderstanding with the hotel staff. Who? – a wide field there. This girl was one for striking up casual acquaintance. Laetitia – doesn't that mean 'joy'? Well named! Joygirl is what she was.'

'You're rather silent, Castang,' said Greene jovially.

'I'm eating. And listening. The judge of instruction is alive to these arguments; they are his. He's an experienced and able magistrate, and rest assured he'll not be premature in any conclusions. He will be very anxious to hear yours. I feel pretty safe in saying that he'll ask to see you tomorrow. The Judge and his family, by the way, Mr Greene, you were going to find out what you could about them for me.'

'Good gracious, there's not much I can tell you. High Court so he's a knight, and due soon probably to move up, equivalent of your Court of Cassation, which would make him a lord. Apart from that I looked him up as I promised in *Who's Who*. I copied it out,' searching in his pocket for a piece of paper. 'The information would mostly be rather arcane to an unEnglish ear: I mean the clubs he belongs to and such.

'Marlborough; Trinity College, Cambridge. Wartime service Fusiliers, called to the Bar – means became an advocate – such a year, took silk, that's rather technical, I'll try to explain.'

'Don't bother,' muttered Castang, adding silently 'black rod' to himself. Gold stick; Unicorn Pursuivant.

'Married Rosemary, daughter of: you have all that. One ess, one dee, likewise. Decorations and distinctions. Hobbies country walks, botany and birds, interesting if not at the moment helpful. Flat off Sloane Street and a house in Egham.'

'Egham, Surrey?' asked Castang casually.

'That's right. Are there others? May well be, I suppose; it's the only one I know, though,' emptying his glass. 'I'll give you this if you want it. Sir James Clarence Gregory, you got it all from his passport.'

'Where have I been hearing about Egham, Surrey? That's right; Miss Mary Johnson. Now that we've Laetitia I'd forgotten her.'

Mr Larkins, who had been meditatively eating a few fried potatoes that had been left in the dish, one by one with his fingers, cleared his throat.

'I remember, Castang, you used the words fortuitous or gratuitous earlier on. I wasn't quite happy with them at the time though I didn't know why. This girl Toth, who we're agreed is a bit of an odd customer, one wondered what she was doing here. I didn't think much of it. The Loire country, the châteaux and all that, a centre for tourism. And you said you'd found traces of her around Caen, that's Normandy, right? –

122

another natural tourist centre. So that could all be pure coincidence, though I did wonder whether she might have been following this family for some obscure reason. Her giving that phony address does bear that out in a way. You've just seen it: the Judge's address is available to anybody who takes the trouble to look it up. Public knowledge. And she was a sort of journalist. It makes one wonder whether she was trying . . .'

'To get alongside him for some reason?' suggested Townsend.

'To try and get an interview for something she was writing?' asked Castang, who had still not mentioned Monsieur Robin.

'On holiday?' said Greene doubtfully. 'Why in France?' Larkins looked at him thoughtfully: if a little vexed at his talking too much, Castang thought, cop enough not to show it.

'Our Judges, Mr Greene, aren't as you're aware much given to granting interviews. It's pure hypothesis, but it is a possibility. To gain kudos for herself or her paper she might have had hopes of striking up a casual acquaintance, which does happen while on holiday, when people are more approachable than at home.'

'I get it,' said Townsend. 'A plausible young woman could catch him in an unbuttoned moment and chat him up.'

'Off the record surely?' objected Greene.

'Nothing's off a record if you announce yourself as a journalist.'

'Did she even do that?' wondered Larkins. 'I've experienced it myself. An established journalist won't break the rule: he can't afford to. If he once printed something unauthorized he'd be dead. But these fly-by-night freelances, living in hope of something they can sell to a scandal sheet, very often aren't scrupulous, and an acquaintance might be contrived abroad, where English people are more thrown together, which would be unthinkable at home.'

'Isn't she going to a great deal of trouble?' asked Greene.

'They often do, when they're after copy. But as I see it there was a fortuitous happening, in Mr Castang's sense. Say her eye was caught by the car on the ferry: a bit of snooping would enable her to identify the passengers. She thinks it worth following up.'

Castang was more impressed than he showed. He knew there was something in all this, whereas they didn't.

'It's worth following up for us, perhaps. But why should he be good copy, the Judge? Is there something special about him?'

'He might have presided over a trial recently, cause célèbre of some sort,' offered Greene. 'We can look it up in the news-paper files – but you'd know, surely?' to the two policemen. They shrugged.

'Not one of ours,' said Larkins, 'but he's fairly well known. He's a hard Judge. Good luck to him, I say.' It struck a chord in Castang.

'Dishing out death penalties?' he asked, interested.

'We don't have them any more. He's the sort who would, if he could. They aren't all marshmallows.'

'We have the same problem. However, none of this gets us closer to knowing why she was killed.'

'Of course not,' said Larkins briskly, 'but I've heard nothing yet to deflect me from my opinion that a woman in possession of firearms may have had criminal associates, and it seems to me at least plausible that whoever killed her may have known of her interest in the Judge, and sought perhaps to create an embarrass-ment, out of some revengeful spirit. It would be interesting,' with meaning, 'to know Monsieur Richard's views.'

'He's probably back by now,' cursing him inwardly. 'You're going back to the Consulate? I'll get him to ring you, the mo-ment I catch him.'

27. Monsieur Richard's Penitence

Castang sat disconsolate in the office with his hands in his pockets. Richard nowhere to be seen. Cantoni and his three toughs who comprised the 'anti-gang' squad known officially as Search and Intervention were sitting uproarious in their office, drinking beer, having arrested no less than three of the bank hold-up villains. Another was in hospital with a wounded hand, sounding fairly innocuous until you knew that he'd been hit with a ·357 magnum and knocked clean off his feet. No, it hadn't been a cowboy operation: that had been the only shot fired. A fifth villain had fled and made good the flight, but they weren't bothered about him. The eldest villain had been twenty-three, and two nineteen. They were a lot gayer than Castang was, in the hilarious sense.

Lasserre was in his office. As Richard's second, and co-ordinator of all the day-to-day work – he was a kind of chief of staff, responsible for communications, equipment and technical resources in general – he knew all about the sources of Castang's irritation.

'Haw,' he said with vulgar bonhomie. 'She went to interview the Judge about death penalties, and he gave her a practical demonstration. Most convincing – Richard'll be delighted!'

'Where the hell is he?'

'I've genuinely no idea, but stick around; he'll be back.'

There was a slight noise and he looked up. Richard stood in the doorway, watching him with a faint grin that seemed like malicious enjoyment. Furious, Castang leapt up.

'My dear boy,' lifting his hands in surrender, 'I am quite desolate. Je suis confus. My heart bled for you.'

'No no – these pirouettes of yours, you pick them up from the Prefect,' whose bland roundnesses, tones of deep concern, and soapy skill at saying nothing were notorious. 'Not good enough. You put me out on a branch, and saw it off. The English are furious. To them I'm just an understrapper.'

'Hush,' with his finger on his lips. 'I don't blame you but that's enough. I am truly penitent; I will make amends: I promise it you. It's perfectly true I've been all this time with the Prefect, but I had to stay until Cantoni gave me the word. The Minister had bawled him out, and he was looking for victims. I told him about the English and he said they could get stuffed.'

125

'Stop Being Funny.'

Richard stopped at once, shut the door, and sat on the witnesses' chair opposite. A penitential seat; a tangible proof of willingness to amend.

'I'll be quite straightforward with you: these English are being a bit funny. The Minister, in his words "mentioned the matter" and the Prefect had said "We don't want any bother" – notice the "We". So on the English side somebody quite high up has asked for the door to be bolted. Now there was a lot more stuff no concern of yours. Take it from me: I couldn't get away, and I got handled roughly: he has a nasty side. I got a considerable amount of useful work done, in exchange for an undertaking that there'd be no slip-ups. "Bavures" was the word used. Now I've a free hand for the rest of the day, because Cantoni made a good job. I'll do anything you want: fill me in first.'

'This becomes interesting,' when Castang had finished. 'This Laetitia – she always sounded so; she is. Good: salient points: one, she used a phony name, with the Judge's address. Two, she spent the night with his son; we can't prove it, but it's so. Three, she chatted with this Robin in Caen about death, and violence, and firearms. Four, a new one, she had firearms in her flat. Five, her car was found, but not her clothes. Six, no trace has been found of a companion or associate. Good, let me do some thinking about this. This chair's appalling; come back with me.'

Installed in his own chair he lit one of his small terrible cigars, black Brazilian things that were full of gunpowder, for which the phrase 'villainous saltpetre' had been invented.

'Fausta, phone the British Consulate. I must go barefoot to Canossa, through the snow. I don't want them here, I'll go there. Some satisfied vanity is a necessary preliminary to successful anaesthesia. They must be given the illusion that I'm in a box and about to be sawed in half: arrange that, will you.

'She certainly wanted to get alongside the Judge. She lost no time, you might think, in getting alongside his son. So little that there must, I think, be a previous contact or acquaintanceship in England. They won't tell us that, but it's of no consequence.

Can we view the episode with the boy in Caen as a preliminary, a sort of rehearsal? Mm. This terrorist stuff is all balls: if she were gunrunning or stuff like that she wouldn't come hawking her mutton in a police bureau, even if this Robin were more of an ass than he sounds. Yes, Fausta?'

'They'll be delighted to see you, and won't you come to tea?'

'Tea!' said Richard, as though it were some rare exotic brew, 'yes I'd like that very much. Will I stop I wonder at some cakies shop on my way? Perhaps, yes. That Prefect gave me a hamburger for lunch, damn his infernal cheek.'

He was in no hurry to jump up and run for the cakies. He was saving his energies for the ordeal to come. He swung his chair and began gazing out of the window, which looked out on to the courtyard; three plane trees and a lime, all still naked, and the regional service of Jeunesse et Sports across the way. A sunny spring day with a drying wind.

'Nice weather,' he said to nobody in particular, in an extinguished voice scarcely above a mumble. 'Good for ... fishing.' Castang mystified. He knew nothing whatever about fishing. Neither did Richard. But a bright, glary, gusty day in March, surely ... No comment was needed; Richard had forgotten about the weather and was now staring at the big wallmap of France.

'Mm; Tours. It's not really all that far. Yes. You'd do it in a morning quite comfortably, as long as you didn't dawdle. Yes. You wouldn't go out of your way a great deal to look at pretty castles. What is it Stendhal says? Set off south of Paris and la belle France is a gigantic dollop of the world's most boring countryside?

'Mm, the distance would be thought relatively trivial, if you were one of these hotcha rally drivers like Orthez. But across country, and we notice that the autoroute goes the wrong way, as they invariably do. Several nationals, with straight bits, the sort where there's always an on-coming truck, and it's just too narrow to pass the one that's holding you up. Unless you're Orthez of course.

'And some – relatively few – twiddly bits.' None of this

sounded at all like the head of the Police Judiciaire, but he did sometimes have these gaga moments: Castang waited patiently for it to pass.

'You see, Castang,' still talking to himself, 'there come moments when one has to do something silly. Be responsible, and prudent, and sensible, and they'll give you a Legion of Honour, but you stay in your box.

'It's not a question of odds. I never bet, I'm not interested in odds. I don't suppose for a second anything will come of this. But if it did, we'd no longer be in a box.

'Pleasant occupation too. Not like sitting seventy-eight hours outside a bank waiting for someone to come—and hold it up.'

'I can see,' said Castang, 'that you've got some vile pastime in mind, but I still don't know what it is.'

Richard put the cigar out and went to wash his hands. He explained over the running water.

'And you call that making amends. I go fishing, with Orthez of all people, and you go tea-drinking with the English.'

'Just like Martha and Mary,' said Richard.

'Tomorrow morning. There won't be light enough to do it today.'

'Start now. We've very little time. Start from this end: Tours have started from theirs.'

'Nonsense.'

'Or they will, as soon as I speak to Philippe Benoît on the telephone which is now. Fausta, get me Commissaire Benoît at Tours, and follow it up with a telex. What is more, Castang, he'll make a great deal less fuss than you're doing. Go see Lasserre, for the equipment. Go on. Move.'

Amends! thought Castang, going in search of Orthez. Penitence!

28. Orthez

'Yes, I know,' said Lasserre, 'the old man gave me a buzz. We've some shallow-water equipment, and can get more from the gendarmerie. Deep-water stuff we have to borrow from the fire brigade.'

'Need frogmen,' said Orthez.

'No-we-do-not-need-frogmen,' said Lasserre as to a small child.

'Well, if we've a wet suit I can dive.'

'I can't have it laid on before tomorrow morning,' paying no attention. 'And to see exactly what water there is, how deep, what sort of currents there are, we'll need an engineer from Ponts et Chaussées. In your place, Castang, I'd take a car and spend what light you have today in reconnoitre. If I understand the old man's thought there can't be that many places. Stopping for a pee and hiding it in the bushes? Or hurling it over the parapet as you speed past? And the bottom counts, huh? Stones or sand, whatdyoucallum, pebbles, gravel, and you've relatively clear shallowish water. But if there's mud or clay, and our Diver here goes leaping over in his wet suit – is that what you call it? – all he'll do is make the water more opaque than it is already. I'll get on to Ponts, and an underwater team for where it's deep, pray heaven that won't be needed, but if by tomorrow morning you've pinpointed the likely places from the point of view of the fella, that might help a lot. I'll phone the garage; they'll have the stuff ready for you.'

'I'm not clear yet,' said Orthez once they were on the auto-route, 'exactly what it is we're looking for.'

Castang, who was driving, had a moment of irritation. Typically Orthez who never knew anything! In the same moment he realized that the remark was sensible and simple, not stupid. The matter had been discussed between Richard, Lasserre and himself. Orthez didn't know because he hadn't been told.

129

'A bundle of clothes. Possibly weighted, or equally just balla-sted with boots and a handbag. A raincoat. Maybe all together, maybe in driblets. We've a description, and could get an identi-fication because she was seen in Caen. They came from Tours, and along this road. If they had anything to do with her death and there's nothing to show it, the boss thinks they might have ditched her clothes. If we find them it would show it. Quod erat demonstrandum.'

'Erit,' said Orthez, 'future tense.' Castang gawked at him, in some astonishment.

'Didn't learn much,' said Orthez with simplicity, 'just a bit at school. Stuck in my head, though.' Castang reflected that he hadn't known anything ever stuck in that head, and it was as well to know when you were wrong.

'They came this way all right. Boss sent me to check where they said they'd tanked up.'

'That's right, I remember,' slowing to turn off the autoroute. 'D'you want to change places – you're the better driver.'

'No. I'm good at this. You watch the road, I'll keep an eye on the countryside.'

And he was good at it; an extraordinary eye for the terrain. He would say 'Stop' and as Castang was backing up 'Looked a likely corner' and there would be a nice bit of woodland with a handy dip to it where one was hidden from the passing traffic.

'Can't be sure it was a watercourse.'

'That's right.'

'Be easier going the other way. But if you were in the back, looking out the side, it'd be this way.'

'I reckon.'

'I've never been in a Rolls-Royce.'

'Neither have I.'

There were plenty of watercourses, and bridges crossing them, but as Richard thought, not that many suitable for dumping parcels. A bridge in the middle of a village, surrounded by eyes, will tempt no one.

'Stop,' said Orthez. 'Or we won't work back while it's still light.' And he'd judged it just right: night fell as they got back

130

to the autoroute. What did being bright have to do with being a good cop? Not the first time Castang had asked himself the question. He was quite good at things he was good at! Like Orthez . . .

'Wait a moment,' he said, braking on the autoroute approach. 'They didn't go this way. They weren't headed for the town: going to Thomas's place. I saw a signpost,' turning the car and heading back to the crossroads. It was not much more than a country lane, zigzagging through the valley villages, but it was marked on the map, and it would knock twenty kilometres and more off the road through the city, and out again. 'Noddle,' said Castang, meaning himself.

'I'm another,' said Orthez, 'because I used to go fishing along here. I know a good place: the best yet. Because you see it coming, you get me? Stop,' he said, five minutes further.

'Too dark.'

'No. Stop here and pull in. You'll see.' Castang obeyed, switched the lights off, and when his eyes had got accustomed to the gloom he did see.

The hill stream that ran into the river somewhere in the city serpentined here in the valley, full now of winter rainwater. The antique bridge that crossed it made a dangerous narrow S-bend, provoker of numerous accidents until the administration had straightened the kink by building a new bridge fifty metres upstream. The massive stone arch of the abandoned crossing had been too much trouble to bother with, and was in clear view.

'You're right,' said Castang, 'and there's not a lot of traffic along here.' The water dashed under the arch, widened into a pool six or seven metres broad. 'Look in the morning.'

'Shit, it's not over a metre deep and you've a good chance of something washing over towards the shingle there if it wasn't too heavy.' And as Castang hesitated, having no great wish to splosh about in wintry water in the pitch dark; 'I'd like to spit in Lasserre's eye – him and his frogmen,' knowing there was no very great love lost between the two.

'Come on then.' They struggled with the tangled mass of

gear by torchlight. The thickset Orthez clambered grunting into waders. Handling even a shallow-water drag in the dark with only two men is a task they both wished they hadn't begun. There was much cursing when even the shallow water went over Castang's rubber boots and flooded him: more when Orthez struck a rusty bicycle in mid-stream. But he had the knack of handling the chain shackles and wire cables that left Castang's fingers pinched and bleeding. They got the drag in at last after trouble with the willow snags on the shallow side. There was quite a lot of slimy, discoloured and unpleasant booty, resolving itself by torchlight into an old car battery, some plastic sacks that had once contained fertilizer, a quantity of lumps of cement, a broken spade, two rusty poachers' traps and a deal of decaying vegetable matter.

'Fuck it,' screamed Orthez, meeting a coil of barbed wire mixed with old fishing-line and a broken-off pike spinner, all very nasty to handle. 'Hallo – torch, quick.' The sodden, greasy-feeling pouch would have gone downstream perhaps but for the weight within it.

'Go easy,' howled Castang; 'handle it carefully.'

It had once been soft, sweet-smelling Italian leather.

They brought it back to the car, carrying it by the shoulder sling. There was a hunt for the first-aid box all police cars carry. Castang was wet to the waist, Orthez to the armpits. They patched their fingers with plaster and looked at each other gleefully.

'Bit of rock,' said Orthex, 'to stop it floating. But we got it.' He went back for the equipment. Castang could feel it wasn't a rock. He wound some rag round his hand and opened the brass catch.

It was a Luger pistol, heavy enough in the butt to feel loaded.

29. Morphology of the P.J.

A city like Castang's, some three hundred thousand souls within city limits and a third as much beyond, has elaborate and heavy police structures as complicated and rigidly hierarchized as all the other branches of European administration. The municipal police has a large substructure in the 'urban security' brigade which handles most of the crime, even that called 'blood crime'. Blows-and-wounds and even homicides are not a reserved hunting-ground for the Police Judiciaire.

The PJ is a totally separate office, and its provincial 'antennae' in most major cities are attached to the central service in Paris, the well-known 'Thirty-six' of the Quai des Orfèvres which holds the archives, the telecommunications system, and the computer. The PJ is a club, or a caste: a 'péjiste' is not just a flic. An élite naturally, of officers with law degrees and a high level of specialization: a club-of-queer-trades, and a department-of-dead-ends too (VRs or 'vaines recherches' they are called) but the jargon acronyms are less romantic.

While still madly centralized it is less rigid than most European and especially Latin administrations, and less of a bureaucracy. The chiefs of the territorial brigades, divisional commissaires like Richard, have a fairly free hand in organizing their services, and some like Richard, who dislike 'organigrammes' and rigidly-structured pyramids, have surrounded themselves with officers in the varying grades to suit their own methods. Only efficiency counts; there isn't any other choice. The structure of the PJ is nowadays more morphological than purely anatomical . . .

Richard thus had his BRI and VP squads, his financial expert 'Massip-the-Fiddler', and the usual 'mondaine' or morals group specialized in whores and narcotics, as well as oddities like le-père-Bianchi, but they were not kept in little watertight compartments, and Castang while officially a homicide-

133

principal-inspector could find himself doing the antigang treadmill with Cantoni, or anything but the specialized fraud or vice enquiries, as people went on holiday, took overdue leave, or – occasionally – got shot.

One did one's best not to get shot, but there was no way of not getting wet (only Massip the accountant never got wet, and of course the Treasurer-paymaster). So that Vera was unsurprised, and more sympathetic than cross when he got home very late, having sent the sodden handbag to the 'identité judiciaire' lab and left a note for Richard, with soggy socks and trousers. Hot shower, boiling-hot tisane with lemon and honey: aspirin: bed: not so much chat. Mucking about in ponds in the middle of the night, cutting one's fingers, getting soaked, having to send one's trousers to the cleaners (and the treasurer wouldn't accept that as an expense) – these were all habitual péjiste activities. Leaving aside getting shot, much worse happened.

The morphology of the Administration is like all organigrammes, a vast pile of cubes connected with right-angled lines. One can say too that it is an immense mass of gas, custard or ectoplasm: since it hasn't any shape how can it have any bloody morphology? But the PJ is highly elastic. Don't catch rheumatism.

Vera – as an ex-gymnast she had great, even touching faith in massage – rubbed him with alcohol, and in the morning he was good as new. Richard was feeling contented.

'Since the English don't get out of bed early, and neither do judges of instruction if they can help it, I have about three minutes. Good, Castang, and that'll teach you to be an intellectual snob: Orthez was brighter than you were. You've got your proof; and must link it up. There are the clothes still, and the boots: Lasserre's got it set up, and will be furious if it's cancelled: go to it.' Be elastic: be More elastic . . .

For the rest of his 'three minutes' Richard watched them in the courtyard, banging about with their mousetraps, with some amusement . . . Old Castang who'd got his feet wet, but beautifully polished shoes and a crease in his trousers this morning again, and only a strip of sticking plaster to betray him

134

– and Orthez with his loutish look of a football oaf got up in a Sunday blazer . . . the two had got on well together! And here came Davignon, another intellectual type with his schoolmaster air. Pack of bourgeois!

Another annoying business: Davignon's bones had gone to 'Identité Judiciaire' who said flatly they were all wrong. Awaiting yet another specialized report from the Faculty of Medicine, he had two unsolved cases instead of one. Which he had been hopeful about, if not optimistic. An unexplained disappearance could have turned nicely into an extremely strong presumption of homicide: who buried those bones? Whereas now you're sitting there with Vaines Recherches.

He got rid of Davignon, was cheered by Cantoni's arrival with the fifth and hitherto fugitive gas-meter bandit, and further cheered by Fausta: that handkerchief used to gag an elderly woman found battered to death three months previously was quite definitely of Czech manufacture and had only been distributed within the German Democratic Republic. Which was progress, of a sort. Now for the English. Tough customers, and unyielding. What would the judge make of them? And what would they make of this handbag?

Exactly what any defence advocate would make of it. The handbag is meaningless as evidence. If you plant a body in a car, it is no distance at all to planting a handbag in a pond.

'Fausta get IJ on the phone, will you?'

Identité Judiciaire were unhelpful. There was nothing to be made of the sodden leather. The brass catch had been wiped clean, and Castang's precautions set at naught. The contents were exactly what you would expect a woman's handbag to hold, no more, with the exception of a Luger pistol which would make a nice paperweight for Castang. Yes it was hers, had her prints all over it. Likewise the magazine which held four cartridges, likewise a nail file. The papers had not disintegrated during the brief submersion – yes, the time factor would be about right – and confirmed her English identity and her ownership of the car.

'Do we have a telex yet about the car from Tours?'

'Not yet but I had them on the phone. Man's prints on the outside, coinciding with Castang's handling, so they're his. Woman's all over the inside – hers. Position of driving seat fits her, and no sign of alteration like the rear-view mirror. Numerous signs of leather driving gloves, fitting the pair found in the car, presumed hers since they fit her hand. Dust, gravel, etc. consistent with known movements of car. The underclothes found are of course hers. To wit a lemon. If somebody else moved that car they were skilful, lucky, or both,' concluded Fausta, turning over the sheet on her shorthand pad. 'Telex will arrive this morning but place no hopes in it. A note from Commissaire Benoît to say that he continues upon lines hitherto pursued until re-oriented.'

'All right,' said Richard, looking at his watch. 'I'm due to meet the English outside the Palace of Justice, and will be with the judge of instruction if you want me.'

'Tra la,' said Fausta. 'Lunch?'

'They've asked me – the English are keen on lunch. I don't know why, or what good it's supposed to do, but I can't get out of it. There's a general feeling that lunch together promotes fellowship.'

'All right but don't be late. You've these people of Cantoni's, for whom Madame Delavigne has prolonged the hold-at-disposal, and there's an indignant mum arriving at two.'

'Fit Bianchi in somewhere. I've read his report, but I want to see him.'

'I'll fix it,' said Fausta.

30. The Magistrate Instructing

He wasn't by any means as stupid as Richard had made him out. The police are fond of pretending that judges of instruction are a tiresome lot. The reversal of these roles also holds good. They are like the police: some are good, others less good. They are a lot less bourgeois than they used to be, and the police a lot more. In youth they tend to be left wing, and in age to move towards the right, but so do most people. They are fond of emphasizing their independence of the legislative and executive branches, especially when they have appeared subservient. Most judges are . . .

Monsieur Lhermite was thirtyish, tall, well-proportioned, elegant. Old family, evident in the features, as well cut as the clothes and worn with the same assurance and simplicity, and his manners which were excellent. Breeding all over him; no arrogance or affection. Viyella shirt, buttoning. Suit mid-blue, mid-grey. No jewellery but a wedding-ring. Neither distant, nor affable; polite, at listening as at speaking. A reputation for severity, chiefly based upon distaste for cant, and dislike of snivel.

All that, at least, is his best, thought Richard. Though to do him justice his worst is not much worse. When tired and harassed at the end of a long day, and he works twelve hours, he is irritable and he can be silly. I sometimes think he keeps his worst for the police. But not today!

Mr Larkins, despite his experience, was a little nonplussed. Had he expected more anglophobia – or philia? He could have dealt better perhaps with either. His speech was a little too short, and a little too blunt about Roman law.

'Nothing in any law,' said the judge, 'permits me to entertain suspicions. The police may, and do. They enquire of me: is there a case to answer? If a presumption exists, I will examine it. The only presumption existing in this affair is that a crime has been committed. No imputation exists as to authorship. Suppose one to exist. A witness perhaps behaving evasively or in flight; material evidence of apparent gravity. I am empowered to summon such a witness to a hearing. If he refuses to appear, I may presume, indeed: not before. You have a procedure, in your country, whereby if a diligent and patient police enquiry seems to show a case to answer, the papers are sent to the

Director of Public Prosecutions. He may decide upon the written evidence before him. I, on the other hand, require that such a person be brought before me.

'As for Roman law; certainly, it has many unsatisfactory features. So, come to that, does any system. I feel sure I need not remind you that Timothy Evans was tried upon police evidence, hastily convicted and summarily executed.'

'I'm sorry,' said Mr Larkins, 'if I seemed a little too warm or too hasty. Indeed there are many classic instances where the case to answer seemed overwhelming and persons were unjustly brought to trial. I'm so well aware of them that I might have appeared oversensitive. We like to feel – we do feel – that criminal trials are themselves conducted with such care and impartiality that a miscarriage must be very rare. I agree about the Evans case: the Judge at the trial was afterwards seen to be in health whose failure was not at the time apparent – he died soon after. You feel the same as we do. No conclusions on the base of a few superficial material indications.'

'One at least made excellent fiction,' said the magistrate, smiling.

'That concerned two women accused of kidnapping and maltreating a young girl. They lived a solitary and eccentric existence, which lent a certain spurious credibility to the tale. But a presumption, even of some weight, against the holders of office, and office of great public trust and responsibility, meets a barrier. Citing the words of an eminent jurist in your country, such a man is entitled to an initial incredulity, creating a strong predisposition in his favour.'

And with this Mr Larkins had to be content.

The judge of instruction had taken the wind neatly enough out of his sails, thought Richard, offering the pre-lunch drinks. They built up this comedy of the British Bulldog, growling watchfully at any sign of innocent tourists being bullied and browbeaten by blackhearted French fuzz. The – hitherto – unspoken threat, which must if possible be avoided, is to tip off all the English journalists and hold a Press conference letting loose their foxhounds.

138

'Here's to Habeas Corpus,' he said cheerfully, lifting his glass.

'I take it, Commissaire, there'll be no obstacle towards giving us access to the laboratory work upon the two cars?'

'None whatever.'

'I think it's also time that we went over the ground of these various happenings – which as you'll confess are mostly allegations.' Richard made signs expressive of joy: Philippe Benoît in Tours would be less than delighted, but – 'We might find ourselves too asking you for, no, favours isn't the word; facilities.'

'I'm on the spot, of course,' said Larkins with his air of frankness. 'I can appreciate your difficulties – none better.'

'It's the people at home,' said Townsend confidentially, 'who start getting all uneasy. This girl Toth being one of our nationals, they're probably afraid of relatives turning up and making a fuss.'

'It hasn't attracted much attention in our Press,' Richard said, 'after the man bites dog thing the first day. Corpse in Judge's car being thought of as funny. I should imagine that your Embassy people in Paris would be a bit tight of lip? A High Court Judge – he'd not be very pleased at finding his private life the subject of speculative comment in the Daily Thingummy? He was rather touchy with Mr Greene here.'

'I really think that after all I'll go for this steak – what's "poelé" mean?'

'Not grilled: poele is sort of a frying-pan.'

'Rather that than the fire,' Townsend guffawing. 'With lovely gooey sauce – yummy.'

'You must go out to Thomas,' said Richard, 'and have a bash at his grub. Got a good pretext, since all this nonsense began in his car park.'

'Definitely.'

The two cars from the gendarmerie had met roughly half-way. They'd been dragging all morning, finding nothing they wanted, or that anybody in his senses would want. There remained the Loire itself; a nuisance as it always is at this time of year.

Finding a woman's clothes in that, frankly – well, nobody wanted to prophesy. But the smaller, stiller ones like the Cher ...
Castang had learned a great deal more about obscure rivers than he wanted to know.

The gendarmerie, hungry from its exertions, had gone home to eat, leaving Castang and Orthez in a horrible village no tourist guide mentioned or ever would. Horse can be very good to eat, but this seemed a very old horse, nourished on damned stony soil.

They would work back to the starting point this afternoon, but nobody's heart was really in it. Ponts et Chaussées had lurid tales about the Loire's peculiar behaviour.

'Isn't this where they tanked their car that time?' asked Castang staring drearily out at a very wide street with a view of petrol pumps.

'That's right,' said Orthez who was deep, and seemed interested, in the local journal. 'Pump man remembered them, because he'd never seen a Rolls before, and even better because he dusted it hoping for a good tip and didn't get one. They stayed about ten minutes: the two biddies came over here – toilets; I asked – and the old boy pottered up the road to stretch his legs. But the fella there was doing the windscreen, the car wasn't left unattended, and he didn't put no body in the back. Anyhow, as you can see it's in full view. You don't have a body in your pocket, and drop it casual-like in the basket like an empty cigarette packet.'

Castang looked at his watch: a country gendarme hates having his digestion hurried. He strolled out on to the street. The village shops were not inspiring. He loitered across the road: neither was the pump station. Nothing would ever happen in a place like this, unless Duke Mantee turned up with his shotgun; it was petrified. He began to make 'the hundred paces'. The water in the bucket used to clean windscreens needed changing, badly.

At the edge of the service area he stopped and stared at a man who had decided to do his housekeeping while the car was tanked. Emptied his ashtrays all over the deck; typical. The pump man protested. The man shrugged, and walked slowly

140

with a handful of banana skins to the litter bin. Castang stared at the litter bin, which was an old oil-drum. He walked across and stared into it. It was three-quarters full of oily rags, old newspapers and stale food débris.

Orthez was yawning on the pavement, scratching his stomach and getting his shirt back into his trousers. 'Hoy!' called Castang. The banana man took his change and drove off. 'When was the bin emptied?' Castang asked the pump man.

'Jesus, I don't know. Fortnight maybe.'

'Give me a hand,' to Orthez.

'Put it all back,' said the pump man disgustedly. Cops! Halfway down, grease-spotted, filthy, delightful, was a woman's woollen frock in a bundle. With rigorous police exactitude Orthez borrowed the dustpan and brush to sweep up the stale bread crusts. The French will 'saucissoner' upon your tombstone, and still leave all the rinds behind.

31. Vera

He found Richard digesting tranquilly, in conference with le père Bianchi, which gave him a jolt. But one thing at a time.

'Where's the C.I.D.?'

'Borrowed a Consular car and gone off to see Thomas's car park. Maybe they think Laetitia came hitch-hiking with the butcher. They intend to See For Themselves, and they're preparing to throw doubt upon the competence of our IJ lab.'

'They won't, you know. And she didn't.' He displayed his trophy, in a plastic bag from the village Co-op. Richard poked at it with his fountain pen.

'Stinks. Whip it down to IJ then. And wait a moment – it'll have to be identified. What was his name there in Caen – Robin? Fausta – telex to Caen. And get me the examining magistrate on the phone.'

'And if it's all the same to you,' said Castang, 'I'm taking the rest of the day off.'

'Yes, you've deserved that. In those overalls you look like something left over from Le Mans. Tomorrow when you're nicely rested I'd like you to listen to what Monsieur Bianchi here has to tell you.'

'But . . .'

'No, my boy. The judge, you know, isn't going to have these English people dragged in handcuffs across half France. Set your mind at rest. Grenoble got a fright – they lost the boy. But they've found him again. We'll let them come here, in their own good time.'

'Evidence,' said Castang, 'in-con-tro-vertible,' enjoying the word. He was lying on the sofa like the lubber fiend that basked its hairy strength.

'I don't understand at all,' said Vera.

'Neither do I. No one does. It starts with Laetitia, though. An offbeat person, collected offbeat people, like cops. We found a frock in a dustbin and so what? People in cars will throw away anything. But it's hers and a cop will recognize it. She walked into the PJ office of all places, in Caen, chatted up a cop called Robin. He recognized the drawing you made.'

'She had a remarkable face. But – does it mean these people murdered her, or had knowledge of it, or what?'

'There's a heap of texts about misrepresentation and concealment the judge can use. He won't issue a mandate. Like Richard says, can't drag these people handcuffed through half France. Polite notes will be in order, asking them to be so kind as to produce themselves at the commissariat on their way back home.'

'But they'll bunk, surely – the boy, anyhow.'

'What I said. As Richard sees it, the others are surety for his good behaviour: think myself as soon as he gets a summons he'll take to his heels. Richard can ask for a couple of the local constabulary to dress up as ski instructors, do nothing, but watch for him to try; flight equals guilt. It's clear enough, I'd have thought, now: he dumped the body on Pa.'

142

'But why?'

'Don't know why,' said Castang irritably. 'Don't want to know. All this why is the magistrate's worry. Either for cover, as originally thought; only sort of a double bluff, see. Maybe some obscure malice or resentment. Not unheard of by any means. The father being a Judge, much too respectable and self-satisfied for the boy's tastes. How does one know?' sleepily. 'Interrogation will bring it out.' But Vera once started on something pursued it with frowning obstinacy.

'Is the boy supposed to have followed her to Tours? And dumped the frock in the dustbin to implicate the family further? I thought the frock would have stayed unrecognizable, but for this chance of the cop at Caen. It all sounds most unlikely to me.'

'Well, there's a lot still obscure. But that's often the way. An enquiry reaches a stage where you ask people to explain themselves, you ask then seriously because material evidence shows a link. Hiding her clothes and bag shows a purpose to conceal. Not necessarily to implicate. If the boy followed the road from Tours that filling station could be coincidence – the pump attendant remembered the Rolls, but one of those little Triumphs, there are plenty of those.'

'This girl – why did she have a gun in her handbag?'

'Janey, I don't know. She liked guns, had a morbid interest in them, that's clear. Two more at home. Justified it to herself by making a thing out of needing protection, by herself in a car in naughty foreign country. Carrying it around excited her.' Vera made a kind of sniffing noise. 'Woman – leave me in peace.'

'And what are the English going to make of this peculiar tale?'

'Not going to be best pleased, no doubt,' with a note of amusement. 'Richard'll be seeing them: not my job, I'm glad to say. He's been collecting all those English sarcasms – you know, like the Market's chief contribution to England being rabies. Preparing to be devastatingly mild – well, if you persist in sending us barefoot nymphomaniacs with guns, what.'

143

'More to her than that,' muttered Vera obstinately, but she'd been told to hold her peace.

32. Monsieur Bianchi's Geology

Castang was not taken into the examining magistrate's confidence: subordinate officers in the Police Judiciaire are not on chatting terms with judges of instruction. He could guess at some putting together of heads in higher spheres, because really, I mean, even this handbag and this frock, what does it prove exactly? For reasons so far obscure, had this barefooted bitch endeavoured to entice and entrap a member of the Judge's family? This very obscure piece of testimony by a policeman in Caen, apart from being inconclusive – did it suggest a possibility of any misdemeanour of his own? What was there to show young Colin Armitage had ever been near Tours? What could be said with certainty to contradict his perfectly reasonable and plausible claim of having driven from Deauville to Paris?

Tours, bored by the whole thing, said that in their opinion the discovery of the clothes made further investigation on their part, involving persecutions of a lot of blameless folk, needless, no? They were vexed at being asked to pursue with increased zeal the possibility of witnesses noticing the twilight flittings-about of a girl in a red Toyota and perhaps a young man with fair hair and a dark-blue Triumph two-seater.

Mr Larkins had even found allies in support of a complex and ingenious gangster scenario. He was coming round, he rather thought, to a theory of a professional crime, a skilful machination. His associates at the C.I.D. had not uncovered evidence of this Toth female having criminal associations on British soil, but she could well have had such upon the Continent – a word still highly pejorative to the English ear.

He admitted that superficially, professional assassins did not draw attention to their doings by planting bodies in cars. Which in itself pointed to an ingenious bluff, a false trail intensified by dropping bits of clothing in obvious places for a naïve and inexperienced constabulary to discover. Plant one thing, that the most difficult, and you can then plant a lot more. This main road from Tours was used by ten thousand cars a day, any of which could be used to drop things overboard, which you are anxious to get rid of anyhow.

He was merely postulating the existence of possible alternatives to these weird notions the instructing magistrate appeared to entertain – or run the risk of entertaining. Where you have a possible alternative you have an element of reasonable doubt no? And if any reasonable doubt existed there could be no case to answer, surely. Didn't French law work like this? He didn't claim to be an expert himself, but it would be quite easy to ask the Counsellor at the Embassy to consult learned opinion on the matter.

Monsieur Richard quite agreed, upon the principle. Rather though than indulge oneself with hypothetical unknown-persons, for whom there wasn't any evidence, surely it was easier, and not in the least discourteous, to ask the Judge and his family, surely the most reliable and conscientious of witnesses, to testify whether they had any of them ever noticed Laetitia – quite a memorable personality. Running about for peripheral witnesses – his colleague at Tours argued – was not very logical as long as the central witnesses were neglected. Oh quite, they'd made statements to the effect that they'd never laid eyes on the girl before. But that had been in the emotion, even slight shock, of discovering a death. Various small things might have come to mind since. Nobody could conceive of anything injurious in being summoned as a witness by the judge of instruction. No need of the Counsellor, or his learned consultant – the Code is unambiguous on the subject of witnesses.

Castang, spared all this, had found a corner together with Monsieur Bianchi. Not a quiet corner, and agitated by the return to duty of young Lucciani, after a month away with – of all things – jaundice. But Monsieur Bianchi made it quiet.

He disregarded all turbulence, be it physical or nervous. Alarms and excursions weren't his style; there was a Roman gravitas about him. He did not say to Castang 'How young you are' but his eyes said it. Faded and brown, the eyes of a staff nurse Castang had once spoken to, a woman who had closed the eyes of too many others.

The memory clicked into place: she had been speaking about death. A good lesson it would have been for Laetitia ...

'Death,' she had said, '– people die the way they have lived. Some take themselves in hand: those who have always faced their responsibilities. Others panic: they always have.'

Monsieur Bianchi felt in his pockets, put his glasses on, relit his cigarette with a kitchen match (in a neat metal box with a picture of the Cathedral on it) and brought his notebook out. Where had he acquired that? – a sort of diary of Baby's First Year, a PR giveaway by some manufacturer of canned spinach-goo, covered in slogans of mendacious self-praise and full of useful notes about weight and bowel movements. Its shiny plastic binding was carefully mended with scotch tape ...

'Yes,' with a deliberation that would have been maddening in anyone else, 'a district enquiry ...'

Castang had done enough of them to know they were like digging a trench in sandy soil. Go too fast, dig too deep, give even a careless stroke of the spade, and the whole thing falls in on you before you can find some old planks to shore the sides up. Bianchi had dug a trench through Castang's house. And, certainly, the houses on either side. And on either side of that. At the top was a lot of rubbish débris: one could swing with the whole arm, taking off shovelfuls at a time, wheel-barrows full. But it could be with startling suddenness that one reached hard impacted layers of greater interest, primitive stuff from the Miocene or the Pliocene, heaved up near the surface by some volcanic activity. Hereabouts Monsieur Bianchi came into his own. He would tap about – but in a very small way – with his hammer, use his piece or two of simple and primitive field equipment: it was his sense of touch that told him as much as anything. Almost anybody, a boy like Lucciani, could tell

146

the difference between igneous and metamorphic rocks, or impress the ignorant by jargon about the Jurassic, but it took old Bianchi to look at a pebble, taste it with his fingers, make a rapid estimate of its hardness and density, know what to make of its break, know how to find its cleavage point . . .

In the presence of a crime – two crimes, but he believed, like Castang, that they were one and the same – nobody talked. Nobody'd seen, heard or smelt a damned thing. The poor refuse to talk to cops because of their fear of being pushed around by the State. 'Avoir des histoires' means losing your job or your family allowances, being suddenly told your home is unhygienic and your car unroadworthy, not getting your Social Security paid, having the bailiff in. The fuzz knows every way there is of being bastardly.

The bourgeois have different fears, most centring on uneasy suspicions that the fuzz is getting at their income – there is always some – not duly declared to the fiscal authorities. Losing face or losing standing: it all comes down to losing income. To the poor, the fuzz is Might, which has always the means of abundantly wearying out the right. To the bourgeois, who do this all the time, the fuzz is something that might catch them out at it. A Right that was at the same time Mighty; what a horrible thought.

Unhurried by Richard, unpestered by the Press or the judge of instruction or any jack-in-office (in his Victorian vocabulary 'satinette sleeves') Monsieur Bianchi had patiently pushed aside masses of banal quartz, chalk or feldspar, feeling at any less banal pebble with his yellow thumbnail, lifting up his glasses and squinting because of the smoke from his maize-papered cigarette that was always in his scruffy mouth: his razorblades were as stale as his toothbrush. A confidential relationship with the women; it is from the women you find things out. Coming back after hours to catch the men at their least irritable, between their supper table and their television chair. Never refusing a drink but never really drinking it. He had become as familiar a figure in the street as the postman: they'd got accustomed to his being there: unease and hostility had gradually lessened. The

147

problem then was to stop them talking, instead of levering at their clenched molars. Monsieur Bianchi had become an expert on every menopause in the block, every constipation, every little Alka-Seltzer: it was as though he had rummaged in the bathroom cupboard.

Pebble after pebble had been laid aside. A trace perhaps of sodium or fluor, stuff not worth mentioning, interesting only in huge unexpected quantities. Lead or nickel were of hardly greater interest. He was after rarer metals. Finally he had found an interesting pebble. Without the pebble noticing, Monsieur Bianchi had put it in his trouser pocket. While walking about or sitting down, without anyone noticing – or so he believed and hoped – he had taken it out to look at from time to time. A few elementary tests had been made. Specific gravity and density, both quite high. Touch, soapy. Brilliance dull. Crystalline formation regular hexagons. He'd put it back in cottonwool. In a box to keep dust off. He didn't want to fuss with this pebble yet awhile; see what Castang thought about it. No test made on break or cleavage. There were interesting features about it. Radioactive for sure. Oh, probably nothing exotic, nothing transuranium. Something in the high eighties, between polonium and thorium.

The name of this pebble was Goltz.

33. Whiplash

'Hotz?' said Castang, not quite sure.

'Goltz,' with some difficulty through the cigarette. Was he Spanish, or was the old bugger talking Spanish, or what?

'Spanish?'

'Bit Spanish. Bit German, bit French, bit Yugo. Bit everything. Lives in the house next door. You've probably never noticed him. He's not the sort one does. Big, small, fat, thin, bald. Hairy – bit of everything. Shapeless features, that's not easy to remember or describe, or make a drawing of.' Castang saw.

'What kind of car does he drive?'

'A Ford. A big one but not a huge one if you take me. Comfortable not grand. Sort of a chocolate colour.'

Castang had never noticed it and said so.

'En't that what I'm telling you! He's like that.'

Not turquoise matrix or opal, or anything flashy . . .

'Family?'

'Married to a woman who's been cashier in the same bank twenty years. And she doesn't give much away . . . He's a good customer in that same bank, and he has friends there. That's all there is, save a brother, but it's chalk and cheese, the brother. Railwayman! They don't talk, don't see one another. It's a different world. No children. No attachments.'

'What's he do, this Goltz?'

'Mineralogist.' Castang started to laugh.

'You mean he sells pebbles?' amused.

'That's right. Little office in the town; nice building, nothing gaudy. One woman working for him – middle-aged, respectable. Like a dentist and his secretary. Discreet little vitrine in the hallway with stuff to catch the eye, sand-roses and agate; nothing of value! Quiet steady business, making a quiet steady profit. Nothing excessive, and all apple-pie with the tax-inspector. Not a breath or a whiff of scandal or gossip; no drugs or girls or anything. Home or office, clean as a whistle. I don't see much difference between the two, come to that. I've talked a bit to the wife, just because I talked to every tenant in the building and it would have looked odd if I hadn't. Pure routine: were they at home, had they noticed anything, any break in the usual patterns of behaviour? Lemons all round. Perfectly polite, but nothing better. No fear or aggression, neither anxiety nor even curiosity. They just live there. One's got to live somewhere. They like a quiet life.' Monsieur Bianchi spread his hands out, palms upward to show how clean they were – metaphorically . . .

'The Missus does her own housekeeping. Just a simple three-room flat, they've had it since they got married. No animals or birds, nothing to give trouble. Door armoured, and a fox lock. I made the usual remark, nice to see you're careful, and she said quite simply they'd not great articles of value, but had no desire to be vandalized. Office the same – well protected and a good safe. Chose a time he wasn't there – he mostly isn't, afternoons, 'n' said I was the gas board.'

'So what does he do in the afternoons?'

'Easy on,' said Monsieur Bianchi who wasn't going to be flustered. 'It's all a bit too good to be true, you take me. The other people in the apartment say they keep to themselves, always polite but never familiar. No noise, no visitors or friends hardly. Out in the evenings three, four times a week. So what's his hobbies, how does he pass his time? Without his noticing me, natch. Or anyone saying to him after, hey there was a man, taking notes.'

Castang simply nodded. A perfect Bianchi problem; a thing he was good at and even excellent. However colourless Mr Goltz, however discreet his movements, le petit père Bianchi would be as unremarkable. Castang lit a cigarette and stirred his coffee. The old boy had an automatic machine in his cupboard; it stood on his desk while he was working. He didn't bother with any ashtray – used the waste-basket, to the disgust of the cleaning woman. There was ash all over the table, and he was on his fifth cup. Even the typewriter's key-bank was full of ash . . .

'Not easy to get alongside a man like that, specially one that's constitutionally watchful, and so I told Richard. Why bother, you might say? He was all I had, at the start. And he's just too bleeding blameless for my tastes. Plays chess in the evenings, and a good bit of bridge. The only thing about that is the friends he makes. And he makes friends. Doesn't drink, doesn't smoke, but knows how to make himself agreeable, and be hospitable-like, on club premises. Plays tennis in summer: a good mixed-doubles partner. That's him; he's a good partner; doesn't let you down. So he's lots of, ya, they're not friends, but what's the definition? Men who know you, you're a good chap

in the club. All sorts. Municipal, tribunals, business, banks. So
bit by bit . . . The man's a plain dealer in a small steady way,
trustworthy, reliable, blameless. He's also a thief. Legal thief.
Over the years, going back to his beginnings, he buys a house
now and then. Cheap because badly placed, in poor condition,
tumbling down. He patches them up the minimum, and sweats
the rents. Plain-spoken, he's a slum landlord. Nothing outrageous, not what you could call speculation. But twice now
he's made a good thing out of a place on its ground value. Let
it fall down, and when he's got rid of all the tenants sell it to a
property speculator for a little apartment house. Buy in on that
at cost – you get it?' Of course Castang got it: it was a commonplace.

'But never too greedy, never in a hurry, wait well over the
legal limit between buying and selling. Never try and force, be
content to mine it patiently, content with a low percentage.
Nothing remotely illegal. I looked up all his transactions over
twenty-five years at the Registry Bureau. There aren't all that
many. Made a list, took it to Massip. He wouldn't touch it. No
fraud. No difference to playing the stock exchange.

'At this point I was ready to give up. Where's the crime?
Because your old geezer, chap who got hung, Auguste, that's
right, said there was a crime and he could prove it. Well, where
this Goltz is concerned, where, and how?

'But I'd nothing better . . .' Sheer tenacity, thought Castang.
'You haven't a hope, says Massip. He borrows cheap, from his
bridge partners like, and lends dear. He has a good margin.
Nothing to worry him except the usual drawback, he isn't
liquid, like if he wants capital he hasn't any because every penny
is out where he can't realize it quick.

'All right, I'll cut it short. He's got two houses adjacent, in the
old quarter behind the Saint-Paul. Both damned rickety. He
succeeds in getting one condemned, that's fine, because there's
a redevelopment programme for the district, the ground's
worth a lot. But too narrow to be right; the street's got to be
widened, you must set your new building back a pace; diagonal,
right? And with the house next door he's stuck. He owns it,

sure, but there's an old couple owns a top floor he can't get shot of, and they just won't sell. So you've got to wait till they die. And they do die. Because there's a fire.'

'But –'

'No no. Years it took. He didn't put any pressure on them, too crafty. They had a court order to be left undisturbed, and he leaves it at that. The fire isn't crude, or too sudden to make a nasty coincidence in people's minds. No high insurance cover. Sure, the company makes an enquiry, they always do. I talked to the adjuster. He wasn't happy, but he got the word from higher up – you see? – to let it pass. Officially the word was they'd queried or refused two other claims in the quarter, and didn't want a reputation as bad payers; their fire business is good and highly profitable. So okay, no enquiry. Adjuster was sore, but he didn't want to reopen it. It's his job, right?'

'And this old couple died in the fire?'

'Right; asphyxiated by smoke from the staircase. I'll tie it up for you. Fire starts in the basement. It's a very old dilapidated house, there's only the one floor tenanted, and squatters or hippies had bust the door. Which our Mister Goltz, usually such a careful man, hasn't had mended with his usual efficiency. The old couple complain, but their rent's real low, which is one good reason they don't want to move. They got clochards camping in the basement. This was a year ago. Last winter. And a clochard upsets a candle or something and sets the straw and junk ablaze.'

'A clochard,' said Castang thoughtfully. 'Ho.'

'Yes,' said Monsieur Bianchi. 'Tell you what. We'll go look. Not that there's much to see. But to give you the picture, like. The pub along the road isn't bad. You like grilled gut-sausage?'

'Yes,' said Castang. He phoned Vera.

'What you got to eat? . . . Keep it till tonight? No, I'm not stuck, it's just that I'm busy with Monsieur Bianchi – you see? – and there's a lot of detail. Okay? He says to give you a Bonjour. Back early this evening, fair enough?'

Monsieur Bianchi wedged the car in just off the street, in

front of the building site, next the wall of rough wooden boarding supposed to keep rubbish from falling on the innocent passer, and the perfunctory-polite notice saying Pedestrians Please Use the Opposite Pavement. Castang trod on a heap of sand like a cat, not wanting to get his shoes scuffed. Bianchi placidly kicked at some plastic sheeting, locked the car on his side and waved casually at the building; the usual pile of open shoe-boxes. The place was still at the basic-construction stage: no windows or balconies in yet; some interior plastering protected by sheets, but things seemed at a halt: the site was deserted and the cement-mixer drooped empty. It had not been too cold to pour concrete for some weeks already, and Castang said so.

'Money,' said Bianchi, rubbing thumb on finger. 'New contractor. Wanted to do it on his own this time, make a real killing instead of seeing all the big profit go to another guy. But like I say he's not liquid. Strapped for cash. Got to raise a fresh loan, and that's not done in a day, even if you've lots of friends. Maybe for just that reason – they're pals, you can't hurry them. But he's wise enough never to be in a hurry. He's got it sewn up this time. It's there, and it'll still be there when he gets back in a week or two.

'All perfectly above board,' he went on, allowing Castang to buy two glasses of white wine and adding water to his. 'For my stomach ... Right, you saw. He has what, twenty-four flats there, from one-room studio to three-room. Nice situation, poor quarter but central and definitely rising in value. This time it's the gold mine. Bank finance, but the building permit's in his name. I looked it all up at the Housing Office. He's moving in on a big killing, and that's motive enough to knock over any witnesses to anything, however small or dubious it might be. You agree? What did the clochard, maybe, or old Auguste, or the two between them, find out? We'll never know, probably, but if we can ... right, it's something maybe pretty trivial, maybe only talk, but if it was enough to hold up the building here, create some waves in the Press, that's too much. He's paying all that time, and he can't afford to pay. He's got to get unfrozen,' holding his tin fork like a fish-spear and stabbing bread with it. 'He can't afford any hold-up. Bank takes him over – friends are only friends, but business is business – and he sees the pot slip away from him. He's bust himself putting the package together, and they'll eat the birthday cake? – way I read it, that's the one thing he can't endure, and motive enough to that kind of man for two assassinations . . . Not so much maybe losing money – seeing others make it, and on his back.'

The place was poor and noisy. Dingy wooden tables, cheap bentwood chairs, a paper tablemat and a waitress with bow legs and a protruding belly. A considerable din; a loud mixture of crude cooking smells. The food came quickly, coarse, plentiful, fresh. The landlord, at the street door, let out a sudden bawl.

'Cop wants to know whose car is parked illegally on the building site.' A groan of derision and whistles came from the assembled company.

'Ignorant little man,' said Bianchi mildly, throwing his fork down and departing with his mouth full. The PJ got as many parking tickets as the Nigerian Consulate . . . Castang was in a good humour. Good local plonk; become a rarity. Grub not out of some foul deepfreeze; more so, if possible. A new Bianchi; not only one that ate, and heartily, but talked, was even garrulous. Was good company. And making out a hell of a strong case. Proving it might be difficult, but straightforward. Not a one step forward and two back while curtseying to the English. He sent the girl for another pot: came from Auxerre, she said; patron's brother-in-law. An unhurried, unworried meal. The case was there, but how to get it tightened up, without this Goltz noticing?

Sunny out, and warm. They had both eaten and drunk a tiny bit too much. Castang put his hand on the warm dusty metal of the car's roof and belched slightly. Monsieur Bianchi couldn't recall which pocket he'd put the keys in and hunted without rancour: there wasn't any hurry.

The first shot was blurred. A deux-chevaux was being started and its motor raced in an enormous clatter, polluting the whole

154

damn street. But unmistakable. Castang flopped on his belly instinctively and never mind that pile of dirty sand. He was trying to make out where the shot came from when the second one scorched him. Perhaps his movement saved his life, or perhaps the tilt of the sandheap. His ear told him a rifle, at close quarters. It hit him like a whip, scoring across his right side just above the liver; the lash jerking him, completing the roll down the sandheap.

34. Pointblank

Hit but not crippled; he could move, and had better, and quick. He could go two ways. The cement mixer was the better cover, and the pile of cement sacks, which would stop any bullet, better still, but both were too far. He went into a violent twist the other way, rolled twice and came up behind the car. Castang had the build for a gymnast, and had been a pretty fair one a few years back, but was slowed by lunch and too much Auxerre. The third bullet thudded into the sandheap just as he left it.

He had his gun drawn by now. The PJ is mostly armed with a modern American weapon, the ·357 magnum revolver worn on a holster just behind the hip. Shoulder holsters are folklore; underarm is where a cop nowadays puts deodorant, not guns. Castang would have been no gymnast without strength in wrist and forearm, but he was lightly built and he found the ·357 simply too much gun for him. His was a less massive but classically simple, efficient weapon, deservedly famous: the ·38 police-positive by Smith and Wesson: four-inch barrel. Two and a half is too inaccurate and six too awkward. Finish blued, not nickelled, the grip real walnut and not lousy plastic. He fired twice two-handed off the back of the car, at the first floor balcony embrasure only ten metres away where he had seen the plastic sheeting move. He didn't know, later, whether he had actually seen the rifle-barrel: he thought he had, and then again he thought he hadn't. A human form, no. The sun was in his eye, and that plastic sheeting is semi-opaque and throws queer reflections.

There was no point in blazing away. He braced himself on the rear wing, holding the revolver level, thinking of rushing the rough concrete steps, thinking he had a very good chance of doing so. He moved to the right so as to get better footing, away from that accursed sandheap. He had forgotten Monsieur Bianchi. Who disliked guns anyhow and said so. But who by regulation should have been wearing one, and certainly knew how to use it.

Le petit père was lying on his back, trying to move, with a feeble flutter of the arm. The face was drawn and distorted, the dry lips open. Something pinkish, like bubblegum, showed at the corner of the wrenched mouth. Shot, thought Castang, or rather feeling it as though he had taken it himself, in the lung.

If the bastard hadn't run at once, and even if he had, there was still a chance of getting him. That is duty. It is perhaps overriding duty but I don't care. I'm not leaving Bianchi here to die. The bastard has made two killings but he's not going to make it a perfect score.

Instinct told him the bastard had fled, the second he found a cop in front of him on his feet and shooting back. He had had the perfect ambush, two sitting ducks at pointblank range, sleepy and unsuspecting. One had had no chance; shot where he stood, with all the time in the world. For the second he'd had to work the action, bolt or lever, change angle; he'd missed. Castang had forgotten that he hadn't missed, but that was at this moment irrelevant. Castang's ear had automatically compared the sharp spat of the second shot with his own two. A ·22 long-rifle cartridge. A rifle is clumsy at close quarters, and the little fatty holding it would be flustered at missing the second duck, frightened and unstrung.

I'm damned sure I can take him, said Castang loudly inside his head. But the wounded cop came first.

156

To make sure he bracketed two more into the window, reloaded swiftly, risked showing his arm and side, retreated deliberately round the sandheap to the cover of the concrete-mixer. Nothing showed: he'd shifted the whore.

He holstered the gun, and turned. A crowd will gather happily for any western, but only when a camera is shooting: there wasn't a cat on the street. The pub landlord was sheltering behind one of his iron tables like he was Rudolf Rassendyll, unaware that a bullet would go through him and it both.

'Get up, idiot,' said Castang. 'Keep the yobboes back.'

The drinkers in the bar sat gaping at him: he was Rupert of Hentzau. He picked the phone off the bar, dialled Police Secours, the Samu ambulance. That came first. PJ next, thirty-thirty-thirty, the Winchester with the stutters.

'Castang, Bianchi's been shot, café Three Crowns, Rue de la Scierie. Richard: Cantoni, intervention.' He stayed where he was. He could see without knowing it the patch of waste ground in the angle at the back of the building, cluttered with the crane, the piles of brick and roofing. The bastard had dropped out there long since, awkward and hampered by a rifle down his trouser leg, but well able to do a stiff-kneed freedom-fighter act to a discreet back street where he would have left his chocolate bastard-wagon. A track like a camel, pretty certainly some witnesses; Cantoni would get all that. The bastard was a gone goose anyhow, now. It didn't matter. Nothing now mattered but what the ambulance man said. He went out to Bianchi, pushing the landlord out of the way. Fellow pointed wordlessly at his stomach; he looked down indifferently. His shirt and the top of his trousers were soaked in blood. Funny, he'd thought it was sweat. He knelt down. Bianchi was breathing. The slime of oozing body-liquids was covering his scrubbily shaved jaw and going down his neck. Castang didn't dare move him, but tried to hold the head up a little to clear the labouring windpipe, prayed. In the distance he could hear the two hoots of the ambulance and the Police-Secours car; the two double hoots, fa-sol and sol-la forcing their way angrily through the afternoon back-to-work traffic.

Richard was there before either of them, looking down into his face, the two blue eyes gone incandescent. Cantoni behind him, feet braced apart, face clenched. They'd all come in the same car. Four ·357 magnums to knock that stupid box of bricks to pieces.

'Out the back,' said Castang, jerking his head. 'Look for a brown Ford. Got a ·22 rifle.' He tried to get up, and slid over backwards on his arse.

'You take that, Cantoni.' Richard's hands were under his armpits, lifting him to his feet. Uniformed cops, machine-gunned to the armpits, were jumping out of the patrol wagon. The ambulance, a white Citroën, bumped softly up on to the pavement, steady on its hydraulic suspension, an inch from his nose. He felt his eyes shutting and wrenched them open. Cops were pushing back the now-emboldened crowd of sightseers. The boys in white were lifting le petit père. Cantoni was gone. Richard was holding him up with golfing muscles.

'Boy, you're bleeding like a main drain.'

'It's nothing at all: he scalped me. Hey-up,' sitting down.

'Sit back,' said Richard pulling his soaked shirt out. 'Here, laddy,' to the Samu intern, 'pad this quick, he's losing it too fast, and give him a shot against the dizziness.' Castang felt the needle, but couldn't bother to ask what they were shooting him with. As though a bullet wasn't enough.

'Glanced off the rib. He'll live. But he's got to come in with us.'

'I'll ride with you,' said Richard.

'Sorry, no room.'

'These-are-my-boys,' said Richard distinctly.

'Oh, all right then. Make yourself small.' Castang's eyes had shut again, but he felt the patrol-wagon brigadier.

'Take the statements,' Richard's voice, clearly. 'Rope the space off. When the IJ boys get here tell them to look for the bullets.'

'In the sandheap there,' said Castang, his head suddenly clearing from whatever they'd slammed into his bloodstream, feeling himself taken by the knees.

'Get his gunbelt off,' said the intern patiently. 'All right, boys
... all aboard.' He heard the motor start.

He passed out, or fell asleep, in the wagon and woke up in
Reanimation – on a table with no clothes on, a needle in his
vein putting power into his elbow; Richard in a chair next him.

'What's all this shit?'

'A cocktail, I should think. Whole blood; maybe some saline
or patent dragonsblood mixed in. Bit of Worcester sauce.
Have you up and skipping in twenty minutes. Can you hold
this mug?'

'Yes, of course I can. Bianchi?'

'Right here. Professor's working on him. He's holding his
own, they say his chances are intact, it missed the big artery.
So we're fairly hopeful. Tough old boy. But if the bullet had
been bigger ... He won't be talking for some while. We won't
get him back, I'm thinking. He's near the age limit in any case.
But it missed his spine, thanks be to God. They'll tell us no more
now, till after the surgery ... Now you. You've nothing much:
like you said you've been scalped and it looks worse than it is.
You lost skin, some flesh, tore some muscle. Apart from the
blood, which they're now shoving back into you, it's nothing
to make a song of. I-am-profoundly-glad-to-say.'

Castang drank his tea.

'I knew it was only a skinner. When they're for real – they
hurt less ... Get le petit père's notes?'

'It was thought of, but they're largely illegible.'

'His name is Goltz. He lives next door to me. He has an office
in the town.'

'That's all right. Bianchi gave me a report, you know. Fausta
will have most of it.'

'Then what are you hanging around here for?' asked Castang
with irritable suspicion.

'To put pennies on your stupid eyes! Lasserre's there; our
Titi will perform; don't worry yourself. When you're up to it
we'll take you home.'

A surgeon strolled into the curtained recess, grinned at him,
took the sheet off, whistled in admiration, said what sounded

like 'Chernonsky' to his satellites, added some instructions in Arab, slapped Castang lightly on the stomach, and said 'No call to write home to Mother. A Cossack hit you with his whip. You've had a Bloody Mary – it can be disconnected now – the girls will clean it out, strap you up, and you can take a taxi. Lay off the early-morning press-ups until it's had time to heal. Take this to the pharmacy,' scribbling on his prescription pad, 'come back and see me in four-five days; it should knit up nicely by then. Okay, Commissaire, you'll get somebody else to do the high diving for a fortnight.'

'Yes,' said Richard abruptly. 'And?'

'No and, I'm afraid, for another couple of hours at least. The Professor will see you then. All right?' He finished washing his hands, looked up, and said, 'I think you've all three cause to congratulate yourselves. Put a pilpul round the chernonsky, girls, make sure you irrigate the wahabee and don't make the axial shashlik too tight.'

'It's like new maths,' said Richard resignedly. 'Probably means mercurochrome and a roll of scotch tape.'

35. The querulous invalid

When a cop gets shot, nobody in the department has much time for anything else. English policemen, Judges and Consular officials might never have existed. Forms go on getting filled in: a variety of paperwork had gone off in the general direction of Nice and Grenoble, and now an examining magistrate was issuing a mandate for arrest against a certain Monsieur Goltz on charges of Blows and Wounds with intent to cause death. With a homicide in reserve until Monsieur Bianchi came out of the anaesthetic, and an Ambush. But frankly, nobody gave a damn about the examining magistrate. Lasserre already had roads, trains and the airports covered, and Cantoni was organizing a manhunt. Commissaire Fabre of the urban police cancelled leave for all his men; the Prefect was coughing up mobile gendarmerie and a Company of Republican Security.

Goltz had vanished. Cantoni found his rifle, his car, and a hole in his bank account. The magistrate spewed warrants; they searched his home and his office, and found a lot of paper, which was sent to Massip-the-Fraud. Madame Goltz was asked to come down to the office for an interview. But Goltz seemed to have had a bolthole prepared. It might take a day or so to find . . .

Wound up in his axial pilpul and a heap of bullshit – he grumbled – draped in Richard's raincoat (the administration did not provide shrouds), clutching a parcel of ripped and bloodstained clothing Castang was ferried home.

'Fine chance of getting that reimbursed.'

'I'll do my best,' said Richard sympathetically, 'but you know the treasurer. "Musn't create precedents",' he imitated a fussy administrative tone, ' "or we'll have them asking for a new suit every time they cross a barbed-wire fence. Think himself lucky Social Security pays his skin back". Well, you'll have a flaming big claim against this Goltz.'

'Don't make me laugh, it hurts.'

He was put in bed, Vera completely tranquil, as always in moments of anguish. He could hear a clink of teacups: Richard would rather have tea to a schnaps any time. Everyone offers you schnaps, but where can you get a proper cup of tea? Answer, from Vera. Richard was talking a lot in a soothing mumble pitched too low for Castang to hear. She'll be upset about Bianchi, he thought, with a hint of self-pity. He wanted to go to sleep. Hell, his bladder was full. Accomplishing the tiresome chore of emptying it was a troublefilled bore. He was stiff and sore, and in a lot of pain.

Oh, the cheap egoism and vanity of the human being. Bianchi was in worse. Much much worse. Possibly – with renewed self-pity – but that doesn't stop *my* pain.

He fell asleep, still cross with Richard and Vera giggling and

161

conspiring next door. Damn it, he could hear them both laugh. What did they have to laugh about!

He woke four hours later, feeling fine, or fine but for this ghastly shashlik, which those cows had certainly put on too tight. A slight headache, and tingles in fingertips, and obscure cramps in one foot, but nothing a couple of aspirin wouldn't fix. What he wanted now was a large schnaps and a cigarette. There was a smell of soup in the living room.

'Back to bed,' said Vera, shocked.

'Nothing bed. All these nourishing soups and broths – Czech medicine! Fellow's shot – put a few spider webs on the place to make sure it heals properly, fill him up with bouillon de légumes. Large Scotch! That stuff from Islay that tastes of iodine.'

'Stop your nonsense,' rather cross at rude remarks about the soup. Men – either at death's door or complaining all the time, when they were simply supposed to stay quiet and let scar-tissue form. He can have the big schnaps; it might make him sleepy. But not on an empty stomach.

'I'll put a pillow behind you and you can look at the television.'

'I don't *want* to look at the television. Let's make love.'

'Idiot,' she said. 'Just remember, if you set it off bleeding it'll soak through to the sheet. Tscha,' in Czech, getting grabbed.

He woke up at the crack of dawn, complaining. Hadn't slept a wink. Got a filthy taste in my mouth. Those idiot girls have put the bandage on all wrong: knew all along they were in-competent. Why does this coffee taste of detergent? Hanging around like this one just gets constipated; sitting on the lavatory is quite painful enough as it is. What are you trying to do, poison me?

Vera began by patient explanations. You slept like a rose. But because it was painful to turn you spent a lot of time on your back. Hence horrible dreams, loud snoring, and that is what makes the bad taste. Your temperature is down: you look slightly green but no worse. There's nothing whatsoever wrong with this coffee. You can't have a shower but shave, do your

162

teeth; you will then feel better. It is biting off your own nose to behave in this irresponsible way. The wound doesn't get a chance to heal if you keep jumping about. Read the paper quietly while I do your bed. I can make you comfortable if you'll let me.

He looked at the paper for ten seconds; it was full of rubbish about Manhunt. He threw it across the room, which made Vera angry. He swore at her: she looked at him with dignity and shut herself up in the bathroom. He looked at the floor awhile, picked the paper up and smoothed it out, folded it nicely, laid it on the table, dressed, with difficulty, right down to his gunbelt and shut the front door very softly behind him. Nobody pursued him or shouted from the balcony. His car was parked between the poplars, a little down the road, in the direction in which Monsieur Souche had found the clochard. The day was cold and rainy; buttoned up in his raincoat he felt like a Michelin-man, a Bibendum with steelbraced tyres all around in layers. Getting into the car was an elaborate affair. When Vera's bottom half was paralysed he used to lift her, but putting even her light weight into a car was a complicated process.

He had pushed her a great deal in the wheelchair. They had together explored the byways of the city outskirts. It had grown enormously, this town. Twenty years ago – even twelve, when he first came here still green and thinking he knew it all – it had been recognizably a provincial French town with the pre-war flavour still largely intact. It had not only doubled in size, since: it had changed radically, become a European city. Now much more anonymous, flavourless, a place that could be anywhere, but it was a change for the better. He had liked – and still liked – the old medieval heart and Renaissance grandeurs of the ancient dukedom, but hadn't at all enjoyed the stultifying mentality of the nineteenth-century town, hopelessly louis-philippard, a monument to bad taste and petty moneygrubbing. France has changed out of recognition and for the better, he thought, getting out of the car: getting out was even worse than getting in. This is no longer a provincial town. It has become a large, very nearly too-large city, a regional capital of a large,

163

varied, interesting piece of Europe. Its bottom half is no longer paralysed. It moves, it thinks, it flexes muscles: it is a good place.

Lasserre looked at him with no particular joy. What was he doing here? There was nothing useful he could do, he was supposed to be an off-duty hero, he didn't enter into Lasserre's organizational scheme, he might as well go back home and get into bed. Lasserre had been up all night. He had gathered all the strings into his hand, unknotted and running smoothly like reins between his fingers. No, they had not yet got Goltz. But they were damned sure he hadn't got away. The place was sealed off and Goltz was bottled. Things were in temporary abeyance while shifts were changed and cops who'd been over twelve hours on duty were relieved. It was only seven-thirty. Before eight Richard and Cantoni would be in, all the necessary explaining would be done and he, Lasserre, who had worked it all out sector by sector and making sure it was quite foolproof would go home to bed. He wouldn't get any thanks anyway; he never did. Castang would do well to go home, too: there was nothing he could do, carting his stomach around like an over-weight penguin.

'What about the brother?'

'Whose brother – Goltz? Don't be a fool: one of the first places we checked. Ridiculous: they haven't seen or spoken to one another for thirty years. What could a man like that have in common with a ticket clipper on the railway? One of Cantoni's boys was there, went over the house and neighbourhood, natur-ally, but pure routine, you could see they were flabbergasted. Come to that they're highly respectable and intend to stay that way. "Haven't seen him and don't intend to" said the wife. If he came their way they'd clear him out of it. But he won't. Knows well enough there's nothing to be had out of that.'

'Where do they live?' out of idle curiosity.

'Down in Saint-Loup. Clear off, Castang, will you; if Richard catches you here he'll blame it on me.'

'All right,' said Castang mildly.

36. Down by the Sally Gardens

Being a cop Castang reckoned he knew his city pretty well. But the outskirts of the city he knew best of all, and for this he had Vera to thank.

Vera had been paralysed in her lower half for give or take nearly two and a half years, after her accident. Paraplegia is a vague term. There had always been, thank God, hope and better than hope of her getting well. Her spine was injured, but not destroyed. She had not, and especial thanks to God for that, been for instance deprived of all functions. A couple of weeks after – it had seemed the end of all but vegetable life – she had been still a helpless lump pushed around the corridors of the University Hospital on trolleys, but she'd whispered to him that she knew she was going to be all right; she could control her bladder and her bowels. The surgery had worked. There had been the terribly long – over six months – misery of the dreadful physiotherapy centre. One looked at all those boys, for most of them were so wretchedly young, who'd been in car crashes, floating now helpless in the heated pool, and one could hardly bear to face it.

And once back at home, in the wheelchair and continually climbing out of it, falling on the floor and unable to get back up, there too had been a long mournful time during which he had become secretly convinced that that was that; she'd never get further. But she had: her first wobbly steps hanging on to the rigging he had stretched across the room had been made alone: he wasn't even there.

During that time, and for more than half a year later while she learned again to walk, she had wished above all for one thing: to get out of the flat; not to be imprisoned, not to allow either legs or head to accept the limit of four walls. On all his free days, rain or shine, and on all the summer evenings until it was dark before he got home, he had piggybacked her down the steps and into the car, gone back for the folded chair and slung it in the back, and driven her somewhere she could 'walk'. In the byways, where people and cars were scarce, where the population was old women, dogs, and men in overalls on mopeds taking short cuts home from work.

The growth of a city is inconsequent, wasteful, untidy, badly planned: all good refreshing healthy things.

A field, a farm, a whole village can get abruptly wiped out. The old place names stay, for a generation or two, while the population that is peasant survives. Marius, searching for Cosette in the desert of the Paris *banlieue*, wanders in the Champ de l'Alouette, the Field of the Lark. But this is not Paris, not even Victor Hugo's Paris, and in the centre of a suburb, two steps from a municipal estate whose concrete fields grow old newspapers and abandoned supermarket trolleys, one finds fragments of village. Vera had this in common with Victor Hugo, the love of the city's fringe. Rusty wire fences sagging under the weight of flowering convolvulus, enclosing odd lumps of waste ground where the giant burdocks are head high among the ragweed, were her delight.

Nowadays a new quarter is planned as an entity, with its linking ring roads, its commercial centres and pedestrian precincts, its schools and sporthalls and its horrid park all complete on paper before the bulldozers move in. But Saint-Loup was not like that. It was higgledy-piggledy piecemeal, built a few yards at a time around brickyards and sawmills and gravel-pits. It was spiderwebbed with rivulets and runlets, as when a bucket of water is spilt on ten square metres of worn brick paving. There were odd outcrops of hideous facades in the mock-gothic of eighteen eighty, there were little alleys of tiny cottages lovingly restored at enormous expense, there were orchards, where the grass grows waist-deep, there were amazing gardens crammed with hollyhocks and delphiniums. There were gardens everywhere.

The planners can do nothing with it. It is an enclave, bound to the city by two dusty wide boulevards stinking with diesel fumes, but by nothing else. On the other three sides and much of the fourth it is cut off from the city though still inside it, by a barrier more impenetrable than wire or water: by the railway lines. The railway age, gloriously lavish and confident, cut great swathes of terrain half a kilometre broad, filled it all with branch lines and loop lines and spur lines: there are high embankments, deep cuttings, massive trestle bridges. Nine-tenths of it is now unused, and will never be used again. But the SNCF, which never throws anything away, keeps it all. Who knows, it might come in handy.

No municipality, however large and powerful, can do anything about the SNCF. It is a republic within a republic.

Day after day Castang had wheeled Vera through these little paths between nettles and thistles. Along the railway lines in summer grow an amazing variety of wild flowers. The winter-bare ballast grows a scarlet fever of poppies, a frenzy of fox-gloves, exquisite wild chicory.

The SNCF has the biggest and most beautiful garden in Europe.

Castang stopped the car where a magnificent wide street lined with lindens, with another double row down the middle, came to an abrupt whimpering end before a railway bridge just wide enough for a double cart-track. The city had had vague hopes for the last twenty years of getting across to Saint-Priest, the next quarter beyond, but had given up trying. He walked to a little bridge across a waterway where the village women, thirty years before, had still washed their clothes. Castang spat, in the water. He wasn't making it any more polluted than it was already.

Along both sides of the water, and of all the little waterways, lay gardens. Les jardins ouvrières; segments of ground belonging to the municipality, sometimes the state administrations like the railways or electricity. Pop art, Vera who loved them said; in the true sense of the word. Nowhere else does the good side of France show to such advantage – the passion for individuality, the feeling for proportion, the craftsmanship, the instinctive taste. She could never understand how the interiors of their homes could be so horrible: here, there is never an ugly thing.

167

There are no plaster gnomes, here. Even things in themselves ugly, corrugated iron or asbestos sheet, are here beautiful and good. Every summerhouse, all made of builders' junk and obeying nothing but the owner's fantasy, is a shout of joy.

One must look at them all the year round. In summer when every fence is thick with climbing roses, every terrace roofed with vines, one can do hardly better than guess at hidden delights. In the early spring, when everything lies bare, even last year's tat and empty beerbottles, the beauty is more humble and more touching.

Hardly anything was out yet but crocuses. The willows along the waterside were growing their soft green fur. The green prickles of the daffodil spears showed along the paths. There was a good contrast to the dark firs growing up the steep railway embankment.

Castang went to the pub, a wretched hut bravely called the Green Hunter, with an outside lavatory and a little dusty space between two plane trees just big enough to play pétanque: as funny and as lovely as the rest. There are six thousand of these gardens in and around the city. Near fifteen hundred in Saint-Loup – an enormous area cantonned into six or seven parishes.

There was no one to be seen; he could have pinched the whole pub and loaded it on to his car. Eventually he found an old woman, cross, deaf and smelly but who knew everything: there are always old women.

The way went under the railway bridge and petered out abruptly. There was a car graveyard, adding an autumnal rust to the landscape; a collection of the gigantic cotton-reels on which insulated cable is wound. A path, or bicycle track, led to a signal box of great architectural exuberance, perched like a watertower, overlooking a one-time shunting yard. The path became wooden ties, black and slippery, to cross the rails, and under a metal bridge carrying a main line. Castang followed it, and came out upon an extraordinary scene. A hundred metres ahead lay the twentieth century, the autoroute junction raised on stilts, sloping down into its cloverleaf pattern that allowed the eye, intent upon its tight curve, no leisure for the driver to stare at the countryside. Castang had driven off there a few hundred times without ever seeing the picture that now lay on either side of him; a Corot.

Another of the little streams ran the other side of the railway: the willows on its further bank were enormous, curving over the summerhouse shacks. They would need no further shade in summer: the stone steps each owner had made to the waterside and his punt landing were mossy and squelchy. One owner, doubtless Mr Jeremy Fisher, had converted his whole terrain into a watergarden and his shelter perched aquatically there-upon as though afloat.

The path to the front gates of these gardens ran at an angle to the water so that the slices of terrain grew shorter but deeper. A few hundred metres of this, the gardens now on both sides so that his head swung from left to right like a tennis umpire, and he found one that was an orchard. There were no veget-ables, but nicely mown grass; the trunks of the fruit trees nicely whitewashed. Vera, being Czech, could have told from the bare branches the apple, pear and plum: his ignorant Paris-bred eye could only distinguish cherry. There were no flowers, but the summerhouse by the waterside was covered in climbing branches intertwined that would be rose and clematis. Vera, a Redouté student, said that one saw amazing old-fashioned roses in these gardens that no nurseryman now sold. Castang, who did not know a banksia from a malmaison and found the door solidly padlocked, was chiefly concerned with getting over a high thorny fence without ruining yet another pair of trousers and without the wound, harshly burning under the tight strappings, breaking open afresh. It took him five good minutes, but there was nobody there to yell at him. He got down gingerly, treading on the daffodil spears; a pity, but there were lots and lots more. He walked slowly across the new wet grass. When he got to the hut he unbuttoned his raincoat and put his pistol loosely in his hand. He wasn't going to need it, but it might save exertion that would hurt his torn stomach-muscles.

'Mr Goltz,' he said quietly.

37. Meaningful ongoing dialogue

'Mr Goltz,' he said again. 'I'm alone here. I've no desire to run after you or shoot at you. You shot at me and caused me some damage. I'm sore and I hurt a lot, but I'm not feeling all that vengeful. So I'll come in, if I may.' He climbed the step, clanked at the stiff old latch with his left hand, pushed the creaky door, and came into a darkish sweet-musty atmosphere of fear and rotten apples. Some of these huts are complete cottages, and even have sleeping quarters, but the railwayman lived only half a kilometre back across the track, a ten-minute stroll, and had not bothered with more than a roof over his head, for when it rained. One room, at once kitchen and bedroom, if an old divan made it a bedroom; one lived and ate on the terrace facing the waterside, shaded by the willows, quite alone and private, but wouldn't one be bothered by insects? So thought the town-bred Castang, but nobody here is concerned by so trivial a detail. Goltz was not only town-bred but a bourgeois, possessing none of the skills needed to make himself at home in a shack. Without clean cuffs and creased trousers he was deflated. He'd even kept his tie on. Castang put his pistol on the table and sat down.

'Damp,' he said, 'and at night still cold. You didn't dare light a fire? Well, it wouldn't have lasted more than an hour or too longer. Today, quite certainly, Monsieur Cantoni would drive up and come busting in upon you with rather less ceremony than me. This is your family when all is said. You both discovered that with some surprise. So I argued. So Monsieur Richard will be arguing. Blood is blood. I'm talking of yours, not mine.

'I got here first only because I was wounded, and being kind of out of action didn't have a lot of details to fuss about.

'Your brother is technically guilty of harbouring a fugitive, concealing information, conspiring to hinder the instrument of

170

law – that's me – but probably in the circumstances the judge won't make a great thing out of it.

'You're in trouble, to be sure. There's Monsieur Bianchi, whom you shot. He isn't dead, and unless some queer post-operative infection gets a hold of him he'll be all right, once he gives up smoking. So that one isn't homicide. There are the others, which are. That'll be my business, with Monsieur Bianchi laid up. Old Auguste, huh? And the clochard, whose winter quarters were in that house you burned down. But I don't want to talk: it tires me to talk. Walking tires me too. Have you got the padlock key? I don't fancy getting over that fence again. It's cold as hell here too. So come on then, will you? I'll phone for a car from the pub.' Goltz looked like Jeremy Fisher after he had been spat out by the big trout because his macintosh tasted nasty. Draggled. The man still hadn't said a word. But what was there he could say?

Castang felt a moment of extreme fatigue in the pub. He was used to that; it was the reaction, the let-down of tensed nerves. Still – looking at this . . . rag – it was an anticlimax. What, the entire police resources of the city afoot for that! He asked the old woman for a glass of red wine, turned shruggingly, half-reluctantly to the man who stood quietly by with bowed shoulders, giving no trouble.

'You want something?'

'I don't drink.'

'Cigarette?'

'I don't smoke.' Castang mumbled something inaudible, picked up the telephone, said the fewest possible words in his curtest voice to the switchboard. By the time he had finished the second glass and smoked the cigarette down to the filter Lucci-ani was there with a car. He looked curiously at the hangdog couple as they climbed in, produced a pair of handcuffs: Castang shrugged.

'Stop at the Rue des Acacias. Back under the bridge . . . left, here. Wait for me.'

There were acacias, pruned to give shade to some scrubby waste ground where the children played. Houses on only one side: an oddly English-looking terrace of cottage-type poky little houses whose windows were too small, built before the war. Railway houses, for railway employees. Little wooden gates, minuscule 'front gardens' with tiny gravel paths and absurd 'lawns', all immensely neat and well-painted; all the net curtains spotless. Number sixteen had a 'tunnel' from the gate to the front door, to make a pergola for the climbing roses. Number seventeen had lilacs.

'Madame Goltz? Police Judiciaire, Castang.'

'What do you want? They were here yesterday. Didn't you believe me then? What do you pester us again for?'

'Look in the car.'

'You better come in a moment. I'm not going to talk on the street.'

Tiny houses, but space wasted. A 'hall'. Living room next door. Kitchen built out at the back, bathroom added later. Upstairs, a tiny landing and three tiny bedrooms, parents, boys and girls. Fresh wallpaper with a pattern of roses on a trellis. Hadn't they enough roses, then? He wasn't asked further than the hall. Room for the two of them, the man in his raincoat, a bit bulkier than usual around the middle, and the woman in her kitchen apron, thickened too around the hips, but a handsome woman: plain but well-shaped features with character in them, and kindness.

'My man is away, on stopover. Back this afternoon . . . You got him then. Where was he?'

'Hiding in your summerhouse, on the allotment.'

'The softhearted fool. Letting himself be dragged in. I should have guessed. He was queer last night before going. I thought it – that he was just upset. That *crapule* . . . well. Now we'll be in trouble.'

'You didn't know?'

'No. When the cop came, I had no idea. If I'd known I would have lied, to cover my man. I would have known, today, even if he hadn't told me. Well . . . I suppose I'd have done the same. If it had been my brother. When all is said and done.'

'They didn't see each other.'

'Never once. New Year, All Saints, nothing. Never, even at our wedding. He despised us. Fair enough. We despised him. But at the end . . .'

'That's all. It's finished now. You'll likely get a summons from the judge, but only as a witness probably. I can't be sure but I doubt that the court will want to make trouble for you. Judges are human, too.'

'Yes. I suppose their families would stick together, too.' It was a remark that stuck also in Castang's mind, as he went back down the tidy path bordered with brick to keep the gravel off the grass.

Richard was in the office, looking tired and pale, but in the newest of his working suits, and with a bow tie, as though to put out more flags.

'You all right, Castang? I understand, but don't reopen it; that won't help either you or us. . . . Sit down, you. Take the cuffs off, Lucciani. Get your pad. Take the shorthand. Ask Fausta for four cups of coffee, Castang, will you? . . . I am the divisional Commissaire. You are Goltz, Etienne. Correct? You are, as Monsieur Castang has informed you, under arrest. There are serious charges against you. Some of these I leave aside momentarily. For the present, the accusation against you is that you committed an act of armed banditry, lying in wait for two police officers, firing shots from ambush, gravely wounding Inspector Bianchi, whom I may tell you is still between life and death in hospital, and slightly wounding Inspector Castang here present. Do you admit to the authorship of this act?'

'I suppose so.'

'You suppose so. Well. Whether you admit it or not is of small importance. Your weapon was found with your handprints near this scene. Eyewitnesses will testify to seeing you running away. There will be no trouble on that score, I can assure you, no matter what statements you make, retract, or attempt to cast doubt upon. Whatever the feelings of the persons in this building towards you I tell you formally that you will be treated exactly the same as any other supposed malefactor: that is to say you will be interrogated by Monsieur Castang here

173

or such other officers that may be designated for that purpose. Whatever the outcome of that there is evidence enough to pronounce your formal indictment on the grounds stated. After you have made your statement you will be presented in due form to the instructing magistrate, Madame Delavigne, and the matter will then be out of my hands, I am glad to say. Have you understood this? Don't just nod; your answer is wanted for the records.'

'Yes.'

'Very good. You'll have more to say, my bonhomme. That is not a threat; no brutalities are tolerated here. Can you manage this, Castang? You'd prefer to, I think. Very well then. Go home when you like.'

Castang stood up, clumsily.

'Come on,' he said.

He sat again heavily in his own chair, feeling tired and feeling unequal. Silence gathered. Lucciani waited quietly with the pad on his knee. Goltz sat and did nothing. In the silence Lasserre opened the door, stood there, looked at Goltz, shrugged and went away again, closing the door for once after him. Castang dragged words out of himself.

'Lucciani, you'll do the preliminaries afterwards, the identity stuff. Just note the time and that I cut straight to interrogation on fact . . . Are you hungry?'

38. The dialogue becomes too much of a monologue

'No . . . I had bread, sausage . . .'

'Thirsty?'

'Thirsty . . . yes . . .'

'A beer? Mineral water?' suggested Lucciani.

'A bottle of . . . orangina . . .' The two policemen looked at one another – orangina! Nobody would clip him over the ear. Nobody would even speak harshly to him. A bag of bones . . . one had scarcely the heart even to conduct a standard interrogation. Orangina . . . for a six-year-old, and even then . . . don't drink that sticky stuff, dear; it'll only make you thirstier.

'We'll have to send out for that.' One could see why Goltz passed for unnoticeable. Even trim and smart he was an effaced person. Now that he was grimy and unshaved, the suit creased, the shirt limp, he seemed more shrunken and insignificant than ever. A bag of bones . . .

The office boy brought a tray from the pub across the way. Two bottles of a fizzy, vaguely ersatz compound. One supposed there was some orange juice and pulp in there somewhere, together with the approved colorants and additives and synthetic citric acid. Beers for the fuzz. A salami sandwich nobody wanted. Lucciani ate it finally: that boy was always hungry.

'Why did you shoot at me?' asked Castang suddenly. 'In any circumstances such a – a silly thing to do.' One spoke as to a child, an unlikeable, podgy, awkward child, none too bright, unpleasantly sly and cunning, that smelt bad, given to nervous farting.

He'd felt hemmed in! Followed around, leaned upon, closed in upon. By quiet, slow, mild Monseigneur Bianchi brushing ash off himself and taking his glasses off to polish them. Inconspicuous as you could wish and persecuting, lord knows, nobody, but Goltz, preternaturally suspicious and always frightened, had seen him as a tiger. And suddenly there were two tigers. He'd been mousing around that building – would it never be ready – when could he shake up his last bit of credit, get an apartment smartened up and furnished as a showpiece – then maybe he'd get something sold. He had plenty of frozen capital but it was liquid he needed desperately. Bianchi had been right, all the way.

'You admit then, the shooting?' Incredible. He'd seen them go in the café for a bite, leaving their car. He'd gone home and got a gun. He'd get rid of the tigers. Good grief . . .

175

'And you admit the assassination of the clochard – I forget his name. But you know, very well, who I mean.'

'He was blackmailing me. He wanted money.'

'Yes. And Monsieur Auguste?'

'He was blackmailing me, too.'

'Watch your answers.'

'He threatened to denounce me.'

'Not quite the same, is it? In fact, he did denounce you.

'You admit, then, finally, to setting the house on fire?' It didn't really matter whether he did or not. He'd retract it all later, or his lawyer would do so for him. But why was he such a poor thing?

'Tell me about yourself, Monsieur Goltz. Your early days, for example, your youth. The beginnings, if you like.' Colette Delavigne, whom Castang knew quite well and they were by the way of being friends – she was more Vera's friend than his – they hadn't seen so much of each other recently – Colette was the instructing judge, and she'd ask all this. In much greater, deeper detail, and she'd call for medical opinions. Two at least, and the defence would call for more. But he'd ask it, too. One has the right to be curious, about a man who has just missed killing oneself and a colleague.

Right, again. An unpopular, and even then nasty little boy. A currier of favours, a seeker after popularity and aggrieved at not getting it. A sucker-up, to the chiefs. Not gifted at either academic work or sports, a child disliked, and at best patiently put up with, by its professors. But who'd wanted so much to have some social standing. One needn't be liked, if one was respected. The brother was liked. Slow and clumsy, too, but a patient honest boy. As a front-row forward he put his head down and shoved. And was generous. This one – generosity was a foreign language.

'The pattern of your existence, Monsieur Goltz, as observed and traced by Monsieur Bianchi – this shows a liking for male company, a preference, a seeking out even. Do you agree? Why is that, do you think?'

But of course. Women had never been interested. Indeed,

176

instinctively they had felt that this was a personage to shun. And on his side: fear again, mistrust. The shrinks would go into that; the mother; the grandmother; the early efforts made, perhaps, at seeking prostitutes. Some wounding remark. That little thingy you've there isn't much good, is it? What's the matter then, can't you get it up?

'And your wife, then, Monsieur Goltz.'

'She's always hated me.' It was too dreary: Castang felt almost too tired and discouraged to go on. No integrity, no honesty. No bottom, no centre, no sand. Sitting there sucking at that orangey pap and looking at nothing with those blank little eyes. That is the being still shaken by the thought of the chase, the manhunt. The knowledge that everything has gone wrong, everything is ruined. Being alone in the cold and dark, in that shabby little hut where others were happy but never him. The half-ashamed, half-contemptuous, three-quarter-unwilling shelter and food and forced advice of the brother. Sure, you can stay here the night. I'll come back tomorrow when I get back from Metz. But you can't stay, you know. It wouldn't help. Think it over, sort yourself out. You better go to them, freely, because they're sure to get you. Don't worry – I won't mention it to my wife. No!

But a day or so in jug and he'll be quite chipper again, with ten thousand systems of defence, and complaining about the food. Goltz. One hawked it up, and spat it.

'I more or less walked out on him,' admitted Castang. 'Excused myself; said my scratch was troubling me. Which I suppose was true. Couldn't stand any more of it. Lucciani can finish it.'

Richard was in his usual attitude of meditation, chair pushed back and tilted, foot wedged against the desk, face downcast and chin on his collar. He pulled up his trouserleg to scratch.

'No trouble getting him to talk?'

'All the trouble in the world getting him to stop, and all about him. And one's no wiser at the end. Colette Delavigne might be able to make sense of him; I can't.'

'That pesters you still. This mania for understanding . . . If

177

he were interesting I could sympathize. He isn't. He's too dim a drip to be a horrible bastard. I have no feelings whatsoever about him, and my wish is to get him out of this building as quickly as may be. The English family left Cannes this morning, on their way home. Slow and dignified. Like one of those Tour de France stages where nobody is concerned with giving a show, because of hanging on to what one has. All right? You can go home. You've done a good job. But forget now that it happened in your house and that you took it all as a personal affront. Time not to be professional. I hope that Lucciani's understood that I want nothing but a sequence of facts. On such a day I shot old Fuckdust here. Never mind why. All there is in reality is an enquiry into the financial tangle, and when the judge calls for a supplement of information, that's Massip's job.'

'There's nothing consequent, nothing coherent, and no centre.'

'Go home,' said Richard patiently.

Under the plane trees in the courtyard, still as leafless as in mid-winter, he met Sergeant Townsend, heading like him for a parked car. The C.I.D. man was in two minds about a diplomatic pretence of not having seen him, decided that this was silly, and walked over.

'You got shot, I hear.'

'That's right. Nothing very damaging.'

'I'm glad to hear it. On human grounds, you understand me. You brought the fellow in, I was told.'

'Yes. Our figures for percentages of serious crimes solved are much the same as yours. Over ninety per cent for homicides, even taking political interference into consideration.' Townsend considered this, and decided to let it pass.

'There are worse things than being shot, in the course of an enquiry. You've seen this morning's papers?'

'No.'

'The English papers don't get in much before lunch. Well – I hope your Monsieur Bianchi's going to be all right. By the way, Commissaire Lasserre, the sous-chef or whatever his title is – am I out of line in thinking him a considerable bastard?'

'The opinion is shared in numerous circles, not all of them criminal.'

'Ah. I rather thought as much. We've got to get back to London. It's not clear whether there'll be grounds for further enquiry, on our dossier. In case I don't see you again, Castang, here's to a speedy recovery. I speak for old Larkins, too. You might be thinking him a bit of an old cunt. But we're all professionals, right? We aren't dealing in animosities.'

'No,' said Castang, wondering what he was on about. 'Have a good trip.'

'Same to you,' in an ironic tone, strolling off.

He hadn't expected anybody to be at home in the Goltz household. He waited dutifully after pressing the bell, and was turning away when a voice on the intercom surprised him by saying, 'Yes? What is it?' Sounding toneless, but one can't judge on voices heard over intercom systems.

'Inspector Castang. PJ.'

'Oh yes,' without interest. The catch clicked and he walked in.

On the landing a woman was waiting, wearing a kitchen apron. She looked at him with indifferent eyes, a slightly irritable boredom, as though he needed a signature for a registered letter claiming an overdue payment and threatening proceedings.

'I'm cooking my dinner. But come in. I'm only just back.'
He looked at his watch, amazed to find it twelve-fifteen.

'You went to work?'

'Of course I went to work. People rely on me.' She went on grating celery. A cutlet lay on the table ready to be cooked. Castang had no answer to make.

'I came simply to inform you that your husband has been found, and arrested.'

'It could only be a question of time,' turning the gas down as a saucepan came to the boil.

'He's at the present under interrogation in the Police Judiciaire offices. This afternoon he will be presented to the examining magistrate, who will sign an order committing him to the local prison.'

179

'That's to be expected, I suppose.'

'Yes. The judge will allow you to see him for a few moments. It's Madame Delavigne. You'll have to ask her, whether visits are allowed.'

'What would we have to say to each other?' wiping the table neatly.

'That's,' said Castang, 'for you to decide.' He felt very tired, and even normal curiosity had drained out of him. He couldn't even be bothered looking around him. There was a farmhouse clock with a loud tick. It was the one thing he observed during his call. 'It would be a help to him, no doubt, if you made up a parcel with some things to wear, to wash with and so forth. You could take it around to the Palais. Or, of course, the prison concierge will take care of it.'

'Yes, I'll do that. Is that all? I want to get this meal ready,' shutting the refrigerator door and turning round with a lettuce.

'That's all. You'll be hearing from the judge, with a view to giving testimony.'

'As long as she realizes that I too am a working woman with my living to make,' running the tap on to the lettuce leaves, 'and doesn't expect me to hang around in passages. You seem rather stiff in your movements. Are you the one that got shot?'

He turned around again, slowly.

'The one that got slightly shot. Another day or so, and it won't show. It might leave a slight mark.' But she was putting the lettuce leaves into a basket, rubbing oil on a grill for the cutlet. It looked a dreary meal.

'As long as it doesn't show,' without raising her eyes.

Castang got back into the car with hardly any pain or effort. He didn't feel jaunty, but he was profoundly relieved at getting rid of the Goltz family.

Vera too was making celery salad. He looked at it sadly, not wanting to say it took his appetite away, a little.

'Give me a kiss,' she said. 'I was a bit of a pig. But so were you. Are you staying home?'

'Yes. I found him. In the brother's summerhouse. In one of the gardens along the railway line in Saint-Loup.'

'They're so pretty.'

'Yes, it was a surprise to find so much already out.' He hoped she would leave it at that, but Vera was a girl who had no tact when there was something worrying her to which she couldn't find the answer.

'I can't make the man out. Why did he shoot at you?'

'I was in his way. He'll have it all justified in his mind. The world owes him a living. He'd already killed two people, just because they were a bit of a nuisance. He didn't even stop to ask himself whether there might not be a considerable uproar at two cops being shot. Or whether the ambush being laid in a building he happened to own . . . it's a sort of insanity. A sort one could plead? . . . you'd have to ask Colette.'

'Only a moral insanity,' said Vera dryly.

'That's right. So how do you judge a person who doesn't follow rules because he hasn't any rules. Except a devouring need to acquire whatever; wealth or position or influence. Who thinks no more of the persons in his way than a hyena devouring a new-born cub.

'I suppose the hyena's controlled by some natural selection, or why isn't the veldt overrun with them? Maybe they have difficulty in breeding . . . so do these Goltzes, fortunately. No children, and the wife is so only in name.'

'Poor wretch,' said Vera, leaving it open which.

'Poor Colette,' retorted Castang.

'She's bound by law, but she's controlled by her own common sense.'

'Her reputation in the Palais varies, but it's said that Madame Delavigne doesn't get led easily up the garden path.'

'Goltz in a garden,' said Vera, trying to picture it. 'A strangely incongruous sight. Nobody expected to find him there. Which is why you did.'

39. Stage Arrival of the Tour de France

Commissaire Richard, a Ram born on the fourth of April, had little in common at first sight with his subordinate Castang, a Fish born a month earlier (and what is more irritatingly fantasist than a Fish?) but they had an important bond; a sense of the ridiculous. On (generally important and pompous) occasions they caught one another's eye and had to suppress giggles. Richard's small spark of wit was remembered by both men: the arrival of Mr Justice Armitage in the city did – idiotically – resemble an arrival of the Tour.

It creates a spectacle for a crowd that has sat for several hours waiting for something to happen. Intoxicated by the breathless gabble of blow-by-blow commentary on radio and television, the crowd will break out into frantic applause at the arrival of the scout cars and the motorbike outriders of the police. The wobble of the sprint, three hundred metres in a straight line, takes twenty seconds. Is this what we waited all day for, patiently sitting in the blazing sun? The uninstructed turn to their neighbours, and wives to husbands, like little Peterkin. But what good came of it at last? Can you tell why that was a famous victory?

The stage winner, sweaty and grinning, mounts a rickety podium to be embraced by a pretty girl and handed an enormous bouquet. (Who buys those flowers? What happens to them afterwards?) The rider with the yellow shirt of the leader mounts in his turn, for his day's clean shirt. Frenzied applause. And all the riders of importance, and several who have none, are instantly jostled by a raging torrent of reporters, phallic microphones a-tilt and shrieking silly questions. When will you attack? When will Blouc and Bloggs and Bobby attack? The experienced riders deal with this as to the manner born.

This circus is part of the Tour, and no Tour-lover would miss it for the world. Portable radios and little television sets litter even the PJ offices in the month of July. Once in a while,

182

when the Tour passes our city, we are there in the flesh as well as in spirit.

It began when Castang, supine on a sofa, sent Vera to buy a lot of newspapers, including English ones please, when she went to do her afternoon shopping. Castang-the-Fish should have felt thoroughly ashamed of himself at idle wallowings while devouted wifey hobbled bravely forth upon her crutches. He should have been pushing the supermarket trolley, courageously suppressing twinges round the midriff. But the truth was that Vera liked going shopping.

Riotously funny, the newspapers. As on any day of the Tour, they abounded in wisdom and insights while remaining impenetrably ignorant, imbecile and given over to platitude. Blouc, we learn, has been carried literally in an armchair to the foot of the Alps. Bloggs (who suffered a punctured tyre) has been overwhelmed by a veritable catastrophe.

Le Monde began querulously by asking why an affair of this importance has remained for so long ignored by the public: Castang put it crossly down needing sterner stuff. *Figaro* in polished prose thought it all rather strange and hoped piously that light would shortly be shed. *Humanité* was not greatly interested, since the Police Judiciaire were the puppets of the Minister of the Interior, who was just an old fascist, and an English Judge was certainly another. The local paper spoke of a veritable lightning-stroke, and suggested that Monsieur Richard must be literally thunderstruck by these startling revelations, which were calculated to literally split-infin stun the unhappy public, itself veritably swamped by municipal scandals (see our Regional Pages).

None of this was any good. Nothing in fact in the least out of the ordinary and not a hair twitched. Gentlemen of the English, would you care to fire first?

This was a disappointment, too. *The Times* was faintly funny, with an air of it being rather too easy to be witty upon this subject. The *Daily Telegraph* was pained at these slurs upon international amity, which could only serve conflicting and divergent interests – though Our Paris Correspondent was rather knowing about the habits of Parisians when weekending in luxurious fleshpots along the lecherous Loire.

It was only when Castang reached the vulgar newspapers, those Nancy Mitford said were once thought suitable for nursery reading, that the fur began to fly. Albion howling for French blood. To be sure, *France-Dimanche* made exactly the same insinuations about Brit Royals, practically any week. The Germans were relieved that for once it wasn't their incompetent cops, but slipshod and Französich are more or less synonymous.

To get the real juice one would have to wait for the weeklies. But it was a good start. No Tour reporter, discovering that Bobby is veritably diminished by boils on his arse, would have done better. Castang rang Fausta. Richard was out but she had enjoyed it all no end.

'When is the Tour due to arrive?'

'This evening, I think. Last heard of in Lyon.' Eat up your nice pudding, children.

I'm well off out of this, thought Castang, telling himself luxuriously how ill he was: isn't there some nice Europa-Cup football on the television this evening? Cops too, when brought down in the penalty area, roll around in pretended agony, grimacing and howling.

In fact the arrival was a peaceful affair, and something of an anti-climax. The Rolls-Royce deposited its passengers in front of the Hôtel d'Albion. Mr Justice Armitage walked through the lobby with a particularly unforthcoming expression: the service at the desk was as smooth as could be. Rosemary, accompanied by the baggage-porter, drove the car down the ramp to the garage and went up with him in the freight-lift, skipping the lobby altogether. Patience, carrying the small luggage, stopped at the desk long enough to say 'No visitors, and no telephone calls' in a clear English tone carrying enough to be heard by all the hangers-about.

Mr Martin Greene had been closeted for nearly three-quarters of an hour in the manager's office. He had emerged with his usual rumpled look and harassed smile, and made it known

184

that there would be a Press statement in the small conference room. His voice as always was quiet and apologetic.

'I only wanted to say, or rather to ask – to beg, if you like – on behalf of the family that their privacy be respected. These are perfectly innocent travellers who have had the misfortune while on holiday to get entangled by unhappy coincidence in a brutal crime which has only attracted interest because of this fortuitous involvement. We can't altogether rule out malicious intent towards a public figure, but it appears unlikely. Because and only because this point is unclear, the examining magistrate enquiring into the case has, I must say very politely and without any suggestion of pressure, begged the family to interrupt their holiday for a brief pause here, so that their testimony on various points of detail may be used to verify the statements of others. To which the family has of course consented in the interests of justice.

'They've asked me to be their spokesman, to make known that they won't give any interviews or make any statements, on the grounds that such would be improper in a matter which is sub judice, and further that well, frankly, they refuse to be pestered. That's final and conclusive, I'm afraid. They'll be going to-morrow for a private interview with the magistrate, and after that there'll be a Press statement at the Palace of Justice, on the legal aspects of the affair. Sorry, no further questions.'

Commissaire Richard, going home after his working day, appeared astonished to find Pressmen lying in wait.

'What d'you want? They've come? No, nobody told me. Why wouldn't they come? They agreed to; why shouldn't they keep their word? Their presence doesn't concern me. They made brief statements about the circumstances in which this crime came to light, on the day concerned, and then went about their affairs. Now they're on their way home. The judge quite naturally hopes they may provide a bit more light on things discovered since ... Of course; the PJ antennae here and at Tours were given rogatory commissions to enquire: it's our job. We pass on a mass of information and testimony to the judge: his job is to sift it. These people may be in a position to help

185

verify certain statements made. That's all. What are you in a fuss about? I'm given to understand that the British Consulate is issuing the information you want for your editions. If the magistrate tomorrow wants to make a further statement – that's up to him. I'm going home now, so belt up, do you mind.'

Colin, booking peacefully into the Holiday Inn a mile away, went unrecognized through the hall and up to his room, where he met a gentleman in the passage.

'Welcome,' said this gentleman with a friendly grin. 'Glad to see you skipped the official reception committee. I thought a bit of real hospitality might be in order. Henk Boldoot by the way, *Newsweek*. Like a drink? – my room's just down the road.' Colin grinned back.

'Now that's a concrete suggestion. Was there a blahblah?'

'I wasn't there. I guess so. Highball all right? That too much ice? Consuls and stuff – all a bit pompous. Leave that to the English, I thought. The French went chasing the police captain – what good's that to anyone? I've no intention whatever of trying to pump you; the paper thought I might take a looksee because of the unusual angle: my guess is it's a mare's nest.'

'It is. I was amused at the start. My family's pretty proper, you see, and watching them making frozen faces at all these scruffy fuzz here tickled me. I got sick of it, went off to ski. It wouldn't be any use even if you did want to pump me: I know bugger all about it. I wasn't in Tours, I came here for the three-star grub, and landed in the midst of this corpse-discovery lark, which was riotous, but apart from that . . .'

'So you never met the lovely Laetitia, is that right? Help yourself.'

'I didn't see her at her best,' grinned Colin.

40. The Plenipotentiary

A card was brought to the judge of instruction, in an envelope with the rest of the day's post. The card was large, handsome, engraved. George Brooke, it said. Honorary Attaché H.M. Embassy Paris.

'He's here?' enquired Monsieur Shermite. 'Very well. Five minutes to read my mail.'

He rose politely. Mr Brooke was a large man, with a young-ish, healthy complexion and fair hair brushed severely back, soberly dressed.

'Mr Brooke? I'm at your service, but hardly I'm afraid at your disposal. My little book is brimming over. Patients queue, alas, at the door of the specialists. Can I without discourtesy beg you to be brief.'

Mr Brooke smiled, with the perfect confidence of a man who doesn't get sent out to wait in the passage.

'Frankly, I announced myself thus unconventionally in the interests of discretion. I hope that on the contrary your morning appointments may be shortened somewhat, if you will forgive my suggesting a bit of a reshuffle. I am by way of being a kind of extra counsellor to the Embassy, intervening occasionally when there are legal questions.'

'A lawyer?'

'Hardly. I was called to the Bar but don't practise. But let me come to the point. My field is international law and this is a criminal case, on the face of it. I refer of course to this Toth woman. It would be fair, let's put it, to describe me as a negotia-tor. Perhaps it will be possible to save you, and others, the pains of a wearisome formal series of interrogations.'

'You have powers?'

'Oh yes. Full powers. On behalf of the interested persons as well as H.M.G. Which as is natural doesn't care much to see a Judge of the High Court involved in a squalid murder. Even in his capacity as a private gentleman, the Palace of Justice in France isn't really his sphere, is it?'

'Forgive me an instant while I have a word with my secretary . . . I compose myself to listen.'

'Splendid. Then we can speak between professionals. Brutally, Monsieur Lhermite, we'll leave aside what grounds there are or there aren't for pressing charges. It comes down to this: you press charges or you don't: de deux choses l'une. If you do, then I have no rôle to play. The family or any member of it is entitled to legal representation, we engage the services of eminent members of the Paris Bar, who will naturally contest every procedural point and seek, not to put a fine point on it, to make your life a perfect misery,' amiably. 'I leave aside, again, the publicity angle and the dust raised. It would create, simply, for all a most unpleasant situation and that we're anxious to avoid.'

'You suggest that such a step would lead to a miscarriage of justice?' mildly.

'No such thing. I must reject altogether anything that could be interpretable as interference.'

'Then continue, I pray you.'

'Say you don't charge. Since you have not yet decided I do not prejudice your decision. It's plain that once their testimony is taken there exists no further need to keep them here. Pretexts for asking them to hang about become at that stage a slur, on their honour and position, and begin to appear chicanery. Now that as I need not say would indeed be putting other and more momentous affairs at risk, for inevitably at that point there's a political fall-out.'

'We won't speak of political consequences,' firmly, 'since that is construable as intimidation, nor of chicanery, a word unacceptable in this office.'

'I accept the corrections, but maintain the definitions.'

'Your clients –'

'No, that wasn't one of my definitions.'

'The word protégés must be made to suit. They are not absolved from duties or responsibilities by public office held in any country. No immunity – even from eventual judicial

188

pursuit – could be claimed under any existing diplomatic privilege.'

'Agreed. Unless there's a lot more than we know of, which I believe is unlikely, there aren't grounds for pursuit.'

'But I am, by function and definition, the judge of that,' smiling a little.

'Incontestably.'

'The services of the Police Judiciaire continue to enquire, with diligence, into this affair: the woman Toth, no more or less. I mention that because a variety of nonsensical ducks have flapped their wings. Drugs, gangsters, splinter groups claiming political autonomy: hot air. In the light of discoveries, I would order a complement of information. Now I have the right to expect your compatriots to offer wholehearted collaboration towards investigating officers.'

'Are you offering a compromise?'

'Within the limits of my freedom to do so, yes. I don't wish to embarrass your people by an over-rigid insistence on my personal powers of interrogation or confrontation.'

Mr Brooke kept silence.

'Am I to understand,' went on the judge, 'that the family maintains a disclaimer of all knowledge, en bloc, of this woman or her dealings? Because if a previous connection, however innocent, had been suppressed out of embarrassment or anxiety –'

'Severally or conjointly, vigorous refutal of any such.'

'And those are the findings of the C.I.D. enquiries?'

'They are.'

'Very well. You bring your people here for a formal declaration along those lines and I order a complement of information. You hold yourself responsible for their co-operating, discreetly, with Commissaire Richard.'

'Provided that such exchanges do not take place on PJ premises.'

'That's a matter you must take up with Richard. I won't engage myself.'

'Do you propose holding a Press conference?'

189

'I strongly dislike a situation where an instructing judge should be under pressure to seek publicity for his office.'

'The secret of instruction –'

'Don't talk cant to me. Calculated indiscretions attracted the Press here. Construable as attempts to use limelight in order to whip up emotion. I must ask you to forgive me now, Mr Brooke.'

41. Pull devil; pull baker

By a mysterious unspoken agreement all the Police Judiciaire were dressed up smart this morning. Castang was wearing his English tweed jacket, and was only betrayed by a tendency to scratch where his new elastic strapping tickled. His English jacket had been much admired in the office, and Cantoni had bought one like it. If Castang looked, remarked Monsieur Richard, like a racecourse tout with a hot tip Cantoni was infinitely worse. One of those types, he said, who grip recalcitrant horses by the hindquarters, to push them into the starting gate. And what do they do the rest of the time? All decidedly sinister.

He himself was in his politician's suit, and a shirt with cuffs, and an academic-palms tie. If Monsieur Bianchi were here he could have worn his medals, said Lasserre spitefully. Monsieur Bianchi was not allowed to talk, but had received the news about Goltz with an unmistakable sly wink.

Strange contrast, Castang was thinking, turning over in his head the sister-in-law's remark about judges' families sticking together too. Goltz had no integrity towards anything; was a moral anarchist. Whereas an English Judge ... Vowed to the high priesthood, to the most scrupulous and exact maintenance of liberties. There might have been, there might still be drunken judges, sleeping judges, anti-semitic judges, but this was not one ... Fausta was exchanging polished French phrases with Mr Brooke.

'May I try one of your cigars?' he asked Richard. Nobody had ever been known to have this courage, ever. These things, which looked like sticks of liquorice, were supposed to come from Brazil. They had a whiff of saltpetre about them, as though of Infernal Regions. Mr Brooke's angle, that he could enter Hades with impunity but no other English person could, was irritating, but Richard wasn't about to be abraded.

'I fail to understand your dislike of these premises. There's a perfectly discreet back door, from which the Press can be kept at a distance.'

'Commissaire, understand the view of the public. The very phrase "assisting the police in their enquiries", originally an innocuous formula designed to underline our scruples about usurping a tribunal's functions, has become pejorative. Will you forgive me further if I remark that inevitably and since all time the police here have been associated with a notion of secret midnight dealings. Venetian stealth; people – or facts – stifled in cellars.' Castang would have smiled at this interpretation of 'Les Seigneurs de la Nuit.'

'Don't smile,' said Mr Brooke seriously. 'The Affair of the Poisons.'

'I might remark that it was not Monsieur de la Reynie who destroyed the evidence concerning Madame de Montespan. I might add that the same Lieutenant of Police and his successors enjoyed universal respect at a time when English people were arrested, sequestered and tortured by order of the Star Chamber. Come to that, when was it you stopped hanging children for the theft of sixpence?'

'My dear Commissaire. Let's come closer to our own day. The Affair Ben Barka. The Affair of Monsieur de Broglie.'

'It's precisely because I don't want any affair Ben Barka – if you recall, a matter where a highly placed figure from a friendly country was said to have exercised political pressure – that I think these matters must be handled in the open.'

191

'This won't do; it's pull devil pull baker. Will you agree to conducting these interrogations upon neutral ground, with every facility afforded?

'No, I will not. I conduct my investigations here, in my office, and not in the United Nations or the Chamber of Commerce.'

'The examining magistrate has agreed –'

'The examining magistrate has read the history of Stavisky and Monsieur Prince, and so have I. I'm not Prefect of Police and my name is not Chiappe. I'm an obscure provincial commissaire. You seem to possess influence. Go to the Minister of the Interior and have me sacked.'

'Monsieur Richard, you're being theatrical and you know it.'

'Perfectly true,' quietly. 'I've no wish to dramatize this matter. I'll delegate a responsible, able and sensitive officer, to conduct such investigation as I see fit, on ground acceptable to us both. No more. Any further and I lose sight of your motives in thus pressing for discretion.'

'Very well. The Consulate?'

'No. Polarized.'

'A private house.'

'No. A hotel room if you like. And the simultaneous translator as before.'

'And tapes.'

'No tapes.'

'Come, Richard, you know the fallacies of interpreters as well as I do. The classic is the flogging of the dead horse, which came out in perfect French as the swordstroke in water. When the next spokesman picked up the sword metaphor the English wondered what he was talking about.'

'In the first instance my man understands English and in the second he's not going to be talking in metaphors.'

'Then the tape purely as a means of reference until signature of all statements in bilingual version. Once these are accepted by all parties as a faithful version of what has actually been spoken, the tapes can be destroyed.'

'Very well,' said Richard, bored, fanning the smoke from his cigar away from his face.

'Commissaire, I have no dark suspicions of anyone. Enter only the viewpoint of my principals. If a man holding one of the highest public offices in the realm were merely to be brushed with suspicion of involvement in a criminal matter, he would be obliged to present instantly his resignation to the Lord Chancellor. You must approve that. It is as it should be.'

'Quite so,' said Richard, nodding. 'And it wouldn't be my subordinate's resignation. It would be my own.'

So that Castang found himself in a room at the Holiday Inn.

42. Colin

'Did you check on the journalists?'

'They've moved out,' said Lucciani. 'No problem there.' News is a funny thing, thought Castang. Goes stale quicker than fish. Everybody asks what happened, but very few have the patience to wait and ask 'And what happened then?' There were to be sure the weekly papers. But they had been discouraged by the examining magistrate, who had issued a statement so colourless as to have dampened everyone. Castang had some admiration for this magistrate. A figure – any figure – who does not seize an opportunity of getting into print, who fails to preen and display his vanity with the utmost complaisance. To be pleased with yourself is thought the essential prerequisite to success. The Press, quite simply, had concluded that the judge of instruction, having come unwillingly to accept that there was no ground for pressing charges against any member of this English family, couldn't bring himself to say as much. That would have been losing face. A complement of information my eye – face-saving manoeuvre. Commissaire Richard was dividing his time between a lamentable person called Goltz and games of golf. The weather being so spring-like.

The weather was indeed spring-like, and Castang, ribs still sore, had been rather gallant about letting Vera have the car and go out to draw outside for the first time this year. Not as gallant as all that: someone who leaves a bicycle by the kitchen entrance of a hotel is indeed discreet.

'Make yourself at home, Mr Armitage.' Funny name. Was it perhaps 'hermitage'? 'This character looking like a waiter is Monsieur Lucciani. He's a PJ inspector, but for our purposes he is a waiter. He'll get you anything you want, besides seeing we're not disturbed. Monsieur Malinowski you know.'

Colin was relaxed, self-assured, friendly. Good-looking young man. Can understand that the girls find him something to shout about.

'The tapes you know about.'

'Oh yes. I'm well briefed. Well rehearsed,' grinning.

'I've your previous statement here, which saves us all the identity stuff. You gave your profession as designer; that's perhaps a little vague?'

'I work in an interior decorator's office.'

'Law didn't tempt you? Following your father's footsteps? – it's a fairly hereditary profession.'

'No.'

'And you don't know a woman called Laetitia Toth?'

'No.'

'You never met her? Can you be quite sure? Unwittingly. She worked as a journalist, and often for women's magazines. Decorating is a profession in which one often meets a girl like that, without necessarily recognizing or remembering her.'

'I'm quite sure.'

'How can you be so sure?'

'The reason's simple. The police at home made an enquiry. They found no trace of her ever having met me. They're very thorough. So I think it likely we never met. My remembering it or not doesn't seem really relevant at that rate.'

'You mentioned staying a night at a country hotel; you couldn't recall the name.'

'That's right.'

194

'We found it, and the hotelkeeper recognizes you from the description given him. Do you want to query that or contest it? He's a busy man and we don't want to drag him down here on such a trivial matter, unless you wish it.'

'I told you I didn't remember. If he says he saw me I dare say it's so.'

'Under the name of Maxwell, is that right? Why the false name?'

'Is it illegal?'

'It's not illegal unless there's an attempt to mislead a judicial enquiry.'

'Call it discretion, then.'

'Amplify a little. There's no need to be suspicious. You've been briefed to keep your answers short and factual. Warned quite possibly that I'll try and make you talk. You'll see that I've no hostile purpose. Giving a false name for no apparent reason is unusual enough to be thought a break in a pattern. That attracts our attention. We ask about it.'

'Do you ever give a false name, Mr Castang?'

'It happens, yes. For reasons of discretion.'

'Well, then.'

'You didn't want to compromise somebody. Yourself? Your family? Then another person?'

'You don't have to be dense, do you? I don't go about breaking up other people's marriages.'

'Rest assured that we'll be discreet, the moment we realize that it has nothing to do with our enquiry.'

'I don't know her name.'

'Then how do you know it wasn't Laetitia Toth?'

'What makes you think it was?'

'She booked that evening into a hotel in Caen. She didn't occupy her room. She vanished and was no more seen. Until she reappeared in a car in Tours. Leaving some luggage in Caen.'

'I know nothing about that. I saw the body of a woman here – you were there at the time. Long black hair. I didn't see her face then. But I knew I'd never seen her. Some days later I read in the paper that she'd been identified as somebody called Toth. Means nothing to me.'

'Let me get it straight. You admit that you spent the night in this hotel with a woman. You say it couldn't have been Laetitia Toth because this other woman didn't have long black hair. But you don't know this woman's name. All right, so far? You'll agree it all seems a bit weird to the listener.'

'Look, are you doubting what I say?'

'No, I'm not. I'll tell you perfectly openly that the chambermaid who cleaned the room after you'd left received a strong impression that a woman had been there with you. Now you tell me you don't know this woman's name.'

'That's right. Nothing to do with your affair.'

'Since we're neither of us sure of her name we can't be sure of that either, can we? But you're assured of my discretion: you can go forward quite confidently. What she looked like, how you met her, what she said. All about her, in fact.'

'I know nothing about her. There's no need for the old-fashioned moral stuff. We met casually, in the Casino. We fancied each other. So we made a date. All one to both of us, I dare say, if we never met again. So much the better, possibly.'

'I'm not saying it isn't so, Mr Armitage. We wish to disentangle you from this coincidence, that Laetitia Toth was in Caen, and lo, she turns up in your father's car a day or so later. Good; you met this mysterious lady by arrangement in this hotel. Your statement here is that you picked the hotel at random.'

'I admit that wasn't the truth. But see it my way – I could see you asking a lot of questions about where I was, and the rest. So I thought I'd better cover up. A woman like that, picked up – well, I got the impression she'd done things of the sort before.'

'How did she get into the hotel?'

'Well, there was this fire door. I unbolted it – there was nobody about at dinner time.'

'Quite romantic of you – to seek all these complications. You could have booked in as man and wife; nobody'd have said a

196

word. What bothers me is all this hankypanky. It attracted my attention.'

'Yes, well, I thought about this. I came to the conclusion that it was a woman who liked running this sort of risk. Making a bet with herself as it were. Not to be seen, maybe. Romantically silly, I agree. But it made the adventure more piquant, sort of.'

'Is it in your character, to behave in romantic ways?'

'Not at all, I'd think,' coolly. 'But why not let her have her way? I didn't see it at the time. I thought just that she was known at this place, and had a good reason for not wanting to be seen.'

'Very well,' said Castang. 'As you said a little while ago, no need for the old-fashioned moral stuff. Your family – they're built a little along those lines, or would you agree?'

'My father, yes that's true I suppose. Strait-laced and very upright but I understand that. I couldn't see that as anything but stupidity and hypocrisy in anyone my age, but he's another generation, and those ideas were very rigidly instilled in them, and anything more conservative than the Law Society you couldn't imagine. It's natural to them.'

'And your mother and sister?'

'They pretend to be rather large-minded and modern, but the truth is they have quite conventional minds. Still, I have nothing to say about them. They're my family after all.'

'Yes. I see.'

'And, uh. You do see, while on the subject – I mean I have no particular reason to keep this business quiet on my own account, you see. But I'd just as soon know that you won't go and tell them everything I've said. The old man does have his position to protect. That fellow from the Embassy – not my style, but I can see his point. If this kind of thing is made public it wouldn't do him any good, and my mother'd be upset. That's why I gave the false name, really. I often do, at work. Being the son of a judge isn't necessarily the big social advantage you might think. Not in my circle, anyhow. Okay? I've been straight with you.'

'Don't worry: I won't tell tales on you.'

'You do realize – that's why I kept apart from them. On holiday I mean. I just went along here for the grub, and look where that gets me.'

Yes, thought Castang. That does have the ring of truth. And as for the rest of the tale – is it ridiculous enough to be true? We'll see, shall we?

43. Patience

Castang had adopted a very leisurely rhythm. Nobody in a hurry gets information of any real value. To be sure, it is also commonplace police tactics to let people cook . . . Instinctively, also. He had not given it that much thought, but he was still amusing himself with his 'bicycle race' analogy. This stage is against the clock, and a long one. It doesn't do to force the pace at the outset, for fear of blowing up towards the end. He told Lucciani he wouldn't want Patience before that afternoon, and spent nearly an hour peaceably writing up his notes by hand. It took, too, a long time to prepare the script, while Monsieur Malinowski made small perfectionist alterations in English phrasing and polished up his syntax. Lucciani-the-waiter got sent for drinks, awaiting the moment to get stuck in to his typewriter . . .

Castang did not want to phone Richard either, since the call would go through the hotel switchboard. They had arranged to meet for lunch. Both took a quick circular look for any eavesdropping journalists. Neither had much to say. Colin had told a good many lies, but no more than most people did. A twenty-two-year-old boy lies with a youthful effrontery and aggressivity; Colin had kept a remarkably cool head.

'You hear this ridiculous tale,' Castang picking up splinters of bread crust with a moistened forefinger, 'And you'd jump to the

198

conclusion there wasn't a word of truth in it, and I'm persuaded that it's nearly all true. The elaborate dare of not being seen, the whole romantic adventure – that all fits what we know of Laetitia's character. Creating an artificial risk and then having the fun of courting it – it's the same trick as she played with the cop in Caen. A sort of rehearsal for Tours?'

'I'm working on that one. You've no doubt now, that it was her?'

'None at all. But did he or didn't he go to Tours that night? We don't place him with any accuracy. He turned off the Normandy autoroute before Paris and booked in to a motel in the Valley de Chevreuse: Versailles PJ confirm that. From there it's a very easy matter to flip across and hit the Orléans road just before the Chartres cut-off. You've paid in advance, because nobody's to know when you leave . . . If he'd made up his mind to pursue her to Tours while leaving a false trail . . . I don't like it much. Over-forced and over-glib. He's cool, yes, a planner, yes. But it means seeing him as a Ripley, an infantile psychopath. Because putting the body in Pa's car and then arranging to be around in order to enjoy the discovery would be a true Ripley trick. And that, I think, is pitching it a wee bit too high. He enjoys it all so much, and that's Ripley.' Patricia Highsmith's character has become a police prototype for frightful young men who commit psychopathic crimes.

'Do nothing to alarm him.'

'Supremely self-confident . . .'

'Who've you got this afternoon?'

'The sister. Leave the adults till tomorrow, huh?'

'Very strong family solidarity. They must know. The father must realize.'

'Not nice, to be in his shoes.'

It was windless, still. Oceans of sky that was far too blue, floods of sun that was far too hot for March. False, treacherous weather. It would freeze, at night. Outside the huge sparkling clean Johnson-polished window of Holiday Inn was an immature landscape of thin lawn and meagre young conifers that had a nasty artificial look, jaunty as a Swiss tourist postcard.

The sun on the glass made the room so hot that Castang switched the heating off altogether.

Patience was neither plain nor pretty. Her ash-blonde hair lacked lustre but was well cut. Her skin was pale, at its best a pearl but more often pasty. Features a good shape; lovely eyes, nice mouth, nose a bit lumpy. Good figure and excellent legs; very good hands and feet. Clothes like Royalty's, chosen with much straining after good taste: since they are badly cut the result is irredeemably dowdy. The voice of the well-brought-up English girl; soft and clear and impossibly high.

Patience returned the long scrutiny with poise and confidence. Ugly face but not unpleasant. The pale bright eyes were large and not sly. Forehead full of worried lines like a monkey's. Rough dark hair going in all directions. Face all lumps and hollows with both jaws over-developed, but balanced by a wide thin mouth and strong brown teeth. Very clean indeed. Idiotic horsy clothes, but neat and well pressed, and shoes properly polished. Not really unattractive on the whole, and gave quite a good impression. If it hadn't been for being French! One firm axiom was that never, under any circumstances, could you trust the French.

Patience worked in an estate agent's office in the West End. She was a good judge of a house, and a good judge of a customer. When he smiled he crinkled up in a fetching way. Still. A cop. And a French cop, heaven help us. You'd probably get that attractive crinkle while he was busy attaching electrodes to you. She wasn't afraid of that! She was equal to the situation.

'I don't know what questions you can possibly find to put to me.'

'Odd ones,' said Castang, smiling. 'Do you like driving the car?'

'Yes I do. It's a lovely car. Big but beautifully manageable.'

'You've done most of the driving?'

'Turn and turn about, with my mother. She likes it, too. My father doesn't drive often; he's used to having a driver. None of us much likes driving here, I may say. One's heart's in one's mouth. French drivers are simply filthy. Rude and selfish.'

'Perfectly true; they are. Further impressions?'

200

'Of France, you mean? Well, I'd better try and be polite. But we do love the countryside, and the food and stuff is fun. We'd have enjoyed ourselves if it hadn't been for this.'

'Yes, it was bad luck. Miss Laetitia Toth has given us a lot of worry, too. She enjoyed complicating and dramatizing things. But very pretty.'

'I'm not much able to give an opinion on that, I'm afraid.'

'I'm obliged to enter your private life to some extent. I'll try not to be too intrusive.'

'I'll certainly tell you, when you are.'

'You're not married or engaged, I think? You live at home?'

'Yes. I used to have a flat, but now I find it worth it to commute, to live at home. We get on well together, my mother and I. I have my job, of course, and enjoy that.'

'When you marry, will you go on working?'

'No, at that point I don't think I will. I like running a house and making a home. And I think one should bring up one's own children, to a very large extent. I might like to go back to work later. It would depend on one's husband.'

'You'd be an equal partner in a marriage, I think.'

'Heavens, yes. I hate doormat women. In the first place I believe in equality in decision-making, and I've a strong determined character.'

'In the meantime, you're happy to live at home.'

'I see nothing inconsistent in that. I'm as modern or emancipated as anyone, but I've a strong belief in the value of a closely-knit family unit. We've always been closely attached, as a family.'

'Your brother, too.'

'Well, he's a boy, which is different; they have that male need to show their crest and spurs. He makes a bit of a show, because he's still somewhat immature. But he has it, too, the attachment I mean.'

'Fidelity, loyalty – strong characteristics in you.'

'Certainly. And standing up for what one believes in. Make no mistake, I'm fond of my brother. We fought a lot as children, as was natural. And I was the eldest.'

'Police work teaches us too the value of the family.'

'My mother does a lot of social work: you should discuss it with her really. And she had teacher-training. We might be thought old-fashioned because of my father, who can be I agree a bit Victorian. But I most decidedly am not.'

'I'm exceedingly interested. Business first, but it shouldn't take long. The principal stumbling block as you've heard is this business of Miss Toth's clothes strewn along the road. The inference, pretty well inescapable, is that somebody followed you closely enough to observe your movements. Now do you use the rearview glass much, when you drive?'

'But of coursè I do. Not only here; there are frightful drivers at home too, in all honesty. I'm very prudent. We never went fast. This has puzzled us no end. I mean a strange car one doesn't notice, but if it stayed close, following one, throughout a whole morning, one would be bound to notice. I can't account for it. We stopped where we said, for petrol, and we stopped a couple of times to look at the view, and that bridge over the water: well, why pretend, my father went behind a tree, and I suppose I don't mind saying, I did, too.'

'I appreciate your openness.'

'So if a car was following us – we'd have been bound to notice. I can only say we didn't.'

'Is it conceivable, in your view, that one sees a car several times, but because it's a commonplace model and colour, one assumes without thinking that it's several different cars?'

'I suppose that's the only logical answer. We certainly didn't study any cars, except as traffic hazards. The traffic is heavy around towns, light in between.'

'In your earlier statement you felt pretty sure that the car was never altogether unattended. Thinking it over since then, you didn't change your mind.'

'Well, it's terribly difficult being questioned on things that had no great importance at the time, and one starts to wonder. Like being in bed and thinking did I turn the gas out. But really, you know ... We'd have locked the car. It was full of luggage, and one has to be terribly careful everywhere for pilferers. Alone we'd always have locked the car, and turning one locks the lot. That time in Tours we were tired, and the young man with the luggage was obliging, and – wretched man, he must be lying. We'd never have left the car open. It's all too weird for belief. It's been a very great worry to my father, and it's nearly driven my mother batty. You must believe me: somehow there's been a very hateful and skilful trick.'

'If there has,' said Castang,' the investigation will uncover it. That, after all, is what it's designed for.'

44. Rosemary

Vera managed the car perfectly well. It had an automatic gearbox, and the pedal controls had manual doubles in case her foot 'went to sleep'. From the Préfecture Castang had fiddled a windscreen sticker saying GIG, short for Grande Invalide de Guerre, which invests one with various small privileges and considerations; being a police officer's wife might help too. The folding wheelchair she no longer used in the house was stowed in the back of the car: its canvas pockets were handy for drawing materials. To draw the Jesuit Garden in early spring, before its bones were covered in foliage, was a combination of business and pleasure. Since it was one of the city's prides, one might make a kind of album. Nicely bound, in an elegant limited edition, that might make a pretty present for distinguished municipal visitors.

The Jesuit College, now an Ecole Normale for the training of teachers, was a sober and beautiful eighteenth-century building. For meditatings of a peripatetic and recreational nature the Fathers had made an immense garden behind, and being Jesuits had filled it with scientific interests as well as admirable taste. There was even a little Observatory at the far end, abutting on the university campus.

The Revolution declared all this, with indignation, the property of the people, but did nothing with it. The Jesuits, returning imperturbable at the Restoration, cleared up the desolate mess, removed traces of vandalism, and laid it all out afresh in the most modern English style, that of Walter Scott romanticism, so that even Stendhal, who loathed Jesuits, was filled with admiration. A Lamartiney lake, mysterious rocky gorges and a waterfall. Missionaries from the Americas and even China, all great botanists, brought back exotic species and strange essences. By the time the Third Republic flung out all religious orders it was too late for bad taste to make any headway. No ivyclad ruins in phony gothic came to spoil this exquisite creation. The Napoleon III orangery and palm house, in glass and iron Baltard style, was smaller but prettier than Sir Joseph Paxton's. The whole park was now the pride and joy of the municipal gardeners, and intelligently cared for. Vera, doing a sepia of the big gingko being obstinately Chinese, became aware of being watched.

People are nearly always quiet and considerate. Her concentration would have remained intact but for the couple, a tall, elderly gentleman and a dumpy middle-aged lady with an enormous handbag, catching her eye. She knew at once that this was Castang's Judge and his wife. Not only unmistakably English, a rarity this early in the year, but distinguished. She smiled encouragingly.

'This is very clever of you indeed,' said Castang that evening, 'and I couldn't be more interested. How did you manage it?'

'Wasn't difficult at all; English people are always open and easy in public: it's the French who are stiff and forbidding. And they were bored. Museums and galleries are all very well, but when you've something on the mind causing great anxiety, trees and water hook you more than architecture. The fine day tempted them out, just as it did me. And they're charming, cultivated people. We had lunch together.' Castang guffawed happily. 'They didn't want another restaurant meal; we sort of picnicked on the pavilion terrace. The waiter was a bit snotty about my sandwiches – they only wanted salad – and the old

204

boy checkmated him by being very grand and telling him to bring the best white wine. It should have been a "Jesuitengarten" he said – he knows Germany better than France – but we had a super Hospices de Beaune, I forget its name. We enjoyed ourselves. We stayed till four when it began to get chilly. I did no work, but I thought I was working for you.'

'So you were. What did you talk about?'

'Oh, general things. Nationalism, you know. I got very Czech. They're very cautious about Germany, but they like it infinitely better than France. One has to understand the English. France is the traditional enemy: the distrust and dislike is gut, embedded since always. Romans and Normans were just intruders, bringing nothing good to the honest Saxon. You should hear the old boy on Norman law! And Shakespeare – according to him a catastrophe. His hobby is Old Norse; he can quote whole lumps of Sagas by heart.'

'And crimes?' Castang didn't give a rap for Sagas, unless Forsytean and real.

'They're very worried, both. It goes deep. They won't speak of it but it's all the time behind their eyes. She said quite un-self-consciously that they were stuck here as witnesses to a homicide investigation and this was horrid, and she supposed I'd read about it in the papers. I said yes, of course, but I didn't believe papers – so I'm an ally as well as being Czech. They knew nothing of Czech art of course – beer and Jiri Trnka – but when it came to asking what I did here in France . . . I couldn't tell lies. I hope you're not going to be cross with me,' said Vera. Her desperate honesty . . .

'Quite truly, I don't think it could do any harm.'

'I said simply that I was married to a French cop, and the officer who had taken their original statements, so it was normal that he should have been delegated by Monsieur Richard to go on, since he was the only one in the department who could carry on a conversation in recognizable English . . .'

'And then,' said Castang woodenly.

'It brought them up short, of course. But they were too polite to comment, and too genuinely nice to be hostile. That's what they are – genuinely nice. He said, rather splendidly, very much the Judge, that he refused utterly to let that colour the feelings of friendly simplicity on which this acquaintance had been based, and that my candour did me honour.'

'So it does.'

'It's no virtue. I can't conceal things; I have to floop them out.'

'Can't you see?' said Castang. 'Honesty promotes honesty. You've done me a thundering huge good turn.'

'I was so afraid I'd made a fuck-up,' said Vera, tears threatening.

'I had the pleasure of meeting your wife,' said Rosemary. 'It was a real and sincere pleasure. I shouldn't say this. It might sound as though I was trying to gain leverage by boasting of a social acquaintance. I understand of course that you are only carrying out your orders. I'm no judge of her drawings, though they seemed awfully good to me. It's indecent, I suppose, to say that I couldn't help my surprise at learning that an artist is the wife of a police officer; it must be a rarity anywhere. But I can't stop myself saying that it increases my respect towards you. I hope you won't think that an unfair remark: I'm not trying to gain any advantage or even put myself in a privileged position. I have to mention it, you see; my impression was that she'd be bound on her side to mention it to you.'

'Indeed she did: she always does; such is her character. No, it doesn't alter things. This can't become a social occasion – I wish it could.'

'I'm only sorry I was rude on our first meeting. But it all seemed so trivial and nonsensical then: you can understand our showing impatience. Now it all seems a horrible trap – all occasions do inform against us. What on earth can I say in answer to your questions?'

'I have very few questions. I must make a *mise au point* – we don't need Monsieur Malinowski to translate that.'

'A clarification perhaps. Or putting things in their proper order.'

'I hold my tongue,' said the interpreter, smiling.

'Of course my wife's meeting you, and enjoying it, doesn't

change my attitude to the job I've been told to do,' said Castang. 'But it can change the approach. To be honest I've covered the ground factually with your children yesterday, and apart from verifying a detail here and there – if I might I'd like to ask more about background. I don't mean the class thing. There isn't that much difference to my thinking. Most magistrates everywhere come from a privileged bourgeois sector of society, which I suppose is upper or upper middle class. The point I'm trying to get at is that on both sides of the Channel there's a tradition, isn't there? Of service to the State, I suppose. Of integrity – or loyalty to ideals? I'm not sure I've got the definition right; I'd like to hear your wording of it.'

'Yes, of course. I mean yes of course both ways: you're right and it exists. Or did: we seem to be in danger of losing it nowadays. That tradition, or so we like to think, of devotion to the public weal was what built an empire. Truly we didn't think of it as commercial grab. We were brought up to believe that we owed ourselves to an ideal of responsibility: a dedication almost religious. That sounds quite laughable nowadays but I assure you it was so.

'I don't know much about the subject,' cautiously, 'but I take the point. Responsibility. We – it's general police thinking so I'm not expressing a personal feeling – deplore the decay of individual responsibility. Everything now gets shoved on to the shoulders of the State.

'Leaves us trapped, somehow,' Castang went on. 'How does one get out of it? I mean that one wouldn't want to go back, even if one could. Having no medical insurance, or unemployment protection, or paying university fees: it's unthinkable. But the more the State does the more we want it to do, somehow. It can't take over all a family's duties.'

'I do agree, indeed,' said Rosemary in a cocktail party voice: bright and artificial. Her round cushiony face was handsome; strong large bones behind it, excellent skin. A high natural colour, unlike her daughter's pallor. Fine-grained, the skin, and expensively cared for. The multitude of minute creases only showed up in this strong light. A queen-mother face.

'Responsible means answerable,' he said flatly.

207

He regretted it the moment he said it, because that was the moment he lost her, and it was visible. Was it just the tone, a bit too schoolmasterly?

'The etymology of this word – you there, Jenkins, in the corner. Don't assume that backward expression. Commonplace French verb. Anybody? No? Répondre. Of which the Latin root is ...? Nobody? Oh dear.' Apathy all round. What was the old cunt blithering on about now?

Or had he backed her too abruptly into a corner from which there was no way out.

'Bit of a play on words, rather.'

The tension was broken and so was the thread. He felt in his pocket for a cigarette.

'Lucciani, you might get us some coffee, perhaps. Would you like some, Lady Armitage?'

'I think I would, rather.' He snapped the lighter, turning his papers about.

'I'd like to go over this timetable.'

'Oh,' innocently. 'I thought we were finished.'

'There's an awkward gap that bothers us,' explained Castang politely. 'We lose sight of this woman, alive, at Caen, and we catch sight of her again dead, here.'

'I never laid eyes on her either way,' said Rosemary. 'You'll simply have to take my word for that.'

'Of course,' said Castang. 'She was driving a small red Japanese car. Here's a colour photograph of it.'

45. The Col du Galibier

Castang's bicycle was – how far up the hill? Half-way? The switchback hairpins are innumerable: they all look the same and one had long lost count. Nor do you get off for a rest and a picnic, and a leisurely survey of how high up you are by now among the Alpine summits. A hill stage in the Tour is an effort greater than you yourself had known you could call from your body. There is an end somewhere, and a man to hold you up as you fall off your bicycle, and give you a drink of water. But you don't know where it is. Four more turns in the switchback? Six? Eight?

Hill is not a word with a precise meaning. The high passes of the Alps are strategic roads, made wide enough for guns. The slope is around twelve per cent. The bends are blind, elbows of bare cliff on the one side and abrupt precipice on the other. On the inside is a rough-paved gully to carry off the rain and the melting snow. The surface nowadays is smooth, in fair repair, and there should not be too many potholes: there are still plenty of nasty things that can happen on the way to the summit.

In a mountain stage there are two, even three of these severe tests. The Galibier is the classic. It is over three thousand metres high. Go up – or down – this and you can say you know how to ride a bicycle.

The Tour covers four thousand kilometres around widely varying French countryside, but it is won and lost on the high pass.

Commissaire Richard was not there today, at lunchtime. He had gone to Geneva to have lunch with a Swiss cop. There was a bank account containing, it was rather thought, ransom money from a kidnapping. Castang left Lucciani to the hamburgers. The day you propose to climb the Galibier you are careful what you eat and drink. Don't take any speed pills, either.

The police driver, with a medium size black Peugeot saloon, brought him Mr Justice Armitage at two-fifteen p.m. precisely. Mr Malinowski had eaten hamburger with lots of Old Mother Riley's Cannibal Sauce over it, but he never belched and carried a toothbrush in his pocket; simultaneous translation has many pitfalls, not all etymological.

There are two ways to climb the hill. One can stand upright, the points of the feet upon the pedals, looking straight before one, in a series of darting accelerations. Or one can glue the behind to the saddle, head right down between the elbows, choosing the one steady rhythm and sticking to it.

'Comes the time,' said Castang, 'for direct speech. No way of evading it any longer.' The Judge was lighting his pipe, a thing he had not done before with the cops around.

'I don't like this job. It makes a fool of me, and nobody enjoys that. How does a minor police official go about discussing points of law with a man of your position and experience? He can't. But when he has to, he does.'

The Judge listened peacefully for the translation, puffed, and said quietly,

'I'm not on the Bench, here. I'm a private citizen. I take your point, of course: a man such as myself can never be wholly private, even at his own breakfast table. The problem is familiar; every Judge has learned the lesson of it. The poet Kipling had a knack of expressing truths succinctly, in verses often vulgar, but striking. A man of my generation grew up with many such, which come apt upon occasion. Thus:

I would go without shirt or shoe,
Friend, tobacco or bread,
Sooner than lose for a moment the two
Separate sides of my head.'

Monsieur Malinowski had a second's trouble with the last line, but Castang followed simple English well enough.

'Good, but I'm obliged unfortunately to create a confusion between them. On the one side I've something personal to say. Addressed to the person. On the other, a policeman talking in technical terms to a magistrate, upon a judicial point.'

'Making a submission, we'd call it. Try that one first. You need not hesitate. Respect for a submission is the first of our duties.'

'We sometimes find, in examining patterns of anti-social behaviour, a form that disquiets us more than most. It's undoubtedly medical as well as legal, so we call it sociopathic, or a pathological attitude to society, though I think no country accepts it as a defence in terms of legal insanity. One can say

210

medical since people showing this behaviour obey various definitions. They are of high intelligence, bright and attractive personalities; charming, frank, sincere, reliable and open.'

'Pattern within judicial experience, certainly; the engaging rogue.'

'We still don't know what impels them towards crime: compels is a matter of degree. They seem to have a need to take risks. They have powerful self-confidence, a certainty of success which means they do suceed, often. Like all criminals they are vain: self-admiration to the point of narcissism. They get high marks too on cunning, slyness, plausibility . . . Cool-headed and quick to improvise. Able to explain anything, always in that winning, open fashion. They would never dream of admitting guilt, for they have no conscience of guilt, and a vanity above such concepts; guilt doesn't apply to them. All their concern is towards not getting caught. They aren't all that frequent, but they aren't all that rare either, and they seem on the increase – not a medico-legal oddity any more. They are generally called immature, because they seem unable to resist satisfying their desires. A cop learns to fear them, because under interrogation they show no disquiet, do not become confused or anxious. They'll run circles round him, and laugh. They know their rights, and how to take advantage of them. Even before a tribunal an indictment against them often rests on circumstance. They were around, they had opportunity. Means, maybe. Motive, maybe, as far as one really understands what motivates them. Like a financial interest. But it's often something no normal person could accept as an inducement to crime.'

'That's the submission? Hypothetical, so far. Doubtless the second leg of your argument has to do with that.'

'I don't know your son well. On a slight acquaintance he presents some of these features. That's disquieting.'

'You must present your evidence, you know.'

'Circumstantial only, which weakens it very much. We think it certain that he made the acquaintance of Laetitia Toth, and spent the night with her in a hotel near Caen. He went on to Versailles; she to Tours. We think she decided to approach you, to put perhaps some pressure upon you. The only thing we know for sure, and that wouldn't be thought of much weight nowadays, is that she was a few weeks pregnant. Your own strong views about abortion are however on public record. As a motive for suppressing her, assuming a threat of disclosure or scandal, it seems lamentable. Motive though isn't always a good basis for enquiry. I think that's where the English police officers went perhaps astray, putting too much emphasis on *cui bono*.'

'Not a great deal. Is there more?'

'Some – in my estimation not conclusive. Somebody, who can only be a sociopathic personality, thought it amusing to sow a lot of false trails to implicate your family. To our mind that removes all possibility of a professional killing: nobody'd take these fantastic risks of being noticed. Put the body in your car for a start – but plant clothes and stuff along the road . . . It would cause – and did – great embarrassment and humiliation. For reasons obscure, so far, to us. To my mind – I'll be open – it's shown by his arranging to be around at the time the body was likely to be discovered, once it was not, by a silly coincidence, found in Tours. He seemed amused at the discovery. Acutely disturbing piece of luggage for a Judge. Small but exquisite embarrassment for the French police and even the French Government. With quite simple resources, an international incident is created. It's not a homicide, it's a vast black joke. This is sociopathic in concept and execution. To our mind.'

'I'm bound to point out that your premises are exceedingly fragile. You don't even place your presumed author at the scene.'

'I'm only too aware. I haven't had time, but time might not help me.'

'You presuppose an acquaintance of at the very least some weeks' standing, and a physical relationship. No trace of a meeting has been shown to exist.'

'With respect, I don't think my English colleagues have tried very hard. I don't blame them. They'd naturally be most reluctant to believe anything that could affect a man in your public position. Your family has the right – I'm quoting the judge of instruction's phrase to Monsieur Richard – "to enjoy an initial incredulity". And policemen of all nations dislike prodding at a situation of potential political sensitivity. We're uncomfortably aware it might have an adverse bearing on our career. We don't have the protection a magistrate has: we can be sacked.

'I believe that all this was present in the mind of the crime's author. He counted on it. I think he counted also on a family relationship. How would any member of his family admit to knowledge or suspicion? He has us all over a barrel. Except, really, yourself . . .'

'I see. Your inference, pertinent if unattractive, is that in these circumstances I must have realized the significance of the discoveries, and faced with the inevitable disgrace and ruin disclosure or corroboration must bring, I chose silence. Is that correct?'

'Absolutely not: I've inferred a great deal too much already. I'm obliged by the circumstances to put it to you formally, and await an answer. No law of ours anyhow obliges you to give an answer. You know as well as I do that on the evidence available, or likely to be so, no indictment could be pronounced. We'd be obliged to classify. A VR we call it: Research in Vain.'

'I see. I find myself thus in the presence of a police officer convinced of my son's guilt in a homicide, and of my felonious concealment of guilty knowledge. A pretty notion you have formed of my family. You then, in order to place me before my responsibilities, tell me of your certainties and compound my burden by skilfully admitting your own impotence to move in the matter. Hm. An extra turn of the screw is that this should all have taken place in France. A country which as you have not failed to observe is not the highest in my esteem. You turn the tables upon me, since I am low in yours. My breath is taken away: allow me a moment.'

46. The summit of the col

The Judge struck a French match, which broke in his hand. Another, which lit and at once died. He rattled the box and looked at it with irritation. Castang kept quiet, secretly agreeing. The manufacture of matches in France has shown a mysterious reluctance to reform evil ways. Petty meanness too, by God; the box is never full.

'Tell me, have you discussed this theory with your colleagues? Or the howdyoucallem, the magistrate of instruction?'

'Commissaire Richard knows my thoughts. He hasn't taken me into his confidence regarding his own. The judge – no. He asked for an enquiry and awaits the findings, which are open to his interpretation. He wouldn't give a lot of weight to unsupported conclusions by an obscure PJ inspector.' Nod.

'There'd be, I think,' went on the Judge, 'a widely-held body of opinion in England, to the effect that the management of affairs here suffers from a grave shortcoming. That an engineer, to take an example, receives a very strong schooling in theory, but the practical realization of his acknowledged brilliance is flawed or faulty with disturbing frequency. As though there were a fundamental imbalance in his thinking? I'm bound to say I've chosen an example I know very little about.'

'It's notorious,' said Castang cheerfully. 'We build magnificent prototypes, and are quite incapable of manufacturing a commercially viable series. The state electricity authority designs a beautiful machine for creating power, without a single second's thought for the effect it might have on the lives of ordinary people, and are most surprised and indignant to be told that nobody wants it. A sort of self-sufficient high-handedness.' Nod.

'A narrowness? A rigidity?'

'That's right. Add a government that doesn't trust its people and won't consult them. Hardly surprising then that the people doesn't trust its government. Not just French, that: seems to be universal.'

214

'To take the sphere that I myself know the best; the law – we are often accused of clinging to absurdly old-fashioned and outworn institutions. We reply that centuries of experience show these to provide a good pragmatic result. The argument for preserving them is correspondingly strong: another example of empirical thinking. Now you – as it appears to us – have been gifted with legal institutions the theory of which seem superior to our own. Yet all too often the result – the decision laid down by the court – appears as confused and confusing.'

'All too true, I'm afraid, and I know someone who agrees.' Damn it, this sounded like Richard talking.

'To narrow things to the matter at hand,' went on the old boy relentlessly, 'though plainly improper coming from one himself concerned, that is my own self. I put it to you that you are vulnerable to this same criticism.'

'I'm aware.'

'You have a theory, and theoretically the argument in its favour could be called strong. But unsupported by evidence it fails to meet the tests a Court – that is to say our courts – would insist upon applying. In fact I am bound to tell you that my own opinion, upon the Bench, would be that there was no case to answer. The Director of Prosecutions, very roughly the equivalent of your Chamber of Accusation, would I think have reached this same conclusion before me.'

Castang began wearily putting his papers together. This old man, stiff as he seemed, was a better climber than he was. Got to the top first, what. His legs felt like cotton.

'It won't get as far as any Chamber of Accusation,' he said. 'If it reaches the judge of instruction it's only in a formal sense, that he voids further proceedings. My own superior, Commissaire Richard, would apply your argument to my summary.' He turned the papers face down and lit a cigarette. What kind of a fist would young Lucciani make of typing this lot up? He'd better do it himself, in sheer self-defence!

Surprisingly the Judge showed no sign of wanting to escape towards the fresh air.

'You have put to me, Mr Castang, a classic enigma, classically described in an excellent book – left alas unfinished – by a

215

writer of much worth, who had some acquaintance with the law: Robert Louis Stevenson.'

'Means nothing much to me, I'm sorry to say.'

'No? *Weir of Hermiston*? You should look it up: it would interest you. Worth the trouble. The name is that of a Judge, a hanging judge, universally known for his erudition and his integrity, but also for his brutal and peremptory manner in Court. He has little contact with his son, a sensitive and imaginative young man, who is one day shocked and even appalled at the apparent callousness shown by his father in sentencing a sordid and commonplace criminal to execution. The young man is moved to public protest, thereby ruining his own promising career at the university. There is here a remote but valid analogy to experiences of mine.'

Castang was listening.

'In a finely written scene the older man refuses, with contemptuous pride, to justify his conduct before his son, and banishes the young man to a remote country existence on an upland farm, where, lonely and confused, and distracted by a love affair with an innocent country girl, the son commits a fatal crime. Here the story ends, with the writer's untimely death. There is some confusion how the tale was to finish. The writer's original intention, as expressed in letters, was that the young man would come to trial in his father's own court. The writer had plans to modify this crude melodramatic dénouement, as we may think. How exactly he would have grappled with the problem is not fully known. We remain uncertain.

'There is no parallel here, Mr Castang, with any situation in which I find myself. Even were I convinced by your theoretical reasoning, which I do not admit, my training and experience teach me, as I have repeated to you, that there is no legal case to answer, and my cast of thought is legalist.

'That much said, I should like to ask of you your agreement, in a sense your forbearance, to allow me to give this whole matter some thought. Do not misunderstand me. I have no enquiries to pursue, or interrogations to conduct, in any private capacity, or parallel to those you have conducted. I ask for some hours of reflection, to postpone if you permit the conclusions of this exchange, for reasons of my own. Have you objections?'

'No.'

'Where by the way is Commissaire Richard?'

'He went to Tours. He wasn't altogether satisfied with some of the enquiries conducted there. Concerning what actually did happen at Tours. That is the pivot of the investigation.'

'I see. You agree then to a postponement for twenty-four hours? Tomorrow at this time?'

Castang mustered a grin.

'Courts allow themselves these intervals to think things over. Agreed.'

Who had actually got to the summit of the col first? For the life of him he couldn't tell.

He climbed on his bicycle, rode back to the office, very slow; the legs were still like cotton. The shortest way was through the university campus. On a wall full of scribble was 'This wall will shortly appear in paperback' and the headline 'Alienation Begins Here'. This message of good tidings would have induced a grin ordinarily but now he shook his head at it. The street facade of the Cité Administrative, recently replastered and in consequence practically virgin terrain, had instantly acquired the usual appeal to Liberate Thingummy, but here the latest, in an attractive purple, was 'Carmen I Love You' to which someone had added 'But start rolling your own Carmen hasn't time' which puzzled him.

47. Lights burning late

'Fausta, where's Richard?'

'Sitting in the train, I should hope not reading Agatha Christie.' Of course; Geneva. No direct flight, and he had tartly refused to take a car. Be back late, and would go straight home. Richard would be no help anyway. He'd say 'Made your bed; lie on it.' Couldn't complain about that.

'Who's Carmen? And why does one have to roll one's own?'

'My dear boy, sharpen your wits. Carmen worked in a cigarette factory'.

'What I need is a drink.' His ribs were hurting like hell. The fresh angry pink scar tickled abominably.

'Well, if you refuse to go to the hospital what can you expect? Sit in God the Father's chair because it tilts back. Take your shirt off; I'll see what I can do.' Fausta could always do everything. She got the first aid box, flattened him like a dentist, swabbed his stomach with ninety-degree alcohol, stinging cold and madly sexy.

'All this old chewing-gum. And pick the lint out of your navel.' The healing wound was tender as well as tickly.

'I'll put a sterile thing on that, and then strap you over. Pouh, that Goltz left his mark on you, didn't he?' A lock of Fausta's hair – everybody in the PJ boasted that she could sit on it – escaped and tickled his tummy.

'Fausta, do that again, but with your bare breasts.'

'Shut up and keep still.'

'Fausta, what are you doing to me; my penis is erecting in a perfect frenzy.' She gave him a frightful slap right on the nerve centres of the diaphragm, at which he shrieked in a hoarse soprano.

'You sound just like Carmen when she gets knifed,' said the horrible girl. He'd managed to piece it together by this time. No provincial opera company could now manage to pay for international stars. So that the Opera du Rhône, and du Rhin, and some Swiss had clubbed together. They did that nowadays; Vera had explained it to him. With a sharp sense of shock he recalled that she was going tonight. A great sexy black mezzo-soprano. And the whole town, enchanted at having a proper tune to whistle at last . . . except for him, of course; he'd been in the Hermitage, when he wasn't Goltzing.

218

'I went last night,' said Fausta. 'It's absolutely super.' Of course. 'José is a poor soft thing; Escamillo's just a stupid stud. But Carmen's red meat. Every male in the city standing on end. That better?'

'If you'd scratch my back it would be perfect.'

'You get your wife to scratch your back; I'm going home.' That late already? He phoned the switchboard, who before going off would leave the line plugged in to the duty officer.

'Who's on guard?'

'Lachenal.' Great big tough on Cantoni's brigade, who would sleep happily all night.

'Leave the line through to me in Richard's office; I'll switch it back when I go.' A quiet afternoon in the PJ office: everybody would buzz off while the going was good. Soon there would be silence, and the small knocking noises of the cleaning woman. Nobody else in the blocks worked late: once the madonna of the mop and bucket was through only the concierge would go whistling on his rounds to check windows and radiators with his dog padding beside him. He wouldn't bother with the PJ offices. Used to lights burning late there.

The sun was setting, throwing a sinister red light into all the offices on the courtyard side. Patterns in the bare plane trees, and a chilly white mist rising from the ground. You got it like this in spring sometimes, and autumn more often: tranquil open skies, clear and windless, out of which the sun poured down all day. Only when the twilight fell abruptly, hustling through to night, did you notice how near you were to winter. At the moment the night lords took over. He reached for the phone and dialled his home.

'Don't know when I'll be back; I might be latish.'

'Oh. Well, that'll be all right, I'll leave you the soup.'

'Why, are you going out?'

'Didn't I tell you? I'm sure I did; you can't have been listening. I'm going to *Carmen*.'

'Oh . . . no no, okay, no problem.' He felt somehow aggrieved, as though she had no business to be going to *Carmen* when he was in the shit.

Might as well make himself comfortable. Richard's chair was padded and well designed: you could lie back in it. You can raid Fausta's cupboard, make yourself some coffee, or tea: there are even drinks there. If you run out of cigarettes Lachenal will have some. If time hangs heavy you can read Richard's files; you can even listen to his 'electronic notebook' which he had kindly left upon the desk, and which would be full of phrases in various states of polish for letters and reports to dictate to Fausta next day . . .

Richard would not be back now. Once off the train from Geneva he would go straight home even if he hadn't been held up. He'd be in at eight in the morning, fresh and attentive then, with a sharp ear for Castang's affairs. But there were a dozen files on his desk. Castang knew nothing about the Swiss affair, which Richard was handling himself, but it was just as important as a piddling homicide of some ridiculous girl who'd been asking for it. Much more, in fact. The Press had gladly abandoned these English people to concentrate on the kidnapping.

Anyhow Richard had distanced himself from this business. No blame to him. You couldn't expect him to be dictated to when witnesses would kindly consent to make statements or submit to interrogation. Richard was ready to back him up, and would, if need be, even though he had not been happy at the 'tactic.'

'You're on a roulette wheel,' he had said. 'You're not even betting red or black: you're betting a number. You're disregarding the basic rule of procedure which says get the odds on your side.'

'I can't see what one has to lose. There isn't any proper evidence. Sawing on and on might I suppose produce a scrap but can you see anyone signing extradition orders? – of course not. With that Larkins sitting there all little condescending smiles, and this Embassy type just waiting to throw half the Paris Bar underneath our feet.

'We've a tacit admission right now that we've no grounds for charges. There's a chance perhaps of making the boy over-confident. Won't get anywhere by acting stupid and waiting for them to contradict themselves. While putting the whole thing on another plane . . .'

'Go ahead then,' Richard had said calmly. 'You never know your luck. In a situation where you've no leverage anyhow . . .' What Richard really thought he wasn't saying.

' "A crime has been committed. You know this, knowing that I know it. Is that going to have any effect upon your family solidarity?" '

'Exactly,' said Richard. 'You expecting the Mafia to drop in and tell you all its troubles? Yes yes, my daughter is keeping bad company, and what's more she hid the body in my car; now how'd'you like that?'

'All right,' said Castang. 'You've only to send Lasserre to conduct these interrogations.' Richard didn't say anything; just stared out of the window. But you could see 'Lasserre . . .!' forming in the balloon over his head. Pow! Whoof! I've got it all straightened out for you, signed your Friendly Neighbourhood Spider-Man. Lasserre won't hit anybody; leastways, not after he's been told not to.

Or Cantoni. We Corsicans, we may have a reputation that is sometimes deserved, but truly we don't go attaching electrodes to people's bollocks. Truly . . . Ol' Lachenal here just a nice friendly rugby player. Big baby, really.

The phone rang.

'Castang.'

'Ah, you're there. I'm at the hotel. Mother and the sister were window-shopping, tea-drinking, strolling. They're finally in, gone up for a bath or what not, going to have a bite here in the restaurant, and they asked the porter to get two tickets for *Carmen*. Okay?'

Dammit, everyone was going to *Carmen*.

'Where's the Judge?'

'Seen no sign of him at all.'

'All right, you may as well see *Carmen* too, since everyone else is. Fausta says it's super. Make friends with the fireman!'

The next call came almost at once.

'Your Judge is going for a nice long walk. Went back to the

221

hotel, took an overcoat, scarf and gloves, stick, didn't say a word to anyone.'

'Where?'

'Along the quays. Foggy. Cold.'

'So you dropped in the pub to have a warm? I don't want him lost sight of.'

'No, I'm in a call-box. He walks slow.'

'All right, don't get too close. But he's an old man; I don't want him mugged by some little rigolo.'

'Understood. Just that I've no transport, see, and if he suddenly jumps in a taxi or something I'm stranded.

'Anything like that you phone in smartish, and we'll pick him up through the dispatcher. He'll stop for something to eat, likely.' And where the hell was Colin? He had to wait another half-hour for this one.

'Ouf. At last. Back at Holiday Inn. Gone up for a shower, or to change. 'S all right, I'm using that phone Lucciani set up, that doesn't go through the board. I reckon on a hot night – he's been asking the desk where the action is. You going to have me relieved? He knows me, by now. Amusing himself, at my expense.'

'What did the desk tell him?'

'Oh, out to the Rancho Notorious, where else? Unless they ask for the candle-lit cellars that's where they send the tourists.'

'Where you been all day?'

'Out touring picturesque vineyards. You know – the cobwebs they guarantee you are three hundred years old. He went through that tasting routine, bought quite a lot of stuff. Walnut schnapps, things like that, a couple of cases. Tapped ma for some ready, at lunch; she signed some American Express cheques. Look, I better keep an eye; he left the car outside.'

'If you're not relieved there, you will be at the ranch, right?'

The ranch was a few kilometres out, down stream, a former fishing inn before the river got too polluted. On summer evenings a riverside 'guinguette' where one could drink in the garden and dance at weekends. Local smart business, smarter than Mr Goltz, doing well with the local riding stable, had turned it

222

into a western saloon, with girls in boots and bare thighs, and silver dollars to gamble with, and barbecue steaks and a little jazz group. Did a roaring trade. Road accidents on the way back had been something chronic until they'd put on a permanent patrol at three in the morning. Master Colin would have an enjoyable time. And the cowgirls were regular, on the books, and well-known to the night porter at Holiday Inn.

The old man was headed that way. But it was a good eight kilometres, too far for him to walk – he'd take a cab. Well, they would see. It wouldn't be a good place for a quiet talk, anyway.

Nothing would happen for another hour. He'd whip across to the pub for a cup of soup – nowhere near as good as Vera's – and a badly needed beer, and a packet of cigarettes. Block off Lachenal first, who'd be working up an appetite by now.

48. Laetitia

The file went back to the beginning, to the time when she was 'the barefoot girl' – even before, to when she had been a Dead-on-arrival, a Jane Doe, a nastily-strangled piece of female flesh of whom there was nothing to say beyond how unusual to find such a thing in a tourist's Rolls-Royce. It was time to take a fresh look at Laetitia. She was the key, the pivot, the fountain-head: no cliché one could think of would dim or blur her importance. She had been the electric current, the life, yes, the vitality that would make it all logical. That's right, logical: it appeared logical at some moment to kill her.

Richard as well as himself had hit this impasse: by police logic the boy Colin was the only serious customer, because forget all the French myths so dear to Mr Larkins. Gangsters or barbouzes and underground action squads, right-wing extremists who assassinate people that have compromising secrets and threaten to spill them. But where was Colin's interest in killing her? There is always an interest, only for a fraction of a second. Fear or relief from pain or maddening tension. If you are going to kill someone purely out of convenience then you're psychopathic by definition. Good, but calling so and so a psychopath simply because you've found nothing better is questionable. Neither courts nor cops like a case built on nothing better than a psychiatric diagnosis.

The pregnancy – they'd been too late to type sperm but it should be possible to type blood. And take a blood test off Colin – Richard had shaken his head. Have to get the judge to order it, and it wouldn't be conclusive.

Castang went on through the reports and transcripts that had been of so singularly little help.

Laetitia alive, at last. Apart from 'statements' thoroughly but deadeningly taken by Messrs Larkins and Townsend, back in England, from the neighbours in Holland Park, through the editorial staff of a woman's magazine, to the travel agency where she'd booked her passage, the only witness they had was that PJ cop at Caen. Who had been an excellent observer, but was it enough? Here was the transcript of a tape, typed out by Fausta. He'd done his best to flush it out. But as often happened, the few joking words, before and after a few drinks with Castang, sketchily impressionist, were more valuable and convincing – and vivid – than this laborious officialese. Paper deadens . . .

'Robin, Jacky, adjunct officer of police judiciaire,' – blah-blah – 'reporting verbally on tape at the request of Commissaire Richard subsequent to' – blah. 'I have a good recollection of the informal and unofficial' – careful man – 'conversation between Inspector Castang and myself. A careful synthesis of the two episodes produces little that I could wish to add, and subsequent analysis does not incline me to take much away. I can conclude that there is no point on which I would prefer materially to alter the remarks I then made, while emphasizing that these remarks were a more or less frivolous summary of fleeting impressions.' Fair enough, boy.

'I do not wish undue weight to be given to any interpretation I may have made in the course of what I can describe as professional gossip, but I understand that the description of the clothes I gave proved accurate, and that she had a pistol in her handbag, a fact of which I was unaware. I think it thus fair to say that my observation of her was materially well founded. I do not pretend to exactitude in describing her mannerisms or reporting her words, but to some factual accuracy. I emphasize that my meeting with her lasted a quarter of an hour, and nothing in it could give me any hint that it would then or at any future date acquire any importance.'

Well okay. Robin hadn't tried to back out or blur over: he backed me up, and does not try to alter my wording. For the preliminary to this had been Castang's putting his own version of the meeting with Robin on tape, including a version of the dialogue (discreetly censored, for which Robin had been grateful). The PJ man in Caen had quite simply 'sent the lift back' for a professional colleague.

It had proved oddly precious. The only glimpse of Laetitia-alive they'd been able to find.

Because Tours had been a dead loss. Commissaire Benoît, prodded by his colleague and brother Richard (equal in rank and seniority . . .) had made a tremendous synthesis of investigations, starting off in the most encompassed officialese about We, Benoît, by virtue of the powers blah, under the rogatory commission issued by blah, consequent and subsequent to blah-squared. It got much better as it went along. Commissionaire Benoît conducting in person the interrogation of the night porter, and coming ominously near losing his patience with this bastard-squared-and-cubed, was as Richard said 'choice', and sometimes wildly funny. But it hadn't got anywhere near Laetitia at all.

Officially, one couldn't get away from the fact that the hotel's car park was some hundred metres from the house, and even visually sheltered from it by trees. Not a garage or even a courtyard. The porter simply pointed to a prominently displayed notice at both the conciergerie and the reception desk, saying that the management refused all responsibility for cars or their contents. The whole affair was thus a dry nut: crack it and there wasn't any kernel. Same thing with the keys.

'You have only to understand, Commissaire,' said the porter patiently, 'that people drive up to the front door, their baggage is unloaded – which we of course do, and if the car keys are given us, we use them to unlock the trunk. But we've stopped offering to park these cars. We found that too many customers attempted to blame us consequently for damage, scratches and stuff, caused by careless parking or even caused days before. We all have good reason to be touchy on the subject – been stung too often. Dishonest customers spoil things for themselves,' virtuously.

He'd never laid eyes on Laetitia! Naturally ... Benoît had pushed him pretty roughly. All night porters have fiddles and dodges ... have been known to let rooms, or allow rooms to be changed, shared, and otherwise 'used' without anything appearing on the book: quite. Pretty young women, unaccompanied, have been known to gain access to private areas of hotel accommodation by the judicious placement of bribes not always monetary: no no, Commissaire, one has heard of such things but believe me they are myths. This is not an establishment for commercial travellers, and being as we are in the depths of the country we are not troubled by light ladies. If guests of course bring light ladies registered as their wives – but in a hotel of this standing, you understand, commissaire, there is a large premium placed upon attending to the customer's small comforts and desires, while maintaining, for the protection of all, scrupulous moral standards. Just leaf through the registration ledger, commissaire, and you will find the gratin, the golden crust, the crisp and flavoursome, the Names. I don't use these ruffianly expressions like bullshitting, commissaire, and let me tell you I resent their use applied to my statements. Look where I was trained, look where I gained my experience; ask these people. They'll tell you: not just no criminal record – nobody with such could hope to keep a position of this responsibility

226

for a single second – but not a breath, commissaire, not a breath.

Benoît had gone quite far, threatening that if as much as a breath came to his ears, he personally would see to it . . . and so on. But a concierge in a luxury hotel is a thoroughly well-carapaced crustacean. You can put him in a pot with water, but getting the water anywhere near boiling point isn't ever easy. You need material evidence, and so, finally, Benoît had concluded (privately, on the telephone to Richard), 'If just one person had seen this woman Toth. If she'd stopped in the village for petrol or cigarettes, in Tours for a meal. I've done all that's human – you gave me her stomach contents and I've checked every establishment serving food in the region. Yes, all camping sites but Jesus, man, in the month of February . . . And a steak . . . she bought it at any butcher's and cooked it herself. This effing porter could have got it out the fridge and cooked it for her but how are you to prove that?'

Laetitia alive, Laetitia dead. Castang took Richard's scratch-pad.

'Service note, Castang to Richard. Has enough weight been given to the following (for PJ Tours)? Reasonable assumption due to weather conditions; the killing of Toth took place under cover (in a car is a possibility but in a hotel is likelier) and reinforced by the following. Elbow strangulation produces well-known physio. consequence: i.e. sphincters relax. This would leave a large unpleasant trace. (Sheets?) Query, has the laundry been checked out, both at chambermaid-housekeeper level, in terms of rooms on hire that night, and at laundry level, where checking and counting of hotel property would take place? This would not be a matter of a coffee-cup on a pillowcase . . .'

Was there any more at all to Laetitia-alive? The English report gave parentage mother-born-in-Nice. Even this had been checked, the more so since the English family were holidaying in the region: almost certainly coincidence but could one be sure? – but no, no trace of any family or indeed any connection, either personal or professional (mother's birth certificate,

227

according to English passport records, gave 'occupation – none'). And the English could be trusted to be thorough at that sort of thing. Mr Larkins too – Richard agreed entirely – was reliably loyal. If he turned up anything that gave a hint, he would not seek to minimise it, however much he hoped that the whole affair belonged to extra-territorial instances.

Laetitia, you idiot girl, with your fascinations about guns and death, criminals and cops.

Yes, agreed the editor for features on the magazine: she had done some work on woman-aspects of crime and criminals, and submitted it on a vague basis of liberation ought to create a steep drop in female crime at all levels from shoplifting up to husband-murder. The features-editor had turned it down, but had said – without making any commitment – that if Letty wished to do more work along those lines it might not be altogether without promise. Nothing commissioned, Inspector, but yes, Letty might have wanted to take it further: she really couldn't say more than that . . .

When Laetitia found out that her new boyfriend was the son of a Judge – did that mean anything?

Laetitia, however banal it sounds, I just wish you were still alive!

49. The Life and Soul of the Party

The phone rang.

'Castang.'

'I'm having a warm, and by God I need it. All the way out along the river to the end of the town. And what does he do then? – about turn like a bleeding route march and all the way back again. Walks well for an old man – I'm ready to pee in my socks. We're Quai des Belges: like you said, he stopped for something to eat. I've a healthy appetite myself.'

228

'Where?'

'Restaurant de la Bourse; you know it? Caught his eye, I suppose; he just stopped dead, took a look at the menu, and walked in.'

'Can you see him?'

'Sure, I'm in the cabin. In the corner, ordering. I'm pretty certain he's picked me up; have to be blind not to, after all this time. But lets on he hasn't, pays no attention. He's taking his time, very dignified – got a little book now, out of his pocket to read.'

'Very well, take a bite; don't make it expensive! Doesn't matter whether he has you marked or not. Just stay with him quietly, do nothing unless he does. If by any chance I'm not here, Lachenal will know where to find me. Okay.'

What was going on there? Not that Castang really expected anything in the least dramatic: balance, detachment and self-control were the base of the old man's existence. Unless that base got sawed off . . . but the Restaurant de la Bourse was not a place in which one did anything dramatic. It might be an interlude. But it had on the whole a calming effect.

He knew it well, and had a good picture of the situation. Solid, sedate, old-fashioned place: there weren't so many of those left now. Plum-pudding Third Republic décor with much dark-varnished wood and panelled ceiling; an inordinate number of gilt faded glasses in which Herriot and Blum had studied their reflections. Large tables covered in coarse white cloths, plush-upholstered banquettes, heavy ornate old silver. The kind of place that still has an old duck-press in the centre of the floor. Sedate heavy food, plain but good. Bourse of what, originally? Stuff shipped by river; wine presumably. The shippers' meeting-place and still very much the businessmen's restaurant at lunch, full of bankers and insurance men eating stew and noodles. Oysters, excellent Chablis. As close as you could get to an 'English' restaurant; the Judge should feel at home there. The business quarter was dead in the evening, but there were always a dozen or fifteen people, mostly elderly, with a family party or two up from the country, working through antiquated Escoffier

229

food and a very good cellar. It didn't have a star in food guides: neither wanted nor needed one. The old lady at the cash desk in black satin was gone, had been gone these twenty years, but the 'youngster', balding and with worried wrinkles, fifty-five now if a day, had looked the same for thirty years, contented with the atmosphere he had always known, in which he had grown up. One of the last bastions of tradition. Couldn't last much longer; the chef in the kitchen was deep in the seventies. If you didn't want to labour through all that cream in the sauce you could get 'a chop and a bottle of claret' and a bowl of real consommé with marrow to begin, and cheese after. The Judge's instinct had not got mislaid.

His daydream got interrupted.

'Castang.'

'Ranch ahoy,' a voice sounding as though it had had two or three drinks. 'Only just got here, really. I picked up back at the Inn, young thingy had a kip I expect, kept me dodging there an hour and more. Getting down to the real work of the evening. Got into a party – French, Swiss – they're all still arguing about what they're going to eat. I slipped out; I'm okay, got some sandwiches in the car. Menu there costs the earth and is all shit anyhow.'

Indeed! Total contrast to the Bourse – a very showy menu full of exotic this from Hawaii and that from Stockholm and all of it dollied cardboard, and a thoroughly salted-and-peppered pricelist.

'Stick to the beer.'

'You're telling me!'

'What sort of impression does the boy make?'

'Nervous. Feverish, noisy. Laughing a great deal. Life and soul of the party. There are plenty of spare girls so he's being kept busy. Perfectly under control so far, but I wouldn't lay bets on how long it would last.'

'Reckless?'

'Yes.'

'Stay close, and stay careful. If he gets into a fight or anything . . .'

230

'I understand, chief.'

'He's under considerable strain all right. Looking for ways to get off the hook, or anyway an illusion. He knows we're treading on his coat, so this is a defiant act, daring us; right? Act accordingly. If he gets off with a girl we'd like to feel close at hand.'

'You're not going to come across?'

'I don't want to; he knows me, he'd take that as provocation. He's a cool character, but he's been drinking all day. Maybe not much and well spaced out, so I can't tell whether he's just letting off steam or whether he's deliberately lashing himself up. Use your judgement; if he shows signs of disturbed or violent behaviour I'll be along: for the moment keep a tag.'

'I got it. For the moment he's just playing. Plenty of money, and buying anything that takes his fancy.'

'I doubt if I'll hold on. Doesn't look to me as though it's going to create any crisis. I'll leave word with Lachenal, but if you want me try my home first.'

With Richard there he might have taken the risk of leaning on Colin, inflating the nervous strain to create a deliberate crisis, but he realized that this wouldn't do. Whatever else, leave no open-ing for any eventual complaints about police tricks. He could not know how accurate his reading was. The boy had chosen a place where he could blow off a lot of steam without it being untoward. The 'executives' of all ages did just that. All day terribly prudent, conventional, intensely respectable; being soft-spoken and polite to their seniors. After duty they wanted to let their hair down, in an atmosphere where they felt safe in doing so. This dump was really a glorified Playboy club, where anxious and constrained little salesmen calling themselves marketing managers could beat their chests and strut their machismo in front of a gallery of vapid females in silly clothes. The Ranch was really terribly respectable. The musicians made a racket, and a lot of animation got whipped up around the dancefloor, and the red-jacketed waiters whizzed about with trays of guff; hot hors d'oeuvres and rubbish on skewers; and the twirly-skirt girls with long ringlets flourished huge, very

231

thick-bottomed glasses full of ice-cubes and just a dab of whisky drowned in bubbles. A few rapid, practised headwaiters pushed up the trolley with grandezza, did their deft juggle with silver lamp, copper pan, wristy stuff with half a dozen bottles, a sheet of flame immediately doused with a watery juice of Maggi and ketchup, and much flicking of napkins. Cheap fairground dazzle: you don't transform the Colonel's Chicken by rattling pokerdice over it. The French and the Swiss – they'd be delighted with Colin. Give them a chance to show off their English. Secretly they'd be despising him – and he'd be despising them. Their girls would enjoy him . . . It sounded all pretty safe on the whole. Castang shrugged, stood up, put things back in his pockets, and decided he'd better go home.

50. The Jesuit Garden

He was asleep. It had taken him a long time to get to sleep, with the familiar symptoms of overtension. Vera had got back late: when you walk with difficulty, and there are a great many cars parked in narrow streets, it all becomes most laborious, but she was still exalted and beaming. *Carmen* had been lovely. And well done. Not oversophisticated. A simple freshness very much to her taste. No damned metaphysical overtones. Yes; he wished a few more of his own affairs were like this. She was very tired, and he got out of bed to make some cocoa, happy to have something to do.

'And your baby liked *Carmen* too?'

'Oh yes, extremely happy. Bounced about at the exciting bits, now very tired and blissfully asleep.' Alas, he had still exciting bits to bounce about for.

'The music goes on in my head. Never mind. Let me just lie still.' And after talking for an hour they had at last fallen asleep.

And he was very deeply asleep when the telephone rang. Cursing was no good. If you don't want to be shaken out of sleep by the telephone be a bank clerk.

'Castang.'

'Barde, chief. Slight drama here. Your boy turned the car over on his way back from the Ranch. I hadn't thought him all that drunk. Overstimulated, say.' Yes. Like me.

'Hurt?'

'Not really. Bit bruised. We're in city limits so the urban brigade has him. He's over the odds on alcohol naturally, driving dangerously. Nobody else involved, which is lucky, but he was saucy; they're taking him in. Why I phoned you was, what d'you want me to tell them? They've sat him in the van while they're taking measurements – skidded all over the shop.'

'No problem, let them take him in and book him. Once he's in the tank tell the brigadier that we'll want him, so make a fuss in the morning, you get me? Big deal about insurance and a long statement, multiply the paperwork, spin it all out. To keep hold of him in short until Richard decides whether to take him in – he'll want to see the judge. Okay?'

'Right.'

'I'm awake,' said Vera's voice in the dark,' so you may as well tell me all about it.'

A bit red-eyed over the coffee cup next morning, he rang the central commissariat. The day shift had just come on.

'That's all right,' said the desk brigadier's voice. 'I've got the file here. Big black eye, cut on bridge of nose, extensive bruising but nothing broken – hm, he was lucky. Lost some skin, lower arm and upper thigh. Urine test taken, tetanus shot given. Speech slurred, vision blurred. Doc wants to see him again this morning anyhow, gave him a fairly strong sedative and he's been quiet all night. May want to whip him down for an X-ray, query neuro-psychiatric examination – that what you want?'

'Do no harm but I'll be getting on to Richard. May want a second expert right away, for corroboration. We want him probably for homicide.'

'Plenty of tin-can stuff to hold him on if you want a pretext. Okay, let me know.'

'I'll be in the office in ten minutes,' said Richard unemotionally. 'Meet me there. I'll handle the family.'

'What are you doing?' Castang asked Vera.

'Who knows how long this will last?' looking out of the window at another sunny day. 'I want to get as much of my Jesuit job done as possible before the foliage gets too thick. Bones with a thin fragile skin.'

'You might have company,' ironically, shrugging into his jacket.

The sun was still thin and pale, but she wanted the morning light. Not that it was doing her much good – the drawing was bad, whether through Carmen's fault or her own made little odds. She tore the sheet off the pad and began again.

An elderly party was standing on the other side of the path. The Judge.

'I beg your pardon; I was staring rudely.'

'It doesn't matter.' She smiled, which seemed to encourage him. He made his mind up to sit down on a bench.

She drew a totally meaningless line.

'I distract you, I'm afraid,' courteously.

The drawing was no good anyhow. She gave her chair a hitch to bring herself closer; never mind the sightline.

'Let's talk,' she said.

'With pleasure. But I fear I speak no French.'

Vera thought about this problem, which was grave.

'Perhaps German!' she suggested timidly.

'Ah. Yes. Ah – rustily.'

'Good, then. Me too. I am Czech. But better one rusty than two clean – I didn't make that very clear.'

'Quite clear enough – I agree. Interpreters . . .'

'And I don't care about exact shades of meaning' – she hadn't spoken German since student days, but it was not all gone – 'we speak about simple things.'

'They aren't always so, alas,' smiling.

'They are for me. I have a very simple mind. Nobody seems to agree much about what's wrong with our world, though plainly there's a great deal. To me, most of the trouble comes from complicating things. But I am a peasant.'

'And an artist.'

'Artists, if they're any good,' shrugging, 'simplify. Look at this landscape. The trees and the bushes are designed by God, in a very complicated and subtle fashion. Trained, modified, patterned by man in an essentially simple way – it's only a surface sophistication. The equation between the two is what interests me. With behaviour it's much the same.'

'You interest me.'

'Of course. You're a Judge. My husband told me a little about you.'

'Obliged to view complicated situations.'

'And to simplify them. "To protect the children of the poor and to punish the wicked". That's what it should be about.'

'Oh, my dear young lady . . .'

'In the case of this murder for instance. Isn't it really very simple?'

He stiffened up, as though about to commit her for contempt, and then said, 'Go on.'

'My husband – no, I don't want to talk about him as a personality. Say the police. They think it's your son. I haven't met your son. But they've built a complicated theory. They're having trouble digesting it.'

'And you have a simple theory?'

'Simpler, in any case. I haven't met that woman, either. But then neither have they, except by accident a policeman up in Caen. He saw her very well, I think.'

'This is refreshing. And what was his conclusion?'

'He just saw her as a threat. To him, at that moment. Cops have an instinct for the trouble maker. Or the trouble-magnetiser,' looking for the right word, pawing in the air.

'Attractor?'

'Good. And that is how I see her. They showed me her photograph and asked me to make a sketch. I'm not a portraitist, and

235

technically it was impossible ... I did my best. But that cop in Caen found it looked like her. I was pleased. I saw her as he saw her, you see,' laughing, but only at her syntax.

He pulled out his pipe and was filling it.

'Pray go on.'

'Laetitia. Joy. You met her, didn't you?' He was striking a match.

'Is that what you think?'

'If you want to know what I think it is that Laetitia was worse than a troublesome person. A dangerous person. Who loved to complicate things, and with them to entangle, to entrap, to entice people. I think that you got her, I've got that wrong, that she got you into a complicated position that suddenly became intolerable – untenable – to yourself. And that to simplify matters in a hurry you found you had to kill her.'

'Really?'

'But if I'm wrong, then you can tell me.' He smoked, thoughtfully.

'You remind me of another simple person whom I know. The Nachrichter. He who comes after the Judge. He who executes.'

'Are you talking of a person – or of a function?'

'This is a real person. He was for many years the public executioner. He wrote a memoir, which many people bought, no doubt for morbid reasons. What interested me was his personality.'

'Yes – executioners interest me too. They must be very hard to find – I mean good ones.'

'Exactly. He was a very good one, and aware of it, and rightly proud of it. And for twenty years utterly reliable and conscientious, the perfect instrument of the law. And then, suddenly, he resigned. Quite abruptly, his life had no meaning any more.'

'Please explain.'

'You see, he had no imagination whatever, which kept his hand steady and his nerves firm. And he had high moral precepts. To him it was not a job but a vocation. It was in the family – his father, and his uncle. The astounding thing is that

236

as a schoolboy, writing an essay on careers, he wrote, as the most natural thing in the world "I want to be an executioner". He was born to it, you see. He was intensely proud of his dignity, his craftsmanship, his self respect. He had, too, respect for the victims. This is striking. Those, you see, who have the nerves for the job, who are neither drunken nor degraded, are frequently psychotic.'

'It's the drawback to capital punishment.' He missed the small irony.

'One. The other is that everyone agrees there must be exceptions, but nobody can agree on what they should be. It cannot be left to individual bias.' He had let his pipe go out.

'And I put you in mind of this person?'

'It isn't ruthlessness. A calm, perfect certainty. He was totally content – for thirty years.'

'A singularly old-fashioned person,' without adding 'makes two of you.'

'I should think he realized that in the end; that time had caught up with him.'

'It's probable,' said Vera. But the Judge was still pursuing his train of thought.

'He says, rather pathetically, that he always tried to keep a human awareness. And then, revealingly, that human awareness involves memories, dreams, fears, and that these are what break a man up.' Vera said nothing.

'What I have not understood is why she hated me – as she plainly did – and sought to entrap me. I have even wondered whether my son . . . but I cannot believe he was aware . . . But it was almost as though he were amused . . .'

'You are rather a bourgeois figure, you know,' she said gently.

'I suppose that I am.'

'I cannot myself help seeing that you were among those that punished – with death – the crimes of blood, so called, committed by the poor. While the authors of economic crimes, men who stole millions from the poor, enjoyed shelter and protection.'

'It is not true! It is true that the borderline between what is right and what is wrong has become fatally blurred.'

'Right, wrong; good, bad; day, night. You know? – an old, wise cop told me not to go out at night. That is the time of the power of darkness. The police do; they have to. They belong, they are part of it. The night lords, he called them. It was a Venetian title.'

'Ah. You believe in the powers of darkness.'

'In Satan? Certainly. Not this modern, morbid superstition, chattering about exorcisms. But if in day, then in night. Look at how many public figures: look at their faces: look how many belong, and how openly. Written on their features.' The Judge looked at her, finding nothing to say.

'I have advice for you if you'll take it,' she said timidly.

'What is it?' he asked. 'I feel sure that it will be good.'

'Go to the police. To my man. To Commissaire Richard. They are not like your executioner. They have imagination – too much. They don't believe in justice much. But they know a lot about good and evil. They go out at night.'

As he walked away down the path Vera thought that the man was oddly like Goltz. Come on, don't be idiotic; not like Goltz ... But yes. Goltz could not understand why people would come and disturb his tranquil existence.

51. Richard's Desk

When the Judge walked into the PJ offices and announced that he wished to see Mr Castang it created some embarrassment. The floor, none too large to begin with, was crowded with fourteen imbeciles picked up after a drug-party. A fifteenth was in Intensive Care after an overdose, and wasn't going to make it.

There was the small and squalid 'confession-room', but this was no place for a Judge. Furthermore it was occupied by Colin, left there alone to meditate.

'You'd better see to this,' Castang suggested hopefully to Richard.

'No, no, interpreters, thanks! Bring him up here – but I'll get in to bed with Fausta. Move up, Miss.'

Castang should have enjoyed this novel promotion to Richard's office, but enjoyment was not at present on top. He had run out of cigarettes, too. And one never knew what to call the man! Every time he said 'Sir James' he felt a fool . . .

Life was full of pinpricks. Try to remember not to scratch your stomach: Mr Goltz is still an imperfect past tense. This morning's news of Monsieur Bianchi was satisfying: he was complaining a lot about enforced immobility.

A PJ cop at Richard's desk is The Doctor. Whatever he is told, and no matter how many lies, he is unsurprised, interested, sympathetic. But the consulting-room confidences are not as easy as those made on park benches.

'This is without interpreters,' said Castang. 'You'll have to forgive any little clumsiness.'

'I've been talking to your wife. We got along in German, remarkably well. I don't find this a handicap; your English is good.'

Castang's smile was faint and mechanical. What has Vera been getting up to?

'I'll abandon preliminaries,' said the Judge. 'Explanations have a way of needing more explaining.

'I find myself in a position I cannot support. Whether or not you guessed as much; whether or no your suspicions, expressed yesterday, were largely pretence, designed to put pressure upon me – no matter. You owe me no explanation either. Perhaps you're as anxious to avoid them as I am.'

'If I understand aright, you confess to this crime. Is that correct?'

'I cannot place my family in this . . . I also need the
239

opportunity to regularise my – professional position. Can you allow me a brief private interview with Mr Brooke?'

'That can easily be arranged.'

'I don't know where to begin. If you wish to question me I will reply to the best of my ability.'

Castang nodded and took a piece of paper.

'This doesn't have to be formal. If I make notes, it's to keep myself from confusion. An instructing judge, eventually, would put precise questions and expect an exact answer. For the present I'm concerned to verify. You see, people have admissions to make, but they aren't always . . . understand; I'm not suggesting you'd mislead me. But there are several different kinds of truth. Some are only true to the speaker's own mind. You understand – I need factual, verifiable information.'

The Judge smiled a little.

'You need not pick your words with such care. False confessions made to police officers are within my experience. I wish to make a point. I do not seek to protect members of my family. Equally, I cannot allow them to be placed in jeopardy by attempts to protect me.'

'Which has been the case?'

'If we put it hypothetically – ?'

'I should think I could get you assurance that they would be immune from pursuit, if false information stops at this point.'

'Of that I freely assure you.'

'Then they will not be harassed.'

'I should like to see them freed of all blame.'

'It's a legal point. I'm only a police officer. If they were in – a complicity, a conspiracy beforehand, then it's up to the judge. If you're worried only about silence or suppression of knowledge, maybe just of suspicion – then I can reassure you. Family loyalties wouldn't make people accomplices.'

'The legal definition we use is "accessory." '

'I haven't the power to make bargains – that again concerns the judge of instruction. I'll give you my word on this though: your family, whatever they knew or guessed, kept silence out of loyalty to yourself – is that it? No more than that?'

240

'My daughter Patience got rid of that car; knowing and suspecting nothing at that moment. I promise.'

'Ah, I see. Nobody will hold that against her, and I don't want you to think that I'm trying to trick you by dangling inducements in front of your nose.'

'Having spoken to your wife, I can believe you,' with simplicity.

'It's as in England,' said Castang sadly. 'We are governed by a severe and scrupulous code of behaviour. There are crooked cops.'

'Also, Mr Castang, in Great Britain.'

'Let's begin with this point,' said Castang. 'It explains much that worried us. Your daughter drove the car down, and parked it in Tours?'

'I told her simply that the car belonged to a friend of Colin's, who had asked us to see that it was put in a place of safety to be picked up later.'

'Which convinced her, after the discovery of the body, that her brother was the author of the crime.'

'I'm afraid that might be so.'

'Shall we go back to the night before? Would you like a cup of coffee? Or a beer?' asked Castang hopefully, longing for one.

'I think I'd quite like a beer,' said the Judge, who was becoming human in Castang's eyes by great bounds. Castang snatched Richard's telephone.

'Send across would you for four bottles of beer and a packet of cigarettes for me . . . Where were we? Yes, the night before.'

'I think we have to go back further still.'

52. Richard's room

Behind the office-boy kicking the door open violently to bring the tray, Divisional Commissaire Richard came slipping in quietly, and sat humbly in the corner. He had probably found that the department, which was to say Fausta, functioned better without him. Drugs bored him – too many dopes involved – and could be left to Lasserre. He knew about as much English as Vera, enough to listen intelligently and keep his mouth shut.

'Am I inhibiting you, Castang?'

'Not in the slightest,' tempted to put a foot up and tilt the chair back, but restraining it. 'To Bayeux?' paying for the beers.

'Ask Fausta to make me a cup of tea,' said Richard austerely.

'To Bayeux,' agreed the Judge, tasting the beer, finding it not too cold, nodding approval.

'I admit that I thought so. Two or three people found her face familiar but nothing could be proved. In the early evening she left her hotel in Caen and was not again seen. It's only twenty kilometres.'

'We were looking at the famous tapestry. It's in an ordinary room. People standing about – concentrating of course on the walls. She put a piece of paper into my hand.'

'Do you have this piece of paper?' colourless.

'Fortunately or unfortunately, I do.' Crumpled envelope. Half sheet of ordinary hotel paper. Bold legible handwriting.

'It should not be difficult to get this verified as her writing.'

Dear Sir James,
    As a close – I should say a very close – friend of Colin's it is of great importance that I should be able to have a word with you. I realize the need for this to be discreet. May I beg of you to meet me in the hotel car park this evening around nine-thirty? I shall not keep you long.
                                        LT

'What made you keep it? – you took pains to get rid of the other traces.'

'It was in my inside pocket. To tell the truth I forgot it until a day later. Then – I thought it better to keep it than destroy it. It turns out to have been wise.'

'Very much so. Go on, please.'

'You will have seen then that car park, or better courtyard. It is dimly lit, and people walking to and fro are not noticed. My first instinct – of prudence – was to disregard this rather silly mysterious message. But it occurred to me that Colin might have done something foolish. And, I suppose, vulgar curiosity . . . However: I told my wife simply that I proposed to take a stroll, to digest some good claret. She went up to bed.

'I recognized her, having seen her of course in the Tapestry room. You may believe that that was the first occasion. I asked her, fairly curtly, what she wanted. She suggested getting into the car. I said I preferred to walk. She agreed, but after a few minutes complained of getting wet: there was a slight drizzle, and it was not cold. We turned into a sort of café. She asked for a drink; I did not want one. I accepted a cup of coffee; she took, I think, brandy.'

Excellent, concise, conscientious witness.

'She was direct. She said that she had had an affair of some months' standing with Colin. I find this to have been quite untrue, but had no means then of confirming it. She said she wished to marry him. She played anxious to please and be accommodating. She said quite sensibly that she had not wished to be sprung on me – to be introduced suddenly to the family without some warning. Hence this discreet approach. I was puzzled, and somewhat put off, by her air of mystery and her obvious tension.'

'A speciality of hers,' said Castang dryly.

'I wondered what caused this. I was – puzzled. A little intrigued. I suppose I was a little stiff. She said she had more to tell me. I said that I was tired, and wished now to go back to the hotel. She begged most insistently to see me again, and explain. I said that I wished to think this over. She asked me not to

243

mention the meeting as yet. She asked where I would be next day. I told her – very foolishly – the address near Tours my wife had picked out as attractive. She left. I must admit that she intrigued me. There was plainly more behind this than she had said – I wondered what . . .'

'It's possible that she was in two minds,' said Castang. 'We'll never know, but it is possible that as a journalist she wanted to find out what a Judge was like, in private life. She wanted a pretext for getting close to you – but it's of small importance now.'

'You may be right.'

'At that moment, plainly, she felt confident of having her hooks into Colin. She spent the night with him; it's quite certain. He'll have to fill that in for us.' Prudently, Castang suppressed the fact that Colin was downstairs 'meditating', with a plummy eye and a hangover . . .

'Yes. Well, I must come to the point, there's no help for it. The next day we drove to Tours. We had there a lighter and more digestible meal but I must accuse myself of drinking a little too much of that attractive Chinon wine. It must have contributed to recklessness.

'I repeated to my wife that – my excuse of wanting a stroll. She was tired and – a little irritable. She said that she would have a bath, take a sleeping pill, and go to bed at once.'

'Can we put it,' asked Castang gently, 'that you felt you had a certain freedom to stay out?'

'I think,' determined to be honest, 'that you can.'

'Please go on.' Richard was cat-quiet in his corner. Fausta, slipping in with his glass of tea, was equally noiseless.

'Nobody saw me go out.'

'If I may anticipate for one instant – did anyone see you go in? After? Purely a confirmation – the night porter swears he knew nothing.'

'Later? No. His light was burning above his desk, but he was not there. The door was open.'

'I beg your pardon. The pig – but guilty only of negligence.'

'He may,' said Richard sweetly, 'have been entertaining a friend.'

'The car park – but you are aware – is some distance from the hotel and screened by trees. It was a cold, foggy night, much colder than it had been in Normandy. She was in her car.' The Judge rested his forehead on his hand for a moment. 'What in heaven's name possessed me?'

'Everybody, even after she was dead, remarked upon her extreme vitality and great powers of attraction.'

'Yes. Perhaps. And powers of darkness.' Only Castang recognized a 'Vera' phrase. But he wasn't denying it.

'I proposed, as before, a stroll. But it was really too cold. I did not want to sit in her cramped little car. Half mechanically – I tried the door of my own car. I must ask you to believe – this was a genuine coincidence arising out of misunderstanding. My wife and I had both thought that the baggage porter had locked the car.'

'I accept it. I see how it came about.'

'I proposed getting into the car. Since she still complained of cold, I spread a travel rug for her.'

'Ah. No matter. A detail, no more.'

'I think I cannot adequately describe the events of the following hour.'

'You need not, though I'm afraid the judge . . . don't bother for now. Can we say that she seduced you, or that you seduced her?'

'I think,' stiff and unhappy, 'that there can be not a doubt . . . she was . . . wearing no underclothes.'

'I'm afraid that she was both deliberately amusing herself, and also quite certainly looking for leverage over you. It had worked like a dream with Colin. How much more ambitious, and exciting, to repeat the experience with his father – and a Judge.'

'May God forgive me. But – I know – payment will be exacted.'

'We'll leave that. I should like to ask you one thing. Was there a moment, perhaps a gesture or word of hers – that impelled you strongly?'

'After – I cannot call it love – she gave an odd, hysterical laugh. She had her handbag with her. She opened it. She had a pistol. She pointed it at me, close to. She said – I can't recall her exact words. But I give the sense – after love, death. Or – Love is a strong sensation. Death is another. I cannot recall.'

'And you . . . ?'

'I was very frightened.'

'Yes indeed.'

'In reflex – I got an arm around her. Sitting – it is ridiculous – side by side, even in a large car – one is cramped and ill at ease. The more . . . I got an arm round her neck. She started to scream. I . . .'

'It's all right,' said Castang gently. 'Let it just go loose.'

'I'm sorry,' said the Judge, standing up shakily, 'I should like to go to the lavatory.' It was Richard who stood up swiftly and took his arm. When Richard came back, and sat down, he and Castang stared at one another, emptily, across Richard's room.

53. Mr Justice Armitage

Castang uncapped the other two bottles of beer, which hissed gently in the silence.

The Judge had washed his hands and face with great care in Fausta's little lavatory which she kept herself so beautifully clean; the working women were, she said, 'sloppy'. He had combed his hair. He had found Richard's bottle of Roger & Gallet. He was in command of himself.

'May I smoke my pipe?' he asked humbly.

'Please do. I have only one more question. Sir James –'

'No. I'm afraid that only Judges have the right to the title. As of now I have no more that right.'

'I have an answer to that,' said Castang with a show of being lighthearted. 'The Spanish find that Man is the most honourable

246

of titles. But to the point – I'm sorry about this. We found her frock, her coat, her bag. But that travel rug. I have to put this bluntly – it was no longer clean.'

'No . . . I rolled it up tightly. I found no opportunity of getting rid of it. It was in the back. Next morning, I succeeded in preventing my family from looking in the back. I had some insane notion of hiding her somewhere. I got rid of the clothes, bit by bit. When we got here – that restaurant – Thomas. I sent the girls on ahead. To wash and tidy themselves – I had a moment, my pretext was to lock the car. I took the rug. There was a flashy big station-wagon . . . I left it on the roof as though it had been forgotten. I hoped it would be stolen; it occurred to me that the surest way of getting rid of something unwanted is to have it stolen.'

Castang and Richard looked at each other. In other circumstances – or without more self-control – both would have begun to laugh. Nom de Dieu! The butcher's Volvo . . . whipped off with the vital piece of evidence in a homicide as well as granny, recently deceased . . .

Light-fingered pickers from parked cars, life is full of little jokes, boys. And little surprises to ginger you up. Next time round will be one with a bomb under its bonnet, wired to the ignition.

Castang stood up and took his beer off the table. Richard sat in his place, made himself comfortable, slipped himself into gear.

'Translate, Castang. Mr Armitage' – Richard wasn't going to trip himself up with titles – 'I am obliged to place you in custody. The regulations state that you should be deprived of your tie, your shoelaces, and anything else that could serve as a ligature. I have not the faintest intention of respecting that. Rather than humiliate you, I rely upon your integrity. Monsieur Castang here will see that dinner is brought you. I will myself go and explain matters to your family, and you may see them in private. One or the other of us – take notes, Castang, we don't need Fausta – will contact the Consulate, and get hold of Mr Brooke. The interpreter, Malinowski – he's due at the hotel this afternoon: tell him to go to the Palais de Justice instead. I'll see the judge and arrange for him to see you as soon as possible, and that any Press statement shall be as brief and undramatic as may be.

'Since you have spoken, in this room, so frankly, I can be frank in return. There is no bail as you are aware on a homicide charge, but the instruction will not be long. We can say with certainty that both the instructing judge and the Court of Assize will take the widest and most liberal view, in the absence that is of any legal chicanery; Mr Brooke . . . I hope he has the sense to see this.'

Mr Justice Armitage thought all this over at leisure.

'You need have no cause for concern on any of these grounds, Commissaire – the last act of my judicial career will be to ensure that justice shall be satisfied.'

'Well, man,' Richard was looking for a joke, 'this isn't the trial of Oscar Wilde, you know.' The Judge looked for a moment as though not about to find this funny, and then his mouth twitched.

'Only, perhaps, his exile.'

When Castang got back Richard had just finished telephoning to the Palace of Justice, and Fausta, in the Judge's chair, was scribbling furiously.

'What did happen to Oscar Wilde?'

'He did about two years in jug and then he went to live in Dieppe,' said the omniscient Fausta.

'Well, there are plenty of worse places. Not exactly Devil's Island.'

'I wish I could go and live in Dieppe,' said Richard putting the phone down. 'Castang, you better go fish out that boy Colin. The judge says he's "not satisfied with the rôle played by this young man" – as though the whole thing was uproariously funny . . .'

'I think he stopped finding it all so funny a while back.'

'Well, they'll all have to do penance in the judge's office and be given a talking to. That Laetitia – if ever anybody begged for trouble . . .'

'And got it,' said Fausta, who had small use for Laetitia. 'But what got into them both? How does a man of that experience come to do something so stupid? What's the diagnosis – I mean what will the shrink say?'

'Anorexia nervosa,' said Richard frivolously.

'No, no,' said Fausta who was being literal, 'that's young girls who won't eat and then find they can't, and waste away.'

'Well, what is the phrase the quacksalver uses, when he hasn't a clue himself?'

'Pyrexia – pyrexia of unknown origin. It means simply a fever.'

Castang, through a hurried lunch in the pub and administrative chores all day, worked on it, and wasn't much further at the end. Perhaps Vera would understand, better than any of them. Getting the fever? – everybody gets the fever, as Peggy Lee remarked. Goltz had got the fever.

When a man of character and great integrity committed a crime . . . well, that is a classic. The man is *bouleversé*. Bowled over? Broken up?

Why do you lose your integrity? A sudden overwhelming disgust, with a world that has lost its own? Goltz, who had the morals of a stoat, was a respectable law-abiding citizen in the world's eye, until provoked by blackmail into killing a clochard. And what, as Commissaire Marchand might say, is a clochard more or less?

Good God, we live surrounded by far worse criminals than that. What are politicians? Des gens, as Napoleon remarked of the members of the Directory, à pisser dessus.

Integrity! Has Richard got it? Have I? Well, we do by day. And we don't by night, as Monsieur Bianchi was wise enough to realize.

Integrity is not enough. The Judge behaved like a perfect fool throughout. No worldly wisdom. That's what comes of living that isolated, artificially perfected existence.

But what the hell is worldly wisdom? Is that what Goltz had?

What were Oscar Wilde's thoughts, walking up and down the seafront in Dieppe?

Not much difference, is there, between being a Judge convicted of murder, or sodomy? – or indecent exposure come to that.

French courts non-obstant, Mr Justice Armitage would recover his integrity by seeing to it that justice was done him.

No hangman would come for him, nor little mechanic with the machine. The English were rather proud of their hangman. More craftsmanship about it that way! But even in the old days – the Home Secretary would have been signing reprieves in a flash, while sanctimoniously breaking the neck of a penniless eighteen-year-old girl who'd killed her own baby in despair.

Less hypocritical nowadays, at least. Mr Brooke aiding and abetting, a French court would hurry the instruction up, and dish out three years (two suspended). Eight months in all, a nice clean airy room, plenty of library books and no low company.

And what do we get out of it all? Well, perhaps we can compromise with integrity just a tiny bit, twisting Mr Thomas's arm.

Towards the end of a weary busy PJ day, Castang went driving out to the village, just outside city limits, that had tempted the butcher into bending municipal regulations – really, the Judge had not done much worse than fail to report a death to the authorities in Tours ... The local brigade of gendarmerie, who had been efficient about the butcher, his car, and his granny, could now take steps to recover a travel rug, of excellent quality and in good condition; slightly soiled ...

After seeing to this, he popped in for a friendly word with Mr Thomas.

'You ought to be in the *Guinness Book of Records*. Has there ever been a restaurant keeper with not one but two cars containing corpses on his parking lot?'

'Hush. Not funny. I'll say this for you though, you kept your word. The Press never did mention my name. When are you and your charming wife coming out for that dinner I promised you?'

'Tomorrow,' said Castang instantly.

'Oh,' a little put out by this promptitude. 'Very well then, I'll keep a table.'

'Be seeing you then,' said Castang, climbing into the car clutching his parcel (one travel rug, recovered from the local dry-cleaners).

Very tired, but relatively jaunty, he looked at his watch. No, too late today to go and visit Monsieur Bianchi. That would have to be tomorrow: the day was fading towards night. Cops would put on a collar and tie, and be bourgeois, go guzzle in three-star restaurants, like lords; like night lords.

Meanwhile, there was going to be a very beautiful sunset.

More about Penguins
and Pelicans

For further information about books available
from Penguins please write to Dept EP, Penguin
Books Ltd, Harmondsworth, Middlesex UB7 0DA.

In the U.S.A.: For a complete list of books available
from Penguins in the United States write to Dept
CS, Penguin Books, 625 Madison Avenue,
New York, New York 10022.

In Canada: For a complete list of books available
from Penguins in Canada write to Penguin Books
Canada Ltd, 2801 John Street, Markham, Ontario
L3R 1B4.

In Australia: For a complete list of books published
by Penguins in Australia write to the Marketing
Department, Penguin Books Australia Ltd, P.O.
Box 257, Ringwood, Victoria 3134.

Nicolas Freeling

'My whole idea,' states one of Freeling's characters,
'was to write about Europe in a European idiom.
Something that has a European flavour and
inflection.' If this was also Nicolas Freeling's
intention, what a triumphant start he has made to
his un-American activities! Here are characters that
are subtle rather than tough; dialogue that echoes
real life; settings (in the Low Countries) exactly
inventoried; and, in Van der Valk, the Dutch
inspector, a detective as human and unorthodox as
Maigret himself.

Gadget

Nicolas Freeling

A gadget is physicists' jargon for a nuclear device: a
playful and harmless word for what we would call
a nuclear bomb.
Jim Hawkins, a minor physicist working in
Hamburg, is kidnapped by terrorists, who have
collected enough fissionable material to make a
big bang. To encourage Hawkins' cooperation they
have also taken his wife and children. Ultra-
civilized living conditions and gourmet food do
not make captivity too unbearable. And Hawkins
has to admit the technical challenge is
fascinating . . .

The following novels are also available:

Because of the Cats
Double Barrel
The King of the Rainy Country
Lake Isle
A Long Silence
Tsin – Boum

More mysteries for armchair sleuths

Even the Wicked
Ed McBain

Although the coroner had recorded a verdict of accidental death, Zach Blake believes his wife was murdered.

She was buried a year ago. Now Blake is back – to bury her murderer. And to get mixed up in kidnapping, drug-running and more murder . . .

Brat Farrar
Josephine Tey

When Bill and Nora Ashby were killed in an air crash their son, Patrick, was so upset that he disappeared leaving a note on a lonely cliff-top. Missing, presumed drowned.

Now, on the eve of his twin Simon's coming of age, a young man turns up at Latchetts. He calls himself Brat Farrar, and says he is Patrick. Aunt Bee, Ruth and Jane all want him to be what he says he is – but Simon has good reasons for knowing he is an impostor . . .

A Question of Degree
Roy Lewis

'Why did her husband confess to having pushed her down a coal mine in South Wales? The defence was soon tearing the prosecution's case apart. Inspector Crow, the intelligent and compassionate detective, has to go out to French Canada to get the final solution and wrench it out of the complicated surround of past and present.

Satisfyingly suspenseful' – Maurice Richardson in the *Observer*